CHERYL'S KIDNAPPING
AND HER ODYSSEY

CHERYL'S KIDNAPPING AND HER ODYSSEY

Roger I. Lewis

iUniverse, Inc.
Bloomington

CHERYL'S KIDNAPPING AND HER ODYSSEY

This is a work of fiction. All of the characters, names, incidents, organizations, and dialogue in this novel are either the products of the author's imagination or are used fictitiously.

iUniverse books may be ordered through booksellers or by contacting:

iUniverse
1663 Liberty Drive
Bloomington, IN 47403
www.iuniverse.com
1-800-Authors (1-800-288-4677)

ISBN: 978-1-4620-4987-5 (sc)
ISBN: 978-1-4620-4988-2 (ebk)

Printed in the United States of America

iUniverse rev. date: 11/18/2011

INTRODUCTION

Cheryl's kidnapping and the Odyssey that follows is a story of obsessive domestic violence.

When love dies individuals separate, but the disengagement is often painful. The parties discover that they were entwined in each others lives tangibly and emotionally. Sadly the fabric does not come apart easily. Sometimes the outcome is not less than tragic.

Domestic violence is not new. Research behind the closed doors of history reveals that dominant males were abusing subservient mates far back in time. Women wore long dresses with full length sleeves and that concealed cuts and bruises. The social code of the time made open discussion of spousal abuse inappropriate, and there was a social presumption that somehow the victim brought the problem on herself. In my time on the judicial bench times were changing. Victims are encouraged to be self assertive and to speak out in their own defense. Women's groups have organized to help and counsel battered women. Perhaps now we live in a better world.

As a judge I was involved in many cases where the violence was also a chargeable crime. The abuse to which a vengeful ex can subject a former lover can be as varied as the bounds of human imagination. Two incidents from my experience illustrate just how crazed the state of mind of the abuser can be.

In a pending divorce trial, the wife was given temporary possession of a house that the parties owned as their community property. The estranged husband was a building contractor who owned his own excavating equipment. He decided that it was not fair for her to have the house by herself and so he drove his tractor onto the lot and bulldozed the house to the ground. Abusers can be very destructive.

In a more tragic situation, an ex husband refused to accept termination of the marriage. He was calling incessantly, trying to discuss reconciliation, but the abused spouse had had enough trial reconciliations and was adamant that it was over. In response, he pleaded for face to face negotiation again and this time indicated his feelings were so strong about it that he would try to compel the proposed parley. Furthermore he said he now had a gun to emphasize his efforts to persuade her. All of this was presented to me in the form of her testimony, and it was a very adequate showing for me to sign an order compelling him to stop contacting her in any way and ordering that he stay away from her residence. Within hours he was served with a copy of the order. That night he went to her house and fired five shots through the door killing her instantly. So much for court orders.

Rolf Burnside presents a unique example. He is obsessed with an almost psychotic urge to hurt his ex wife and further to render pain and financial revenge against her second husband whom he believes was instrumental in destroying the Rolf /Bonnie Gay marriage. But he is not typical. Abusive acting out usually occurs soon after the parties break up, sometimes even before. Rolf is angry from the beginning, but he does not act. Instead, he broods, he plans, he prepares. He incurs great risk and fanatical effort in preparation for his plan. 13 years come and go. But now, at last, he is ready. The plan to subject his ex wife and her new family to a horrid and prolonged revenge begins to unfold.

The geography of the story location is real except for the City of Titusville which I invented. Hawkins mountain appears on the map, but as far as I know the lava tube does not exist. All roads and locations exist, although they have not always been passable for the type of traverse accomplished by Bart Bartholomew. A State Highway runs north through Cle Elum and later becomes a county road ending at Salmon La Sac Campground. It then reduces to rough and bumpy dirt and becomes U.S. Forest Service Road 4330 as it follows the winding course of the Cle Elum River some nine miles ending at a convergence of several hiking trails.

Along its route there are a variety of side roads in even worse condition that nevertheless are the delight of four wheel off-road vehicle explorers in summer and snowmobilers in winter. One of these is the Fortune Creek road which follows the main thread of that creek more or less five miles to Gallagher Head Lake. Fortune Creek flows westerly to the Cle Elum River. After a short but difficult hike east from Gallagher the land surface breaks to the east and De Roux Creek begins its short easterly flow to where it joins the North Fork of the Teanaway River. A trail runs southeast from there to De Roux camp ground and the beginnings of a road which follows the Teanaway terminating near the intersection of State Route 970/US 97.

Except for a few scattered summer cabins and one or two hardy year-round residents, there is no civilization, no electric power, and no telephone line north of Salmon La Sac and the upper reaches of the Teanaway road. In most of the area, the Cascade Mountains rise up on all sides of the roads. Cell tower reception is thwarted by peaks and canyons. Wireless' phones cannot function. Short wave radios may or may not transmit. Satellite dishes do work if you can power up with your own generator.

The story and its characters are fictitious, and no real individual is the basis for any character described.

CHAPTER 1

On October 6 Titusville was quiet. Police officers who had spent the day patrolling its streets had little to do and nothing to report except minor misdemeanors and neighborhood arguments. Graveyard shift had laughingly reported one alcohol influenced domestic dispute where he and she were throwing rocks at each other albeit with no serious hits on themselves. However the combatants did score several strikes on automobiles owned by other people. Numerous shrieking complaints had been called in to 911.

Titusville did appear busy; the principal roads and highways in and out of the town were jammed with traffic and that was normal. Otherwise, not much had been going on. Summer had been arid and warm, warmer than is normal in the Puget Sound area of Washington State. Now temperatures were beginning to drop slowly toward their autumn norms. Today the streets were wet with a light but persistent rain. Titusville was shrouded by a blanket of fog covering the city and about 100 feet up the hills on either side of the Cedar River Valley.

Rolf Burnside drove the nondescript Oldsmobile Firenza slowly along the residential areas west of the Titusville school grounds. For more than a decade, Rolf, with the help of a fugitive character living in India, had letters and greeting cards mailed creating the assumption that he was living in

India Letters came to his mother proclaiming that he was enjoying success there albeit sometimes he needed small loans from her to help in his enterprises.

He steered the old auto over to the curb of Pearl Street and stopped. The sidewalk was bounded by a five foot cyclone fence marking the west boundary of the Titusville schools, Titusville High, and the combined Maude Hellgraves Elementary and Middle schools. The middle school building was closest to Pearl Street. The high school was 100 yards further east, and it was adjacent to another street bounded by a cyclone enclosure some 8 feet in height. Rolf surveyed the closer and shorter fence and nodded his head murmuring to himself, "OK." Then he stared at the higher fence and murmured "not OK."

Rolf was now 38 years old. He had his mother's red hair and grey eyes. He looked older than he was. For weeks now he had been stone sober, but he had to admit that in years past he had probably drank more than he should have and some of that plus a lot of fast food showed on his florid, puffy face with much more folded over his belt. At a 5'-10" height, his 200 pounds was well over what the charts would recommend. He had to squeeze a bit to get under the steering wheel of the compact automobile. And today he was uncomfortable. He was wearing a black wig and cheap black rimmed glasses. The whole get up felt heavy and it itched, but he felt it was necessary because there was the faint chance he could accidentally run into Bonnie Gay. The last thing he wanted was for her to see him and have the India ruse destroyed.

He had been cruising these streets for the past several days. Today he already had spent more time in Titusville than he wanted to. He well knew that if one appears frequently even on busy streets eventually other people will begin to notice. That was the risk, but it had to be taken. The things he had to find out were essential to the execution of his plan. He had considered delegating some surveillance tasks to his co conspirators, Arnie and Bart, but on second thought he had to admit neither of them could be trusted to get the information needed without causing people to be suspicious and to wonder what was going on. No, all of that prep had to be part of his personal assignment as the mastermind of the plan. Besides, he had kept himself concealed from so many people for so long that he was beginning to believe that no one could be as stealthy as he was and it was all kind of nervous, stimulating fun anyway.

Burnside was studying the buildings and grounds of the two adjacent public schools. But he was no educator. He was not seeking new ideas about the layout and design of school buildings and grounds. The most important object of his surveillance was a tall dark haired girl of 13. On one of his earliest visits to Titusville, he had walked the periphery of the school grounds. Whenever he could would engage elementary and middle school kids asking if they had a girl classmate named Cheryl Burnside who would be 13 maybe 14. He kept getting the same answer. The school had several Cheryl's of varying ages but none was a Burnside. Then finally one 7th grader pointed out a Cheryl Comstock. Rolf studied the identified youngster for a moment, but then professed that that was not the girl he was looking for.

It was exactly who he wanted to see. Once she was pointed out, he could see a clear resemblance. She looked like Bonnie Gay; she did not look anything like Rolf Burnside. He quickly walked out of sight hoping that by denying recognition, he would stifle any tendency the informant might have to tell Cheryl about his inquiry.

3

He did look closely at the girl identified and noted that her height and striking good looks would make it easy to identify her again. Cheryl was tall for her age, 5 feet 7 inches and still growing. Still somewhat shapeless she had worried about why she had not experienced a beginning of normal menstrual cycle. With many of her 8th grade classmates rapidly maturing, she took little consolation from the assurances of her mother that being 13, 5 foot 7 and skinny was normal for her family; and that time would bring maturity soon enough.

Cheryl was a natural athlete. As morning wore on to 10 AM she was on the volley ball court with three ninth graders. She obviously was dominating the game. For a moment or two Burnside registered pride and actually smiled briefly because this lean graceful youngster was his daughter. She was born during the stormy marriage of Rolf and Bonnie Gay Burnside. Rolf laughed out loud and had to muffle his own cheer when Cheryl spiked the ball and the girls broke away from the net. Apparently the game was over and Cheryl's side had won. He felt a surge of great satisfaction in this demonstration of skill by what was his own flesh and blood, but then he flushed with renewed anger. It dawned on him that Cheryl's use of the name Comstock probably meant that Marcus and Bonnie Gay had initiated adoption proceedings so that she no longer carried his name. His face flushed full red and he muttered, "Comstock, Hell, I'm the father, I made that kid. That stuffed shirt Comstock had nothing to do with it." For a moment or two Rolf noticed he could feel his own pulse racing and pounding in his ear. His stomach felt sickly. It took a while for him to calm down. Rolf knew his anger was great and that it had lasted so long that he might well be harming his own good health, but the psychosis ran so deep he just did not care. For Rolf, the divorce would never be a thing of the past. It was on his mind every day for the past 13 years.

As he continued to drive around the periphery of the school grounds he was changing his traverse from one street to another and as school bells rang signaling the end of the mid-morning break he reached a conclusion. He would choose Pearl Street. Its easterly edge marked the westerly boundary of the grounds. A five foot cyclone fence marked the division between the grounds and the street. That fence proved to be the lowest of all the fencing surrounding the school grounds.

Now the sun was burning through the fog. He reckoned that he had driven around and around the school area enough times that somebody could be watching. Small matter, these local residents would never see this vehicle again. Besides, he had now carefully studied the whole school grounds as well as the roads that would be used coming in and going out of the city.

He drove on into the city center, found a bridge that crossed the Cedar River and then he followed the signs onto the coupler road which connected Titusville to the cross mountain state highway, SR 18. He followed 18 to its intersection with I-90. Following the freeway he headed east without stopping until he turned off at North Bend. Once he had passed the business section, he turned off the main street to a road running southeast to an isolated and dilapidated old farm house with moss covering its slowly failing roof. Some of its windows were out and the spaces boarded up to keep out the weather. He drove around the house and parked in back.

In fact, there was an adequate parking area in front of the house, but Rolf was especially careful to hide all the gang's vehicles from any possible observers. After gazing across adjacent rural pastures just to make sure that there didn't appear to be anything that might pique an observer's interest, he entered by the back door which dragged on the floor as it was pushed open and then refused to close when he was in and endeavoring to shut it behind him. The weather was now warming so a partially open door was no matter anyway.

The living room was blue with cigarette smoke. He stood looking at three men deeply concentrating on a fresh dealt poker hand. The betting had them all tense and they were stealing furtive glances at each other hoping to glean some hint of the state of mind of their respective adversaries. As he stood there a lean young hound dog appeared from between the legs of the players and ran toward Burnside jumping up on him obviously seeking attention. "Yelper, get down, you clumsy son-of-a-bitch" and with that Burnside brusquely pushed the dog away.

Yelper responded with first a hurt look and then he turned and bounded up a set of stairs leading to the bed rooms. Half way up the steps lay a large black and white cat with scarred misshapen ears and a short tail. He appeared to be asleep, but as the dog thrust his nose into the cat's face, the cranky feline swiped the hound's nose in a manner that would have been painful if the feline claws were set for real combat. However, this was not a battle to the death. It was an act for the benefit of all who might watch. The dog and cat performed as they had many times before. The performance was brief but did feature fierce dog barks and cat screams. No humans bothered to look up and in an instant it was over. Yelper bounded on up the steps, found a bed that looked inviting and jumped up on it. In a few moments the hostile cat seemed to have a change of heart. He sauntered slowly up the stairs and down the hall to the same bedroom where he stopped and stared at the dog for a few moments and then quietly leaped up and snuggled down next to the hound. Soon both were asleep.

The three card players gave nodding acknowledgement of Burnside's arrival and then continued betting. These three were a strange mix. Burnside had drawn two of them into his nefarious plan by promising them great wealth. Their eager acceptance of Rolf's proposal was a clear example of the criminal mind in action or lack of action depending on how you want to analyze it.

Rolf Burnside, if nothing else, was a spell binder, a con artist with the remarkable ability to excite others about his get-rich-quick schemes. He had the natural talent of stimulating his followers, and these two were ready to follow him giving no serious thought of the consequences if the plan came unraveled. A con's master plan of action sounds brilliant to them and once convinced, they never contemplate the probable loss of liberty until they find themselves surrounded by grim faced law enforcement types. Failure of prior schemes and the consequences of getting caught etch little on their minds and the new plan always intrigues them.

The first player, Arnold Robert "Arnie" Sorenson, was not particularly outstanding in appearance. He stood five feet six inches in height with thin blond hair and blue eyes. A rather deep scar over the right eye gave his round face an expression as if he was questioning whatever was being said. His complexion was somewhat dark.

Born in Billings Montana to an alcoholic mother and her heroin addicted husband, he dropped out of school at the ripe old age of 9. He ran away at 14. Lying about his age, he landed a job as a "go-fer" helping in a steel fabrication shop in Great falls. In 10 years he became proficient in metal fabrication and machinist work. Sadly, he had spent the first 14 years of his life where chicanery and fraud were the usual modus to provide a slovenly existence. He was raised in an atmosphere bathed in drugs and alcohol and where the adults in the household drifted from job to job. His father was being constantly discharged from one position after another for absenteeism, insubordination, and for being high or drunk while on the job. Some youngsters of dysfunctional families succeed in spite of the environment, but Arnie was a low achiever.

It was not surprising then that he had no concept of loyalty and honesty owed to whoever might hire him. Soon he was caught stealing funds from the office petty cash box and forging payroll checks at the shop. When the company bookkeeper uncovered the resulting shortages, Sorenson wisely sought to leave town, but it was a winter night when he tried to drive away and alas, he forgot he needed headlights. The City Police took a dim view of that practice, and the city judge was downright insulting. Having been apprehended and prosecuted for the several offenses committed in Great Falls, he served 18 months of a five year sentence.

Upon his release he failed to listen as the parole board detailed the conditions of his release on parole for the balance of the five year term. Then he more or less went underground and Montana records revealed that he was in violation of his parole for failing to report to his assigned parole officer. In due course a warrant was issued but never served. Overworked Montana law enforcement had more important cases to deal with.

At age 31 he was now more mature in his work habits, but he had become a weekend alcoholic. Beginning with red eyes and profuse perspiration on Monday mornings, he would work his way back to health by Friday managing to both survive the hangover and put out the work required by his employer. Then, come Friday night, the pain and gastric upset of Sunday morning last was a faded memory, and another binge would begin. For a while at least, suffer as he might, he did not fail to be at work on time each day. But, unfortunately, every boss or supervisor with whom he worked was unreasonable, favoring other workmen over Arnie. If he did not get fired he quit. Never once did it occur to him that he might be the cause rather than the victim. The end result was that for all of his talents, he never kept any job very long.

For several years prior to what he regarded as his very fortunate meeting with Rolf Burnside, he had worked for independent repair shops in Spokane. He had avoided larger companies even though they might pay more. Larger shops had a propensity to do background checks and investigation would reveal that Arnie's trail was littered with various charges including suspicion of child molestation. The later case would show as closed because the mother of the alleged victim refused to testify and the victim herself, looking fearfully at her mother, would profess lack of memory.

In Rolf's scheme of things, Arnie's shady past was of little consequence. His enthusiastic and unquestioning acceptance of Rolf's plan was of primary importance, and there were elements of that plan where a skilled mechanic with welding and metal burning skills could be invaluable.

The second player at the table was John Parker "Bart" Bartholomew. Bart came into the scheme of things as more or less a guardian of the third player, Gerald "Grunt" Graham.

Bart had made Arnie's acquaintance months before they were recruited by Rolf. The relationship grew out of Bart's Saturday night pool game challenge issued to the clientele of an Idaho bar just across the border from Washington State. Most of the local patrons knew Bart and all of them were of the opinion that they had lost enough money playing against this very skilled master of the bank shot. Then Arnie turned up at Bart's watering hole.

When Bart slyly invited this newcomer to bring his beer back to the tables and engage in a little friendly play with money on each game, "not to take advantage, mind you, but just to make sure the game didn't become boring." Arnie could sense the knowing winks being exchanged around the room, but yes, he would accept the invitation. Well, Arnie proved to be a real challenge. After playing eight games to a four—four tie, it was getting late and they agreed to quit after one more game as a tie breaker. But the bar owner noted that it was closing time and most of their audience had gone home. Retreating to Bart's mobile home park unit, they talked well into the dawn of a Sunday morning. Arnie revealed his shady past, all of which was given nods of understanding and perhaps approval except for the molesting thing on which Bart took a "no comment" position.

Then it was Bart's turn to talk. Bart was 37. At an even 6 feet he was the second tallest man at the poker table. Although still young, his hair had reduced to a brown fringe around the temples. His face was sallow and his eyes were brown and deep set. Overall he conveyed a rather sad expression.

Born in Sacramento, he had graduated from high school with highest honors and entered Stanford University on an engineering scholarship. Following the popular collegiate trend of those days, he slipped ever so gradually into the grip of drug addiction. First it was an honest effort to keep himself awake as he used his slow reading rate to cover text material and lecture notes but then more and more it was less and less the pressure and more an more the insidious compulsion of addiction. He sustained three successive convictions for possession and dealing. That was too much for the school to tolerate. His scholarship was cancelled.

Changing his identity and in complete contradiction to his prior involvement in anti-draft protest rallies, he joined the Navy. That posed its problems too, but the recruiter got his enlistment over the necessary hurdles and the ex-scholar was sworn in.

With the structured life, Bart became a pretty good sailor. His aptitude tests showed him to be a good candidate for communications and he was sent to a progression of schools. Four years saw him rise to the rank of petty officer second class and qualified as a specialist in the operation of a variety of navy communication systems. However during his term of enlistment an ongoing string of scrapes and escapades kept him on the cusp of discharge. Ignoring any thought of future consequences, he responded to a wager by stealing an officer's car. Skillfully "hot wiring," the vehicle he won the wager and capped the caper by taking his companions back to their quarters in style. All that might have gone undiscovered if, in returning the vehicle, he had not lost his way. Two or three drinks too many took their toll. Singing to himself with the delight of having won the bet, he inadvertently drove over the end of the pier and into the bay. Luckily, he was thrown clear and managed to float. The car sank. Unfortunately, the Navy took a dim view of the whole affair.

After his dishonorable discharge, he re-assumed his real name, John Parker Bartholomew.

Bart was now doing moderately well running a small repair shop where he worked on various types of radio and electronic equipment. Aircraft systems were a specialty and amateur aviators used his services frequently.

Sometime that Sunday morning Bart and Arnie began to achieve sobriety and hunger. It was then that Bart revealed that there was another tenant in the old motor home sleeping soundly in back. Bart explained that his roommate was Gerald Graham, age 19 who, as Bart put it, was a likeable halfwit that Bart had nick named Grunt. Halfwit or not Graham had retired at a more sensible hour. As the two older men continued in getting to know each other, the sun began to rise and the talk turned to prospects for nourishment. Gerald "Grunt" Graham arose, wide awake and obviously in a good mood. Arnie was astonished by Grunt's massive size. He estimated this youngster to be at least 6 foot 5 inches tall and probably 250 fairly trim pounds in weight. Asking the men to wait a bit for him to take his turn in the bathroom, Grunt volunteered to prepare breakfast for all three. The offer was readily accepted. Both older men were complimentary; as the breakfast was prepared quickly and was a pleasure to consume. Grunt's earlier years saw him shunned and rejected by almost everyone and he had grown to yearn for acceptance. Now he beamed in response to these words of approval.

Later, when there was nothing left of the meal save the need for clean up, the two older men did their part by falling asleep so as to stay out from under foot. Grunt cheerfully took care of the necessary housekeeping. The trio spent a lazy Sunday with the two older men talking about their past experiences while Grunt, humming to himself, cleaned house, tended his the flowers, and prepared a lunch of sandwiches and a stir-fry dinner. Whatever might be his other intellectual limitations, Grunt was a good cook. The variety of meals that he could produce was limited to those he had been taught years before, but if one did not mind repetition, all of those fifteen or so offerings would be turn out perfectly every time.

Graham's alliance in the scheme was pathetically sincere and was spawned of his absolute allegiance to Bart. In his simple mind, he had accepted the outrageous stories told by Bart and Rolf to the effect that the Comstock's family was a nest of criminals who needed to be reined in and punished for their numerous crimes against innocent people and the American government.

Arnie had moved in with Bart and Grunt. The arrangement worked out very well for all concerned. Almost a year came and went. With two careless and somewhat uncultured males tracking mud, dirtying the bathroom and throwing dirty clothing hither and yon, Grunt was elevated to fulltime housekeeper, laundryman, baker and cook. That meant he had approval, praise and dignity. He was delighted, and he was more devoted to his two housemates than he ever should have been. The two older men shared expenses and did shopping at Grunt's behest. They helped their housemaid with repairs, and things were going well.

Those days were not very eventful, however, they did take in two more tenants. One was a stray black and white cat with a grumpy disposition. The cat's moodiness was off-set by the joyous friendliness of the other newcomer, a clumsy young, brown and white hound. Their respective pedigrees were no more illustrious than those of the men who took them in.

Arnie and Bart continued their Saturday night pool games. Quite by chance, a stranger whose vehicle bore California plates, said he knew the two men were better pool players than he, but congenially he joined their game and dropped some one hundred dollars before suggesting that that was as far as a "friendly game" should go. The pool sharpies reluctantly agreed, and the stranger was invited to follow them home and join in their now traditional midnight supper.

It should have seemed strange to them that this apparently well-heeled newcomer was so interested in them, but both Arnie and Bart were captivated by his story, and they sympathized with him as he skillfully spun embellishments about how the spoiled son of an electronics dynasty had cheated him out of ten million dollars and then added insult to injury by making off with his wife and daughter. There was a strange quirk in Rolf's telling of the story. If either Arnie or Bart would mention his rights as a father, he would deny that he was. Then in other sessions he would refer to her as "his kid." The recruits both thought this ambivalence about paternity was strange. He vehemently denied that Bonnie Gay got pregnant by any other man. Furthermore, his whole personality seemed to be a bit deranged as he continued to rave on about the Comstocks. Nonetheless, there was nothing ambivalent about 10 million dollars split three ways, and the boys signed on for the caper without considering the possible consequences.

Grunt was virtually oblivious to his own strength and he was also remarkably agile; something seldom seen among mentally handicapped persons. He seemed always to be in a happy mood. Very few things upset him, but he also exhibited a sense of insecurity. He was anxious to please anyone who might befriend him. It rendered him vulnerable to just the sort of manipulation that Rolf Burnside could skillfully wield.

Earnestly seeking accolades from others, he would high jump cyclone fences. He would jump a four foot fence from a standing position and he would clear 6 feet from a short run. His irrepressible good humor, remarkable agility and magnificent strength coupled with both his total gullibility and his accomplished cooking skills had led Burnside to conclude that this young man would prove to be priceless in the execution of his plan. Grunt would be on the team.

And so on this day, October 6, Rolf had assembled and carefully trained his team of three. On balance, they were just about the most well suited gang that Rolf could have hoped for.

CHAPTER 2

Now the troops were passing the time of day with a small-change poker game as their commander looked on. At first glance it was a case of two shills taking money from a virtually helpless country bumpkin; but if one were to watch the play for a few hands a whole different story unfolded. Grunt's mind had not been totally damaged. Although his speech was child-like, his brain harbored a mental capability that seemed astonishing in view of its severe limitations. The human brain is even yet just vaguely understood.

Grunt could cast his eyes down a stack of packing boxes bearing serial numbers and it made no difference. There could be two, four or ten boxes he would look down the stack pausing only to read each one and instantly after having read them all, recite the correct sum that would be reached by adding the numbers together.

It was a boon to a poker player. He could do what is the bane of the casino operators everywhere. He could simply count and keep track of cards. Looking at cards face up in the stud game, he could make good deductions as to what cards were still in the deck. Suffice it to say, that at this early afternoon hour most of the nickels and dimes were piled up in front of Grunt with only meager remnants in front of the other two men. Rolf grinned and then laughed out loud as he had done before, and he slapped Grunt on the back saying "Burn 'em good Grunt, teach 'em the game." One more hand and Grunt had swept all the money from the table. His two adversaries grumbled about a dummy's good luck, and it was over for the day.

Grunt excused himself in his always polite way to prepare a late lunch for the gang.

Usually after lunch the four occupants of the dingy, musty smelling old farmhouse would spend the afternoon doing things that they could to ready themselves to execute the master plan, but on this day preparatory work would be on hold. Commander Rolf Burnside gathered them all together around the table for a serious briefing.

Arnie spoke first, "well boss how are we doing?" Burnside chastised in response, "all you characters have accomplished today is to trade some small change around when you could have been packing the supplies into boxes the way I asked". "Hell boss, you said we ain't going to move for a week yet."

"Well, things have changed, Arnie, and we have to put this caper in motion before the end of this week." This was news the gang did not expect.

"Now what the hell?" Bart blurted.

Rolf responded by awkwardly turning to one side of his chair and producing a wrinkled copy of the Titusville Mountain Globe from a hip pocket.

"According to their local newspaper tomorrow is a so-called in service day for teachers and the kids won't be in class. That doesn't concern us, but in the next paragraph it says the State is after the local school district to cover up some asbestos ceiling tile in a storage closet and in two rooms in the middle school building. While that's going on, kids will be having their classes in the old portables behind that high school. The work would start sometime next week and last for three months. If they are on the high school grounds, we're looking at a fence 8 feet high, and there is no way we can do what we planned to do, besides that new satellite police station is in plain sight of where we would have to be exposed. We can't take that risk." Rolf paused for a moment to let that much sink in and then continued.

"So, today is Monday, October 6. No school tomorrow. The move to the portables is planned for Thursday or Friday or they thought it might be as late as Monday. We have to consider that it is going to be Thursday, because if it is we have to go on Wednesday, otherwise this plan is screwed tight to the lamp post for the next three months when the kids are scheduled to return to their own rooms. That puts us into winter and you can see where the complications come up then.

"Furthermore, I don't want to be on I-90 any later in a week than Thursday because the word is that the Governor of the State is all upset about an article on speeders printed in the Seattle Times. It criticized the State patrol for allowing a tolerance of as much as ten miles or more over the posted speed limits on freeways. The word is the State Patrol will be on a traffic emphasis going after both speeders and seat belt violations. We just do not want to make any more work for them."

Grunt was tickled by the mental picture of being stopped by a patrolman and he giggled, and that in turn brought a withering stare from Rolf. "Gee whiz, Boss" Grunt continued seriously, "we are going to have to move fast." "Brilliant Grunt, brilliant. D-Day is Wednesday that's it; it's locked in so let's figure on it. I would suggest you guys get busy packing all the stuff that isn't up there already. We're going to have to run a marathon tomorrow. It is going to take three loads.

Rolf Burnside had spent many hours thinking and rethinking what would be necessary to execute his plan. Ultimately included were three 5 gallon propane tanks, a whole truck bed load of miscellaneous groceries, most of which were canned goods which could be consumed over a period of time without any worry about spoilage. There were staples, sugar, flour, box cakes, salt, pepper, syrup, honey and dry milk together with a list of odd, miscellaneous items purchased at Grunt's request so that he could ply his cooking skills and present the rest of the gang with meals as good as anything they could have ordered up in any restaurant. Then, of course, he could enjoy the compliments.

CHAPTER 3

Two hours after Rolf drove out of the city, an SUV pulled off Titusville's Main Street and into the tree-lined driveway leading to the building complex fronted with a sign, "The Comstock Company." It hesitated at the guard station but it was apparent that the guard recognized the driver and waived him through. The vehicle swung into a parking space marked "Mr. Comstock Sr."

Marcus Comstock III, the object of Rolf Burnside's tantrum, was watching from his office window and he smiled as his father got out of the vehicle, closed the driver side door and walked away without locking the $40,000.00 vehicle. In a moment or two the older man, Marcus Comstock Jr. now in his 77th year, first knocked on Marcus III's door and then walked in without waiting for his son to respond. Marcus III spoke first, "Well, how was the game?" "Shit" the older man responded. Jr. grinned "when you gonna give it up old man you know you can't break a hundred to save your backside." "Never" his father shot back and with that he dropped his rain soaked trousers on a visitor chair which was still warm from being occupied by a prior occupant. "Besides, I like the walk. It gets me out of my cramped little office where I labor long and hard hours under terrible conditions to make my only son rich." "You love it you old curmudgeon." "What do you mean old?" was the response apparently without objection to the term curmudgeon *per se*.

Then the older man changed the subject. "How did it go with Navy brass?" His son looked at notes he had taken that morning. and then he spoke. "Navy wants a full field test to take place somewhere at sea. Tentatively, they would choose the Bering Sea near Rat Island and Adak Island. They want the Comstock sensor incorporated into the guidance system of their favorite attack missile. Then they want to shoot at it with all of their anti-missile rocket ordnance and they tell me that if any one of the anti's scores a hit they will regard the test as a failure and send us back to the drawing board. And they are firm on that even though they admitted to me that if it can dodge 75% of their anti stuff then that's way better than any missile they have now."

The older Marcus had 56 years of experience at Comstock. Two weeks after college graduation, he assumed supervision of rebuilding after a disastrous fire destroyed grandfather's original woodshop. He had more faith in the company's good fortune than his son did and he surprised the younger man, registering no dismay at the Navy's all or nothing announcement by saying "Well, we have been working with our little toy for years. You and I know it has been a good little bird dog. It finds oil deep in the ground for Raynar. The Airforce and the commercial airlines are delighted with its navigational genius and over all I have confidence that a better device will not come along for a long time. Let's go with their test. What's to lose? If the attack bird is shot down we go back to the drawing board as they are going to require us to do anyway. If it survives the potential for future military contracts and civilian applications will keep this company going until you are as old and maybe almost as wise as I am."

"Braggart," the son retorted. "OK let's do it. I guess I should have more faith in our bug than I do. But for success it is going to have to bob and weave like a lightweight boxer. Oh! and it was subtly hinted that if we get a contract, national security requires that our phone will be tapped, our mail monitored even for months after any final completion date."

"Well," the older man responded, "we could live with that you know. We don't have anything to conceal unless my kid has a secret life he is not telling me about. They may snoop into our development secrets, but any leak and ultimate use by another company would feel the wrath of our patent legal counsel come down on them. We can live with the navy's domineering ways and suspicious distrust. They are responsible for providing the best possible protection of our national interest and we can tolerate all that. After all we have lived with Raynar, haven't we?"

"I guess," Marcus III mumbled "but government spooks give me the itch. I know they have been nosing around already." "Be nice to them" his father counseled. They are just doing their job and this enterprise does become involved with our country's well being." "Yeah, thanks for the lesson in government father dear now go home and change clothes. Old men are vulnerable to pneumonia." "Stuff it," his father grinned and then took his leave to do exactly what his son had suggested

CHAPTER 4

Marcus III watched out the window to see his father depart the grounds and then he signaled for his floor supervisor to report to the head office. It was time to bring that person up to speed on what was happening with navy negotiations. In the five or six minutes it would take the supervisor to be at his doorstep, Marcus III sat, closed his eyes for a moment and remembered Raynar. That experience changed the younger Marcus's life for the better.

As early as the 1960's, Ray Burnside could see that the glory days of Texas crude were going to end out there somewhere in the future. He was a self-educated wizard in the techniques employed to discover new fields of the black gold, and the rest of the world was relatively unexplored. When his father retired and could no longer resist his efforts, Ray reinvented Raynar Drilling Company, dropping the words 'drilling company" and amending the company name to the generalized "Raynar Research and Development Company."

What they would "develop" would be the discoveries of new oil fields throughout the world. In the early years, aerial surveys and a good understanding of the geology that is likely to contain oil sand was sufficient. But the easy finds were made early on and now there was fierce competition world wide. Again, thinking way ahead of his time, Ray

Burnside studied intently learning all he could cram into his head about electronics and sonar and all the related new and developing technology. He read every page of every publication about the latest in oil exploration. Later he contributed ideas through the various journals and he even successfully patented some search tools of his own.

After the tragic loss of a firstborn, the Burnside's family increased by twins, boy and girl. Both of them sought to be active participants in the company. Knowing his own self-made man status had its limitations, Ray urged that the twins defer their entry into the exciting world of exploration and take five years or so to master all the relevant subjects and to become lettered participants in oil exploration geology. The twins followed their father's advice, and when they joined the firm, Raynar enjoyed great success.

Meantime a third child came along who was named Rolf in memory of an uncle of that name who had been part of the original company. The twins were Ray's pride and joy. They soon were well known persons and admired in the oil world. With Rolf, family and friends agreed that genetics went "crosswise in the chute" somewhere. To begin with he did suffer a weakness of chronic allergy. His mother arguably was a bit overindulgent of this condition, haunted as she was by the loss of the first child to multiple bee stings that were ignored too long. "Rolfy" baby played his mother's concern like a fiddle and the indulgence grew as she continued to ignore what the boy's father could clearly see. The kid was becoming an accomplished con man in adult life. Mother saw to it that life was made easy for him and when the father tried to intervene, it produced such a storm of marital discord that eventually he became disposed to just let it happen saying, "the damned useless kid is ruined anyway."

Rolf knew he was a mamma's boy and a wretched failure, but as he matured he developed an air of superiority and arrogance to cover it up; and so it was a smooth, good looking, persuasive, golden-tongued fraud who descended upon and began to charm a young raven-haired beauty from Galveston by the name of Bonnie Gay Cottrell.

She was fun. She loved to tease. By the 80's gay was a word dictionaries defined not only as a mood of effusive happiness but also as being of a homo sexual orientation. When she met strangers especially haughty women in high society, she would say in a loud voice, "Hello, I'm Gay."

Cottrells were big in the shrimping industry. They had made their way up to moneyed success the hard way with countless hours of sore, sometimes bloody hands, and always bodies wringing wet with sweat toiling at the lines and rigging of the shrimp boats. They were not crude nor were they like some of the ruffians of that world but they were down to earth people who assumed no false airs. They were kindly and when they saw fishing crew people in distress, they were quick to lend needed help. Most of them recognized Rolf Burnside for the fake that he was. Sadly the beautiful child of Barney and Madeline Cottrell was totally blindsided by Rolf's charm and there was no deterring the romance that sprung up between them.

The wedding was huge. It seemed like half of Houston and half of Galveston were there. With money on both sides, the honeymoon was nothing less than a world cruise with all the luxuries and it seemed as though the princess and her man would live happily ever after.

Unfortunately back home was a thing called reality. Mother Burnside had secretly underwritten a half dozen enterprises for Rolf to own and operate, but, as his father said, "he screwed up every one of them ". He never tried very hard nor did he worry because mamma's checkbook was always ready in the wings. He would tearfully explain how, once again, adverse forces worked against him causing failure. No way was it his fault. Bonnie's uncle, rancher and fisherman, Harry, and Rolf's father, Ray, both offered simpler explanations to mother Burnside, "defrauded and cheated hell, he pissed it away like he did last time!" Rolf was a spoiled brat, and unfortunately, spoiled brats do not fare well when subjected to the heat of criticism. Mama lavished considerable sums on the useless Burnside kid concealing the actual amounts spent by telling her husband they were for an overseas refugee relief program.

The first clouds of marital discord in the Rolf-Bonnie Gay marriage began forming not long after the honeymoon. The homecoming was a direct flight from Honolulu to Houston with the couple moving directly in to a home that mother had provided. As days passed it came to Bonnie Gay that Rolf's primary occupation was digging money out of his mother's checkbook and beyond that, doing little else. Bonnie Gay, born of a happy but hard laboring world wondered out loud how anybody could just lay around the house. And so, Rolf, being already somewhat exposed, took to spending time away from home, allegedly on business of course. Soon there were reports of Rolf sightings in places of ill repute and even the police had made some inquiries. Bonnie Gay began to be depressed and members of both families noticed it, although mother Burnside suggested that she simply was unappreciative of the upper class world into which her son had delivered her.

Rolf was now given to heavy drinking. When he did come home Bonnie Gay was justifiably disturbed by his two week absences and his inebriated returns. The discussions would go on louder and louder and ultimately neighbors would call the police when screams and sounds of breaking glass erupted in the supposed happy newlywed home.

Unfortunately, as the troubled marriage crumbled, Rolf Burnside lapsed ever deeper into the psychotic clutches of what psychologists call the "cycle of violence." He began to harbor groundless suspicions about the faithfulness of his new wife. It did not make any difference how innocent the incident, whether she smiled at the male bank teller, laughed with the appliance repairman or hugged a former classmate at a high school reunion Rolf viewed it as a come on for a prospective dalliance. Finally no matter what she did to pacify him it would be of no avail. He would brush aside her assurances of her innocence. He grew to hate her popularity among their friends, and when they were home alone he would violently beat her.

Then, with Bonnie Gay in tears and sobbing her confusion over whatever she had done wrong, the poison would seem to drain out of Rolf's system and leave him repentant. Thereafter there would be a period during which he would smother her with loving attention, begging her forgiveness promising never to do it again. Persuasion was Rolf's ultimate talent and again and again he would woo his way back into the heart of a woman whose love for him desperately, unreasonably hoped that his latest promise would be sincere. And so the relationship would be a love nest again.

But the cure was always temporary and the unreasoning rage would begin to grow anew. Dangerously, the amount of physical and mental harm being done to her was escalating. In the second year of their marriage Bonnie Gay suffered through this circular wringer several times. She loyally and steadfastly refused to share the misery with friends and relatives. Then on an occasion just after the winter holidays

Rolf bruised her so terribly that she could not hide the injuries with clothing.

She tried to sneak unnoticed into the Galveston area to see the Cottrell family doctor whom she knew would keep her secrets if she asked him to. That was well enough but Uncle Harry just happened to be in the area, saw her drive by and followed until she pulled into the doctor's clinic. When she came out he invited her to lunch and she accepted but seemed to be acting strangely. Finally, Harry figured it out and brusquely pulled up one of her sleeves. The doctor's repair work was plainly evident. Harry demanded that her parents be notified so he drove her to their home and there was a family conference that lasted well into the evening. Unfortunately, Cottrells were not knowledgeable in matters of domestic violence. When Bonnie assured them that Rolf had apologized profusely, they decided to let the matter rest for now. What Bonnie did not tell them was that he had previously apologized more times than she could now remember. Anyway to let it ride was the family decision.

Harry had his own plan. He usually did. He volunteered to escort Bonnie back to Houston and he followed her car clear to the house. Walking her to the door, they discovered that lo and behold, Rolf was home for once and Harry greeted him in an apparently friendly fashion asking him to come to the street and look at a new business venture in which Rolf might be interested.

Rolf followed, but when Bonnie went inside and the door was closed, the burly fisherman/rancher grabbed Rolf by the arm and in an incredible burst of strength, lifted him into the air with one hand and then slammed him against the Cottrell automobile. "Burnside you son-of-a-bitch, no man in our family ever hit a woman the way you hit Bonnie." Rolf opened his mouth to speak but Harry barked," shut up and listen to me and don't say a damn word or I'll reduce you to hamburger right here on the street and tell the cops you got run over by a car. No man in our family ever hit a woman, and I am not going to tolerate some cowardly bastard coming into the fold by my niece's stupid marriage get by with it. If I ever find out you have hit her again I'm coming after you. I know a few well placed people in the police department here, and if I come after you, there will not be a police car come past here until after I leave and they will find you in a condition so bad you won't walk for a year, understand.?"

Burnside, still confident that he could charm birds out of trees began, "Uncle Harry you have to understand that some blame lies with Bonni-." He never finished the sentence. Harry Cottrell struck with a fist hardened by thirty years of pulling the lines on the shrimpers, as well as the arduous chores of ranching. Burnside went down and stayed down retching and vomiting everything in his system. Bonnie was looking out a window and watched the scene, ugly as it was. Why it made her hungry, she could never explain, but as soon as Rolf entered a back door and hobbled upstairs, she quietly called a cab and gave the driver the address of an upscale, late hours restaurant.

CHAPTER 5

Previously Raynar Company had been having trouble developing a new sensor that would make soundings deeper in the earth than what they had produced so far. Reading a trade journal, Ray Burnside became aware of parallel research being done by a firm in Washington State. Raynar was attempting to develop a system that would sense vibrations far down into the earth whereas Comstock was seeking a method of aerial sensing that would reach out farther into the sky. Ray Burnside wondered if the Comstock technology might adapt to underground sensing. In a flurry of phone calls and then a weekend of conferences involving four-man teams from each company at Titusville's Holiday Inn, the eight-man convention forged a cooperation agreement.

Marcus Comstock found himself living in temporary residence in a Houston motel for months. This motel was some six blocks from the Rolf Burnside residence.

The Comstock team worked well with Raynar's technicians. They made rapid progress and soon they had conducted some field tests where oil was known to exist. The sensor was getting "smarter" as various experiments occasionally proved successful. But success was neither instantaneous nor complete. Many field tests failed as the sensor falsely reported oil where there was none and then overlooked known deposits. But slowly improvements did develop through a lot of heated discussions and a lot of changes. Some experiments were thought to be looney but crazy enough they just might work. Lo and behold, some of them finally did.

On the last Friday in January, Raynar and Comstock engineers had worked until well after dark, and as the lights went out for the night, Marcus Comstock drove toward his motel resolved to sleep in Saturday morning. but he was not only fatigued, he was hungry. Half way between the Raynar buildings and the motel was a restaurant. The exterior displayed an upscale appearance and the high priced autos of the late evening diners promised a good if expensive supper. He pulled in and parked. Just ahead of him he noticed that a cab pulled up and a lone female passenger got out and entered the restaurant. She was apparently someone the staff knew and she was seated immediately.

Following the waiter to an area specially set for seating singles and doubles he saw the same person seated in a booth back to back with his. She was a striking woman of perhaps 25 years. Marcus was now forty, but he looked younger. He smiled as he passed her and she smiled back. A real beauty he thought, but strange that she would turn her head away slowly as he walked past.

The restaurant lighting was not bright but it was sufficient against the outside darkness as to produce a reflection of the left portion of that face mirrored in the window next to her. The ugly bruises she was trying to conceal reflected clearly.

After he placed his order, he left his seat and was now standing beside her. Never in his shy social life had he ever been so forward as he was in the next moment. "You must have taken quite a fall to do that," he blundered. And she lied in response, "no it was an auto accident." A few more

31

stilted comments were exchanged awkwardly and then conversation began to come easier. As each of them realized that the other had some connection with the Burnside family they ceased feeling like strangers and the small talk continued.

A waiter, struggling with a tray that held full meals for five patrons, suggested dryly that Marcus might want to get out of his way, and sit down so as to clear the narrow aisle. Later they surprised the waiter by dining together, and after that they left together, driving off in Marcus's rental auto.

CHAPTER 6

It took some time but the lawyers representing Raynar and Comstock finally negotiated a license agreement satisfactory to both sides, and the technical teams parted company. Marcus III went home, but without being very specific as to whether such trips were necessary, he was frequently finding reason to fly to Houston. Comstock men were uncertain what he was doing, but women in the office winked at each other and smiled. Declaring that he felt in need of a vacation, he took two weeks off and flew to Houston and thence to Galveston. He spent some happy and restful time fishing with the Cottrell men interspersed with trips to Houston.

One day toward the end of his stay he and Harry Cottrell were hoisting cold ones as the heat outside became surprisingly warm for late January.

In a serious moment Harry confronted Marcus directly. "you know young fella winter fishing is far better on your Olympic Peninsula where I went two years ago. It would be a lot closer there from Seattle than going to Galveston. There's no secret Marcus, everybody in our family, and I suspect some among the Burnsides too, know that you have been seeing Bonnie Gay."

"Guilty," Marcus admitted as he stared hard trying to see wisdom in the bottom of his empty glass. Harry continued,

"Bonnie loved that useless son-of-a-bitch, Rolf, with all her heart; so much so that she couldn't see what a rotter he was. He beat her up badly and I got wind of it. I confronted him and when he started making light of it I decked him telling if there was a next time I would beat him up a lot worse. That's the night you two met at the El Dorado Restaurant.

"Their marriage was a disaster from the git go. That niece of mine, was smart as a whip about almost everything, but not about that useless pup she married, Why she felt so attached to him and worse yet so dependent on him I don't know, but last fall she was shopping in Houston and ran into a guy she had gone to school with in high school; and would you believe it, this man is a marriage counselor, married and a family man. They went to a restaurant and sat for some time while Bonnie told him about Rolf's abuse. He made some suggestions and then when they parted company, Bonnie gave him a hug in gratitude for his support. Word of that got back to Rolf. He went crazy; he beat her up again; and that is the night she met you.

"By that time that paranoid S.O.B. was using his mother's money to have Bonnie tailed by a second rate private detective who was about as big a drunk as his client. He never spotted you two together, but Bonnie told me about you. Still hot on the trail of the marriage counselor, the detective genius lost the real trail. That's when Rolf confronted Bonnie on the street with a gun and thank the good Lord, that prowler car saw it and tough guy Rolf found himself looking down the barrels of two angry police guns.

"Well that did it; Bonnie was understandably hysterical. She called the family and I was there in a couple of hours. I took her to Galveston and Bonnie the lovable dimwit finally consented to filing for divorce with an immediate restraining order based on the Houston Police report. Bonnie moved out of the family home. We wanted her to come home but now she was working, and insisted on staying in Houston. Well that snake he knows where she works. Violating the order, he follows her home one night and rapes her out of damn meanness. The Rangers put out an all points bulletin, and Rolfy baby just disappeared.

"The divorce could then be granted on the basis of a default against Rolf. He was nowhere to be found. Unfortunately that rape did something that scum couldn't do before. Bonnie was obviously pregnant. The court did not want to finalize the divorce until the child was born so it could make a proper order against Rolf concerning support which is a laugh because he won't pay it anyway."

Marcus had long since finished his drink and he was hanging his head saying "God, it looks like I caused this." Harry responded, "no, he was still blaming his troubles on the marriage counselor the last we heard. Marcus, everyone in the family knows about you. We feel our girl finally figured out how to pick a male that is also a man, but both of you are going to have to be careful. We finally located that marriage counselor by pulling some strings with the licensing department. He holds his conference with Bonnie in confidence, will not even admit he saw her, but speaking in a "for instance" mode, he described a theoretical man who has a set of loose screws in his head that would be a ringer for Rolf. He looked awful grave as he warned us. A guy *like* Rolf can go clear off the deep end. If his cowardly anger builds up too much he can do deadly damage to you two or even any child of his which you might take into a new household, do you know what I mean?"

"Yes I do Harry, what have I gotten us all into?'

"You didn't get us *into* anything Marcus, the damage was already done. She would have dumped him even if she hadn't met you."

All of this left Marcus in a gloomy mood, but it didn't last, the fishing was spare but the family was a delight; and the whole trip was capped off by Bonnie Gay's delivery of a daughter.

When Cheryl was born Barney, Madeline and Uncle Harry and Ray Burnside were delighted. Harry's wife aunt, Sue Cottrell, was a naturalized citizen who had been born in China. When she beheld the newborn, Cheryl, she hoisted her out of Bonnie Gay's embrace, held her high in the air and ceremoniously recited "Cheryl the Cherry Blossom. Our new queen, long may you reign!" Cherry Blossom became a nickname used by some family members and even close friends.

Marcus and Bonnie Gay were married within days of the divorce decree. There were some whispers among acquaintances about who Cheryl's real father was, but the newly weds knew what that answer had to be. Bonnie Gay's had always loved to tease and it was agreed, they never made any serious effort to convince their world about the biological truth.

Whatever gift one of these grand parental folks, Cottrells and Comstocks, would give Cheryl, the others tried to do it one better; and this continued even after Cheryl was living far away in Washington State. On her tenth birthday, Grand Aunt Sue gave Cherry Blossom a solid gold bracelet that was adjustable in size so that she could continue to wear it on into adulthood. It was crafted by a New York Jeweler and just happened to be set with several rubies and emeralds that Sue had spirited out of Communist China in her parents' successful escape to Taiwan. Bonnie Gay demanded possession of the bracelet. A local expert appraised it at $22,500.00. The standing order was she would not wear it except on special family occasions and never, never to school. Well . . . sure.

For years things went well for Comstocks, Cottrells and even for Burnsides as to all except Mrs. Burnside Sr. She wept over Rolf's absence but she also bragged about his successes over seas as she repeated his preposterous stories of spectacular financial killings that he was always just about to close. For all that nobody knew where he was, Rolf had employed an intermediary who could get word to and from mother. Soon mother was a bit happier forwarding money to an undisclosed charity.

Harry Cottrell formed his own conclusion. At Cheryl's Christening he told Marcus "I feel sorry for old man Burnside. That Donna is something out of the slums of Hell. How she delivered those twins to their family is a genetic miracle. It wasn't until that useless pup, Rolf, was born that she succeeded in giving birth to her own kind. I don't know how Ray ever came to marry that drunken slut but it must have been the wildest engagement party of all time."

Because of his total abdication of child support responsibility, Rolf Burnside was ultimately declared a fugitive under a warrant issued by the Texas divorce court system. Bonnie was content just to have Rolf out of her life. Marcus's father brought down the house proclaiming in a loud voice that he was making a toast to his new daughter-in-law thanking her dearly for getting his irresponsible son married off before he turned 42.

In due time, Marcus successfully petitioned in Washington State for the adoption of Cheryl. Donna

Burnside had said that she would disown any child born to Bonnie Gay and hence she was not told about adoption.

Marcus smiled as he recalled the events of those days now more than 13 years past, and then he was back to a present reality as the floor supervisor opened his office door.

CHAPTER 7

No one in the Burnside family knew where Rolf was and most who knew him would just as soon have it stay that way. Comstock was prospering in part from Raynar royalties. Bonnie Gay and Marcus III were happy but bewildered parents trying to understand their dynamic and sometimes rebellious daughter.

But Rolf's presence was being felt by others primarily in California. Banks in small towns all up and down California's thousand mile length were struck by an ongoing series of one man bank robberies. Surveillance cameras revealed dozens of different faces which clerks said were disguises, but the mode was pretty much the same in each heist. The assailant would enter a bank lobby and look around. If a security officer was on duty he would walk boldly up to him and, professing to be a stranger in town, would ask a question about the location of some nearby business (which he had already chosen) and ask for directions. Hence his departure from the guarded bank would occur without arousing suspicion. Not many of the banks he chose employed security guards anyway.

The disguised bandit would walk up to a teller cage with paper in his hand as though to make a deposit and then quietly thrust a pistol into the face of the then terrified teller. In a voice no louder than a whisper he would direct that the teller empty his or her cash drawer, and then he would do the same with any teller in a cage on either side of his initial victim. He never asked for more cash than they had. He would not risk the time and notoriety in robbing the whole bank. He would trade large "takes" for speed and sometimes the whole event happened without other persons in the bank being aware until he had left. Tellers were told he would turn and shoot at them if they made a sound until he left the lobby. It worked, every time. The robber would never pull two jobs in one local area. Individual incidents were plotted by the FBI, and the pattern appeared to be totally random. There was no effective way of tracking this guy.

As the months passed there would be several robberies in a week or so and then there would be a lapse of a month or so and then the sequence started all over again and it went on for years. The takes were small but many and when each incident was added to the total being kept by the Bureau, it rose to $400,213.00. But then there was an incident that seemed to end it all.

It was a robbery that fit the pattern and the robber made his get away as usual. He was driving down a residential street when a UPS driver made a driving error pulling out in front of the fleeing car, and causing was a minor fender bender type crash wherein neither vehicle was disabled. The UPS driver exited his vehicle hesitantly knowing he and his hurried schedule were the cause, but to his amazement, the victim driver pulled back and went around the brown truck with rear wheels shrieking in response to full engine power. The UPS driver did get a good look at the fleeing auto operator, but the damage to UPS truck was small, the delivery man chose not to report it to his employer and nothing more came of it.

However when the collision occurred, there was another witness. She saw an unmasked face and because of his strange behavior in abruptly driving away, she strained to get a good look. She had the sense that something else was involved here. She would try to remember.

After this close call Rolf withdrew from the area and committed no more robberies. He stashed the money in safety deposit boxes using different banks in small cities and towns up and down the Pacific coast. The names listed on bank records for the various boxes were the likes of Robert Salazar, Jim Matthews, Jack Hawthorne and more.

In the months that followed, he was busy almost every day. He took flying lessons and purchased a used, but still airworthy 1946 model, Noorduyn Norseman aircraft. It was old but well maintained. It had the load bearing capacity and the performance characteristics that would be needed in the escapade that was now forming in his twisted mind. Once he had accumulated some experience flying the old aircraft, he sought out and practiced many landings on dirt and gravel runways. He was quivering with fear on the first couple of landings, but after a lot of practice, he became quite skilled and then was satisfied that he was ready. The Canadian built Norseman was designed for use on unimproved landing strips and even dry river beds in Canada and Alaska. It should work well in the wheat stubble of eastern Washington State.

CHAPTER 8

For decades Oxford and Minnie Bowman and their daughter Jubilee were the only black residents of Titusville. The Titusville community was by no means free of prejudice, but Bowmans were well accepted by most residents. Mr. Bowman was known to friends as "Ox, the big and gentle man." To a stranger, hearing him speak for the first time seemed odd. The voice did not seem to match his tall and muscular form. He spoke just above a whisper. Years earlier, the mean, ignorant, Randy Murdoch, and his gang left a permanent mark. The 22 caliber pistol shot that struck Ox's throat during their infamous holdup of his service station permanently damaged his vocal cords.

Daughter Jubilee won a scholarship to attend Columbia University and in response to a dare by her dormitory roommate she tried out as a model. She fit the part perfectly. Matriculating into the world of runways and photo shoots, she put college on permanent hold. However her rise to success required that she spend more and more time in New York, and eventually she would get home only at Christmas time.

Her parents were sad to see her so little, but they were proud of her achievements. Minnie would show off her picture as it appeared in and sometimes on the front of fashion magazines. Now Ox and Minnie were a family of two.

Ox sold the station and its now precious lot of commercial real estate for $1,000,000.00. Ox had always been frugal and neither he nor Minnie indulged in luxuries so that with the sale price of the station carefully invested along with life savings, they could comfortably retire. However, Ox was never comfortable with inactivity. He rewired, replumbed and repainted the Bowman house until he could find no more such tasks to occupy his time. He was active in church and in his Kiwanis club and he was still bored.

But then, quite by chance, he was confronted with a challenge that would stimulate him as nothing else had. He volunteered to be a mentor for middle and high school students, and there he became acquainted with Harold Jacobs. All the teachers, prior mentors and juvenile court officials to whom Harold was known had written him off as incurable, headed for a life in and out of jail, but nobody told Ox. By age 13 Jacobs was well known to the Juvenile Court judges in King County. Truancy, petty theft and acts of malicious mischief had him constantly in legal hot water. School testing revealed him to be bright and academically capable, but none of that was reflected in his grades or deportment.

Background could have something to do with it. His parents were likeable, shiftless drunks who discharged the duties of parenthood with a philosophy of free choice and total permissiveness. When Harold lived at home, he was totally on his own. Subsequent court orders deprived the parents of custody. Adoptive parents came on the scene and they were making good progress with Harold up until the night they were killed by a drunk driver. Harold crawled out of the wreck unscathed but believing that he was destined to go through life as a discard. He ended up in Seattle and found himself accepting food and shelter from the Union Gospel Mission. A new set of foster parents living in Titusville volunteered to take charge of Harold, but he was more than they could handle without assistance and that brought him to the local mentor program where he met Ox.

Harold had long since found that hostility was a usable defense. On this first meeting he contemplated the tall but somewhat stooped black man with an air of contempt concluding that this old duffer could be buffaloed. "So what are you going to do for me nigger?" Harold would later recall the next second or two as a blur and in a move so swift he couldn't describe how Ox did it, he found himself upside down with Ox holding him in mid air by his ankles. This exhibition of strength and agility left Jacobs astonished and speechless.

"What am I going to do you ask. Well I will teach you some manners to begin with," was Ox's simple reply. Harold cried out "hey, you're not supposed to spank me, it's against the law!" "I'm. not, young pup, I just want you to see clearly and since you don't see clearly when you are upright, let's try upside down." Just to emphasize his control of the situation Ox shook his inverted charge like he was an empty sack.

Harold was "street smart" enough to suddenly realize several things: Ox had grey hair, a stooped posture and a squeaky voice but he was every inch an adult who was going to demand no less than respect and obedience. Ox put Harold down on his feet, and with that his mentoring program was underway, and it was destined to last far longer than such programs usually do. No one could say that Ox's response to Harold's hostility was clinically correct or that inverting his body would help in the boy's rehabilitation. Surely the experts would be horrified to know that to some degree he manhandled the youngster and some would seriously suggest that criminal charges should be filed against the man, but Harold would never mention this meeting until well after he was a grown man. In an instant, he was seeing things more clearly after all. Ox's parental instincts were dead on, and in the years that followed the bond between them grew. Grudging respect evolved into admiration and then into a bond of ever-increasing love and mutual endearment.

It was not long before Ox, without consulting Minnie, offered the Bowman home for a foster parent relationship. Despite Minnie's pessimistic predictions, "he'll murder us in our bed," Ox took parental charge of the boy. Ox was no dreamer. He went to school authorities and told them in no uncertain terms that he wanted a call every time Harold rebelled, declaring that each school punishment would be supplemented at home. Ox didn't mention to the teachers that he had already told Harold, "boy, you give them teachers any trouble or any lip and I'm sure enough going to whump you good, understand?"

Fostering kids can be a heartbreak, but Ox's instincts were correct. This boy was made of better stuff and under Ox's loving care and wisdom he slowly evolved scholastically and socially. A black family raising a white kid might have seemed strange to some, but in this case, as the years passed, a family relationship solidified. Six months after Harold was moved into the Bowman house, Jubilee managed to get home intending to give her father's living project an intensely critical once over, but it did not quite work out that way.

The instant they met these two rebellious souls began to take a liking to each other. Jubilee was already old enough to be a mother herself and she told her parents that down deep there might be something good in this kid if they could just reach through the anger, however she was doubtful at first that this would ever happen. Ox smiled at Jubilee and said, "just give me time daughter, just give me time." By Christmas Harold and his big sister began to form an attachment for each other that grew steadily and would last a lifetime. The parents did have a little trouble with the somewhat crude mutual expressions of sibling affection that they developed. Each time the two met they would begin with a warm loving embrace and then inquiring as to how things were with each other they would continue their greetings with him calling her his chocolate sister and she referring to him as her white trash, honkey brother.

Eventually Harold Jacobs became an honor student at Titusville High School. Teachers and juvenile workers who had known Harold in his pre teen years could hardly believe the change. The summer after high school graduation Ox introduced young Harold to his first ever experience in carpentry. Ox had planned for some time that whenever the boy seemed sufficiently grown to then build a summer cabin on the property he owned in the upper Teanaway River country. Without telling Minnie, Ox took up an offer appearing in the classified ads section of the Seattle Times to purchase a cabin site located, as Minnie put it, "at the end of a God forsaken dusty road a hundred miles from nowhere." Actually, it was nestled in a thick grove of trees on a bluff overlooking De Roux Creek near where it emptied into the Teanaway River.

Minnie did grow to like the cabin, but not as much as did man and boy. It was not a very ambitious building measuring scarcely 18 X 24 feet; but that was enough so that Harold Jacobs would experience all the principal phases of building a wooden structure. Harold started with the dirty and dusty shovel work left after the hired back hoe contractor had created most of the excavation. Then Ox introduced him to building simple wall forms and using a transit type level. Later concrete was poured and Harold saw how to set the wooden plates on the freshly poured walls so that they were absolutely level. Once the concrete had set enough that the plates would remain level, the wooden part of the structure could begin.

It took all one summer and most of another before they could occupy it as a dwelling. In seasons that would follow a bathroom, a woodshed, a gravity water system, an oil-fired stove and gaslights were added. From the beginning of this project, Ox and Harold were concerned about incidents of thievery and vandalism that occurred at cabin sites nearby. For their own privacy and a hope of obscuring the building from thieves and vandals, they parked vehicles on the dirt roadway and allowed what would have become a driveway to be grown over with brush. In the mountains at 2500 feet and higher that is a slow process, but in about a decade the cabin became obscured from the roadway. Dental School Student Harold and his adoptive father were working in a project together, and neither was ever happier.

In the ensuing years, Harold Jacobs met and married Carla Shoemaker. In due time there were two Jacobs offspring enjoying the cabin as much as their parents.

Not all was happiness however. Minnie was not aging as well as the robust Oxford. She was eventually overcome by a persistent cancer and died with loving husband, daughter and acquired son and daughter-in-law at her bedside.

Ox could not deal with the many fond memories of nearly half a century with Minnie in their Titusville home. She loved their house and she kept it in immaculate condition. Now that she was gone every room reminded Ox of her presence. She always hummed or whistled as she busied herself with the household chores. By time the snow was beginning to melt in the Cascade hills, Ox could endure it no longer and he spent the entire late spring, summer and early fall holed up in the rustic cabin. He spent endless hours sitting on the porch of the cabin staring into space reminiscing and remembering. Knowing that he would depress himself all the more if he just sat there endlessly, he alternately hiked the mountain trails sometimes being gone from the cabin for 2 and 3 days at a time.

When he would tire of hiking, he made trips to and from Roslyn and Cle Elum to purchase lumber, nails and paint upgrading the cabin to what would nearly pass as a full time home. The mountain retreat was helping him get over his grief and so he decided to spend the whole winter. Knowing that he would be snowbound much of the time he begin laying in stores of firewood, fuel oil, propane gas and a food supply that he estimated would carry him through until the spring melt. He bought canned fruit and vegetables by the case. He stored rice and oatmeal and grits in five gallon tins with secure lids to preserve them from foraging rodents and insects. He buried the waterline much deeper than it had been to resist the winter freeze. The loft held three heavy down sleeping bags and spare blankets. He was set to winter it out.

But it was not to be. One rainy day Harold arrived unannounced and after initial greetings, he began to press Ox about why the changes in the building. Why were the pantry and the back of the sleeping loft full of canned goods, not by the can but by the case? As he pried the answers slowly, Harold began to grasp what Ox was planning to do. Wisely however, Harold Jacobs did not explode with incredulity as he was tempted to do, but rather he sat down at the table and began nursing the hot coffee that Ox had prepared on his arrival.

Slowly Harold began to reminisce about Minnie, and how he, Harold, missed her. He went on about how she had been the mother he never had before. He laughed and got Ox to laugh about the suspicions Minnie held about the juvenile delinquent they were taking into their home. He praised the example both she and Ox had set for him. He concluded saying that he had been busy with his practice. He was so busy, it was easier not to go back to the Bowman house to visit with Ox, but also allowed that there were a lot of memories of her in the home that he just didn't want to face.

Harold probably talked for twenty minutes without interruption, looking intently at Ox as he spoke. Ox in turn looked down at his coffee mug listening and saying nothing. As Harold finished he put his hand on Ox's shoulder, and, it worked. Ox looked up, in tears and then sobbed in a final flushing of grief from his system. Nothing more had to be said. The frenzied preparation for the winter stay had fulfilled its purpose. Ox did not have to think about his grief while all that winter preparation went on save sometimes as he went to sleep when the sorrow would still torment him. Now the memories were sweetened with time and they would torment him no longer. Now he could go back to the family home and take up his life there. Minnie's ghost would no longer be present at every turn. Now she was a beautiful sweet memory and life would go on.

A year went by. Another summer was marked by mutual enjoyment of the cabin by the Jacobs and their growing children on weekends while Ox stayed on for days at a time. And then, once again it was late September and the long warm days began to shorten, and soon they would be closing again. The toilet and the hot water tank were drained, the drain traps filled with antifreeze, and the waterline was diverted from the cabin and allowed to run free into the creek below. Then they closed up, shuttered the lower windows and drove away. The season was over. Each of them assumed the other had bolted the bathroom window, but in fact neither of them attended to that detail

CHAPTER 9

September storms had been nature's bluff. For now, the weather was still good this balmy first week of October. However, Harold and Carla would be out of the country until November and it was agreed that Ox would not return to the cabin alone until the snow melted out next spring.

Minnie was gone and Ox, still vigorous and in good health, was now spending some time with a silver haired widow of some 70 years, named Vivian Turner. She had been married to a highly respected black surgeon who died eighteen months before. A New York clothing stylist named Jubilee Bowman Hazelton, had introduced her to Ox. She was the classic rich widow and a merry one at that. After meeting Ox she decided she had had enough of New York and with a son living in Seattle, decided to assume a more subdued life style in the Northwest. Among those who saw them together it was clear that the fire was hotter than simple Ox realized. Notwithstanding Ox's proclamation that this was just a fling between two old people, it was apparent that she had Ox square in her sights. Dr. and Mrs. Harold Jacobs were delighted.

Harold and Carla had signed up as volunteers to work in a refugee aid dental project treating poverty stricken people in need of dental repair in a Malaysian village They would depart in early October. Vivian had been scheming with them and now as the Jacobs were preparing to leave, they also had plans for Oxford Bowman.

The Jacobs invited Ox and his girlfriend in for dinner. As the foursome indulged in a small after dinner brandy, Vivian thoroughly upset Ox's tranquil reserve with a proposal that she and he join forces and sign up as a couple on a world cruise scheduled to depart from Liverpool, England in ten days. The tour proposed an extensive itinerary. There would be the flight from Seattle-Tacoma International over the great circle route to London Heathrow, a train ride to the Liverpool dock, thence down the coast and across the channel and continuing into the Mediterranean. There would be a number of ports of call along both the north and south shores on the Mediterranean, through the Suez Canal, thence down the east coast of Africa to Capetown and thence successive flights to Rio, Houston and home. It would take eight weeks. Total cost $13,500.00 per person.

Ox could afford the trip, but he didn't see it that way. Harold and Carla embraced the whole idea and immediately assumed to induce Ox to go along. It would be difficult; Ox could be stubborn. He was adamant that he would not accept Vivian's charity. He did admit that for him it would be a new and wholly exciting experience and he went on at some length as to how it would be a great experience for Vivian, but simply more than he could afford. Meantime the Jacobs couple were whispering back and forth in what could have been criticized as unmannerly to their guests, but it only lasted a moment or two.

For a moment more, all four people were silent. Then Carla was up and out of the room, returning with a checkbook in hand. Now Harold was scribbling as Carla watched. When he finished, he glanced silently at Carla looking for her approval. She nodded and smiled.

"Here, Ox, is fifteen grand. That ought to cover most of it." Oxford Bowman reared back in his chair exploding, "what do you think you're doing boy?"

"I'm underwriting the tour Ox."

"You're gonna do no such a damn thing young pup, I'm not rich but I don't need charity. I will do just very well if I don't go on any fancy tour. Who would I think I was, Warren Buffet or Bill Gates maybe?"

"Hush up and take the check," Carla grinned.

"Don't you smart off to me young mother, or I may have to take both of you two to the woodshed and teach you some manners."

Vivian was now silent watching the other three go at each other in a family argument where she wisely elected not to intervene. She was a little astonished at the hostile nature of threats exchanged. She was unaware that such threatening banter between father and son had been normal and usually meaningless since man and boy first confronted each other.

"Ox you are the only father I really ever knew. Don't you remember when I was 13? I was well on the way to a permanent residence in a State penitentiary. You, you kindly, lovable old grump, you saved my life. Everything I am or ever hope to be stems back to the selfless patient years that you, Minnie and my big sister, Jubilee, spent straightening me out. I have been thinking about something like this for several years and Carla and I have talked a lot about how I might make some gift that expresses my undying gratitude to you."

Ox was now hanging his head more to hide tears that he knew were coming. "What you just said to me would have been thanks enough" Ox replied in a now very subdued voice.

"Bag it Ox. If you had told that thirteen year old punk you took in out of juvenile court that he was going to gross nearly One hundred ninety thousand in one year he would have sneered in your face. You're responsible for a lot more than just keeping me out of the jailhouse."

Vivian now moved closer to Ox with a hand on one of his as Carla spoke up, "and I love you too you mean old man." Placing her arm around Harold, she added "you raised a wonderful man because that's what you are too. We are forever grateful to you Oxford Bowman, now take that check before I stuff it in your ear or elsewhere. It's thanks from both of us. You are Harold's father and you are my lovable father-in-law."

Ox was totally stunned. All his defenses had been shot down, and his eyes flooded and what little voice he had left him as he embraced both Carla and Harold together. Vivian beamed.

So, on the morning of October 4, Vivian's son drove his van to the Bowman house and then to his mother's place. With luggage loaded they were delivered to the passenger drop off at Sea-Tac airport to check in with tickets on British Overseas Airways that Vivian had purchased more than four months earlier without once consulting Ox. The Jacobs finished packing and departed the following day.

CHAPTER 10

On the same morning, FBI agent, Roger Caldwell looked up from his desk to see the British Overseas Airways Boeing 747 climbing over the city as it departed the Seattle-Tacoma terminal. A rain storm was slowly obscuring the view of marine traffic on Seattle's Elliot Bay. The Seattle office had not dealt with a big case for several weeks, and he was glad of it. He had had his share of bad and dangerous people and would be happy to end his career during a period of quiet routine with minor cases. He had given his notice to the Bureau that he would retire effective December 31.

Earlier the same day Titusville chief of police Harley Miller was in his office. He was waiting for two people. Harley was the son of Betty Francis Miller who had been chief during the 80's. It was unique, a son following his mother in a public office, but Titusville prided itself in being ahead of the trends in culture and government, and Harley's confirmation by the city council had been heralded with civic pride. It was the first either father and son or mother and son promotion to the same office as anyone could remember.

Miller had requested that an old friend, retired police lieutenant Frank Hart, meet with him at his office and then for lunch. Rodney Griswold had recently graduated from the academy and was hired on as a rookie patrolman and although in his first few days on duty he had made a few dumb mistakes, Miller had a sense that Griswold had the makings of a good officer, but he had a tendency for impatience and making snap judgments. The instructors at the academy made note of it, and now his performance on the force caused the chief concern that he would make some mistake out of haste to embarrass himself and the department.

The chief's mother had been a great admirer of Hart. It was at her suggestion that when new rookies hired on that he then share Frank Hart's story with them. The career of Frank Hart was a classic study of patience and persistence. Hart, after being accused of killing a thirteen year old juvenile without cause, had fought to clear his name in the infamous Randy Murdoch case. It had taken him over a decade. Miller's point was to impress on the young and impatient Griswold that good law enforcement has to include a measure of patience, critical analysis and on-going effort especially with cases that seem hopeless or insoluble. Now the conference was over, Griswold was out on patrol and Frank Hart was saying that he would guess that the young rookie had taken the lesson to heart

Bonnie Gay Comstock was standing in the living room looking out at the same unsettled weather hoping it might clear before she set out on her Monday chores. She also was admiring the clean-up and restoration the landscapers had done. It was now just a year since she and Marcus had decided to purchase the old mansion out of the Maude Hellgraves estate. At her death, years before, Maude left no spouse or direct descendents. Her will specified that the house and grounds were left to several cousins as co-owners. They immediately fell to arguing themselves and never agreed on what to do with the place except to rent it to a series of tenants allowing it to slowly deteriorate.

In the twilight of their years, the cousins decided that they wanted to sell the mansion and Marcus Comstock III was the right prospect on the scene at the right time, and he had the considerable resources necessary to restore what time and neglect had damaged. To restore the old palace to a livable condition required all new plumbing, electrical wiring plus a new heating plant, new paint and new roof. It took twelve months with men on the job virtually every day. The overall cost of the renovation would have purchased a house almost as big. However, once completely renovated the Hellgraves mansion was a rich display of the best building materials money could buy and the décor that was a page out of the pre income tax era. There was the wide, curving staircase, several crystal chandeliers, high ceilings, lush, upscale carpets, wall tapestries, you name it was probably there somewhere. The cost was staggering but Bonnie Gay knew in her heart that until she and her husband were old and decrepit, this would be their home.

Now she was momentarily frustrated. She thought her keys were on the table in the kitchen and when that proved untrue her mind went blank as to where they were. Hazel Phong was in the living room beginning her weekly housecleaning chores. She could hear Bonnie chastising herself about losing the car keys. "In the window sill above the desk" Hazel called. Bonnie chose to berate herself a bit more. "Damn! I drop these keys two feet away from where I usually put them and then I can't see them, I must be going senile." "Maybe you're just very busy," Hazel laughed. "Gotta go Hazel, my dental is at 10:00 and I have to drop Cheryl's old clothes off at the Clothes Bank. She grows so fast it seems like she is out of outfits before they are even half worn out." "A lot of people need those things," Hazel reminded, and Bonnie of course knew she was right. Hazel herself was a refugee in her early years and had experienced enough poverty to sympathize with Americans that had fallen on hard times.

Hazel herself knew she was most fortunate. Born an Amerasian she had the rare good fortune of having an American officer father who knew of her existence and assumed his own responsibility. She had been born into a loyalist family, and when Saigon was under final siege by the North, they would have been executed. She was literally scooped up as a member of a group that managed an escape into Thailand. Her dirty clothes bag and personal possessions included a letter in English her father had penned just as the American evacuation was in process. It would be six years with a Thai family, schooling in a Thai parochial school and ultimately another letter with instructions and an airline ticket that saw her in the United States.

Hazel finished schooling in the Titusville system years before and now ran her own successful cleaning service. Bonnie had used her even before moving into the Hellgraves mansion.

"By the way Hazel, Cheryl may come home at noon. She said there was talk about this being only half a day in school. Classes will be moving into the high school portables because of that discovery of asbestos in a closet that made such a hullabaloo in the papers. At least that's what she told me when she talked me into allowing her to wear old, raggedy clothes. Honestly Hazel, sometimes I don't know whether I am raising that kid or she is raising me. I end up giving into her more times than I like to admit." Hazel responded saying "Well I think mother's can try to rope in their children for fear they lose control altogether. She is going to grow up and she will have to be let grow more and more independent. She'll make mistakes, we all do. She is outstanding in school, Bonnie, and you should be pleased at that. Her father certainly is." "I know, Hazel, ever since we were married, Marcus could not wait to adopt her. They grow closer every day and she and he are thick as thieves when I oppose something she wants to do; whatever hair-brained adventure it is, her father talks down my resistance toward it.

"Ever since she began spending a summer month at her great uncle's ranch she is a total tom boy. As a southerner, I may worry about it too much but there are days when I swear I am raising a Huckleberry Finn instead of a lady. The ranch hands taught her to milk and feed stock and clean out a barn, to make a bon fire, to shoot a shot gun and a .22 rifle. My God she even helped out killing and cleaning fryer chickens and rabbits for market. She's a total tom boy."

Hazel laughed "You just wait, she's good looking and in a little while she will notice the boys because the boys will be paying attention to her," and then she laughed, "you will have a whole new set of things to worry about." "Hazel, you always side with that man and that kid of mine. I should can your ass and hire some housemaid that just answers yes ma'm and no ma'm." Hazel responded with a blank Asian stare and then slowly shook her head in the negative. "No you won't" she answered defiantly, "we're stuck with each other" and with that, both women burst out laughing.

"As I said, Cheryl may be home at noon so when you make lunch for yourself you may need to prepare something for her but make her help," and with that Bonnie was out the door in pursuit of her morning tasks; dentist, clothes bank, lunch with Marcus and a subsequent meeting of the arts commission. And finally there would be golf in the afternoon. She estimated she would be home about 4:30. On October 6, life was busy and happy in the Marcus and Bonnie Gay household.

CHAPTER 11

Arnie had suggested the location for the hideout or camp as Rolf called it. But Rolf was adamant that every miniscule detail of the plan had to pass his critical inspection. Although he was in terrible physical shape, Rolf had walked the entire roadway expressing doubts that a 28 foot house trailer could be towed that far without beating it to pieces, but now that house trailer was in place and camouflaged to near invisibility. Just to be sure that it could not be seen from any conceivable location within eyesight, he had huffed and puffed all around nearby Gallagher Lake, Gallagher Peak and Hawkins Mountain. At one time he was within 100 feet of a small hole on the slope of Hawkins but he did not see it

"Arnie do you have any money or have you let Grunt win it all?" "No," Arnie grinned, "you gave me a hundred bucks. I bought about $35.00 worth of additional groceries that Grunt asked for and I've still got the rest." "OK you work with Grunt and get yourself a lunch or a supper whatever you want to call it. You load Bart's pickup and go up to the camp today alone; it's going to be dark by time you get back Is the truck ready to make the trip?" "No problem, boss, some of the bunkers that the Forest Service put across the road are a little tricky to get over, but it's no worse than it has been, and I can do it again. Boy I sure would be glad to have Grunt with me so I don't gotta fix my own dinner either!" "So suffer." the Boss responded. And Grunt grinned. Bart was the only person that he felt absolute loyalty to and Arnie's plight seemed funny to his childlike mind.

Arnie was headed out by 1:30 PM with the Monday load, and with the extended light of summer, he returned just before total darkness. As evening drew on, the loading of the second segment of supplies began and was about half done when Rolf called a halt for the day. As a result, the tension let up a few hours.

Bart queried, "What's next, Boss?" Rolf was a bit exasperated by the question and he sighed with impatience but then he answered, "Just as we have planned, Bart, Arnie will make it a double trip tomorrow. He should be able to be back here the second time just about dark. Incidentally, Bart, if you want those two mutts of yours to go along, tell Arnie they better go up on his last trip. And by the way, Arnie, regarding that money, as you come back through North Bend the second time tomorrow you gas the Dodge full up, OK?'

Arnie responded, "got it Boss."

"In the meantime, you and I, Bart, are going to Seatac Airport to get the rental. That should not take more than two hours total. We abandon our old car in the Seatac parking lot and drive the rental back. That will leave us with all our supplies up there at camp and ready to roll from here Wednesday morning."

Shortly after full dark, Burnside centered his attention on Bart concerning the details of some electronic and radio equipment which neither Grunt nor Arnie understood. They were content that Bart said it would all work exactly as planned. Arnie, however, used this diversion of Burnside's attention to ease back out to the pickup with one last corrugated paper box which he placed toward the front of the truck bed and carefully covered with other objects before drawing a tarp over the whole of the load. Arnie knew he would be driving tomorrow's first load, so this was the time. This particular box had its contents wrapped in several bath towels appropriated from those supplied by the landlord, but if one shook it hard enough, there was a muffled sloshing sound.

"Bart, tomorrow you'll get your good clothes on as we talked about before, tie and all and for cripe sakes shave. You don't look like an out-of-state business man, you look like a bear"

The foreshortened schedule and the earnestness of Burnsides presentation was now raising the level of excitement by leaps and bounds. Again the criminal psyche was plain to see. None of the participants gave much thought to the dire consequences that would befall all of them if the plan failed. The specter of long prison sentences or even the executioner needle did not rise to the surface of their excited states of mind. They were more like a football team the night before the big game, primed and almost ready as October 6 came to a close.

On Tuesday, October 7, the plan went as the boss directed. It took a while to load the large Dodge pickup, but everyone seemed eager to help. They were all willing, driven by the accelerating tempo as zero hour was now just hours away.

On the last trip Arnie again was alone but this time the pets, Yelper and Boomer were in the front seat on the passenger side. Yelper was watching the road go by and apparently finding that very entertaining. Boomer remained on the warm floor boards curled up and sound asleep for the whole trip. Traveling east on I-90 the big truck made its way from the North Bend interchange to a county road called "Bullfrog Road". He took the Bullfrog exit and went up and over the freeway north easterly past the entryway to Suncadia, the new, 7000 acre upscale multi-golf course, recreation and summer home area. Beyond there he came to a roundabout intersection and from there went north through Roslyn, Ronald and past the seven miles of Lake Cle Elum's easterly shoreline.

The pavement stopped at the entrance to a Forest Service campground, Salmon La Sac, and he continued up a dirt traverse signed as Road 4330. It was made up of about 50% drivable dirt grade and 50% of seemingly endless pot holes and washboards. With the first few bangs and bumps through an early sequence of pot holes, Boomer stirred and shifted his position, but he showed no alarm. He had ridden many times on diverse off road journeys with his master.

From Salmon La Sac onward, Yelper was an intense observer, whimpering from time to time to express excitement and interest. From prior trips, he knew that such terrain would be populated with rabbits, raccoons, skunks and red squirrels all of whom God had created for hounds to chase.

The usual Fall rains had yet to get serious, at least not on the east side of the mountains; and so the road was dry and dusty. As some of the dust worked its way through the cab Yelper sniffed and shook his head, and Boomer hissed and then yowled in disapproval. But there was little relief for a while as the road got worse. Finally Arnie turned right off of 4330 onto a winding, twisting passage, which more or less followed Fortune Creek easterly into the mountains to its several origins. It was called a road for lack of a better term.

It could be described as little more than a wide hiking trail. This was four wheel drive road with steep grades and wash outs gouged across its grade by spring snow melt. In several places high mounds of dirt had been placed across the road barring all but hikers and all but the most high centered four wheel vehicles. Arnie and Bart had driven this route a number of times in making preparations for what was to come. A number of obstacles had been rolled, winched or chopped out of the way, and this time the traverse was going faster than a man could run.

A short distance uphill from 4330, access on up this nameless side road was barred by a yellow steel gate locked and apparently secure. In the winter, snowmobile drivers would navigate around it on the trail that was groomed for their use, but now there was no snow and the gate was a bar to most vehicle travel. The gate was chained to a yellow post driven deep into the hard mountain soil. Arnie stopped and with a little exertion lifted the post up in the air. Then, holding the post in his arms, he walked in the quarter circle described by the gate as it swung opening the roadway. Weeks before, when there was only the faint light of pre sunrise he had driven in here and had used his burning torch to cut the post just below ground level. Pounding a smaller steel pipe into the portion of the yellow post still in the ground, placing the upper portion down over the smaller pipe, replacing the dirt back to its original level and repainting so much of the post as his torch had scorched, he had the gate so it could be opened without the key although it appeared securely locked.

Arnie followed the trail easterly almost three miles to where several small forks of the creek come together to form its main drainage. He then crossed the creek and continued on southerly another almost equal distance. He then crossed the South Fork of Fortune Creek and entered a patch of dense woods. This was the camp where the gang would make their headquarters. It was fully concealed to all except someone who might push through the thick brush and stumble on to it.

The camp consisted of several tents and a rickety, mold-encrusted old 28 foot house trailer of perhaps late 1950's vintage. Years earlier, Arnie had purchased it from an elderly widow for one hundred dollars. Getting the old relic some 6 miles over the vehicular Hell that it had to travel, demonstrated just how skilled Arnie and Bart were at off-roading. They had mired or ditched four wheel rigs many times before and that held no fear for either of them. With a fine touch of the throttle and what Chicago gangsters used to refer to as good driving hands, they could negotiate the worst of roads. Using the winch mounted on the front of the Dodge they could continue when there was no road at all. They were never stuck for very long.

The brush was very thick. Bart, Arnie and Grunt had spent a day cutting an internal clearing which made room for all portions of the camp. They had been careful to retain higher limbs of the surrounding trees so as to leave a canopy. The camp was invisible from the air. Arnie's smaller, but more nimble four wheel rig was parked under a nearby tree. He had suffered a broken driveline coming in and the plan was to simply abandon it where it stood.

Arnie worked until he was perspiring profusely in the unseasonably warm fall weather. He unloaded the truck bed placing all items about in the manner that the boss had told him to. Yelper, for all that he was interested in this wild place full of animal scents, was somehow inclined to simply watch with wonderment as Arnie walked rapidly back and forth with the various boxes, sacks and even some barrels of stores.

Finally Arnie picked up Boomer and threw him into the old house trailer and closed the door. Then he called for Yelper and the dog came obediently to him whereupon he picked the animal up and threw him in the old hovel also. He had already filled their water and food dishes, placed a sandbox and, lastly and most importantly had ditched the gurgling mystery box. Yelper went to a window and, watching the truck drive away, looked hurt and confused.

Arnie drove the pick up back toward Forest Service Road 4330. He maintained remarkable speed lurching onto the service road in 48 minutes. Hours later he and Grunt could be seen parked behind an old garage on a remote secondary road near Titusville. As they sat and waited, Arnie took one last reassuring look at the fuel gauge. It registered almost full.

Previously, more than an hour had been spent polishing, grooming, almost completely detailing the old Oldsmobile Firenza. The culprits did not care about its appearance. The purpose of the project was to clear it of any finger prints. Then, the Olds was to be seen driving through the town with a driver and one well dressed passenger. Leaving North Bend it turned west on the freeway melding into heavy traffic and eventually wending its way into a parking spot in the Seatac Airport parking complex. It was unlocked and the keys were in it. If prowlers stole it and abandoned it somewhere, so much the better. Anything to throw the authorities off the trail would be helpful.

In a short time, Rolf could be seen standing among recently arrived airline passengers. Directly, a clean shaven man in a business suit was to be seen driving a bright red Ford Crown Victoria toward Rolf and gliding to a stop. Rolf jumped in and the red Ford joined the outgoing auto traffic. No one in Titusville paid any attention to a Red Ford. No resident saw that rental car was driven into the old garage nor did anyone notice that the doors to the garage were securely closed and then that four men climbed into a large Dodge pickup and drove away.

Months of planning and even practice sessions were now done. Tomorrow, Wednesday, October 8, was the day. The plan, though daring was feasible. The rental car was in place at that old abandoned garage, the sugar beet sack had been placed in its trunk, the camp was ready, the Norseman was parked at Renton Airport, all was in readiness. The die was cast.

CHAPTER 12

With daylight now fading, conversation at the old house reduced to a minimum. All of the men except Grunt seemed to be deep in their own respective thoughts. The dollars they could net with a successful ransoming were more than Arnold Robert Sorenson and John Parker Bartholomew had ever seen leave alone have. They had both had their brushes with the law, but none of those experiences was in the magnitude of first degree felony. Neither of them had thought about that much. Up until now, everything had been planning, dreaming, practicing all under the spell binding direction and leadership of Rolf Burnside. Doubts that they should have had before this now began to disturb their thinking for the first time. And Burnside was tense as well. This was no longer a fun dream. It was reality and it was scarier than Rolf expected.

Tonight no one had much of an appetite for Grunt's good cooking. Plates of food were left half consumed, and Bart had to patiently reassure Grunt that his cooking was as good as ever but that the men were quite tense tonight. Grunt was surprised and queried, "are you scared?" "Well, maybe just a little bit, Grunt, just a little bit, but it's going to be OK, you don't have to worry." Ok then, Grunt would not worry.

Later, not feeling up to the usual poker game, they bedded down early, but the relief of slumber would not come. They were tossing and turning in their beds with tension and apprehension.

The severity of penalties for what they were going to do was worrisome, this just had to go right and they needed to be lucky. Grunt, in his ten year old level of reflections, was excited because tomorrow he was going to be the center of their attention. The whole beginning part of this was going to be his, but he could sense the other men did not want to talk, and he kept his feelings to himself. Tomorrow, he would be instrumental in bringing a very sinful family to task for their many crimes against humanity. Somehow, he was a bit disturbed that a young girl had to be involved and held by them, but, Bart assured him it was right and if Bart said so, it was so. He slept well, snoring loudly.

Rolf Burnside had been very busy with details of the caper and training his crew. Now he was going to execute the plan. In this final night of rest, he couldn't sleep any more than Arnie and Bart. Over and over again he mentally reviewed his grievances. That damned Harry Cottrell, humiliating him that way. He became angrier still as he imagined in his mind that Harry went home and bragged about what he had done. "I'll show him, I'll put a contract on him and let him be found face down in the street or some alley," he declared out loud. "You call, Boss?" "No, Arnie, go to sleep." Burnside's pulse pounded in his ears as his blood pressure rose. He reaffirmed to himself all of the resolutions that he had verbalized to himself in the past decade. He was going to "show that stuffed shirt, Marcus Comstock, who thinks he's such hot stuff and knows so much. Damned Comstock is not going to steal my woman away. She's not his and she never will be. He is going to know. I am going to hurt him and hurt him bad. And that goes for her and for her whole damned family too And I'm going to get that private detective or counselor or whoever sweet talked Bonnie Gay into leaving me and then divorcing me. And I'll get her and him. Maybe after I get the ransom, I'll just put a bullet through somebody's head just to show her." In all of his planning, this was the first time he had ever contemplated doing bodily harm.

The pent up poison seemed to flow without let up. Rolf Burnside's mind set was so consumed with hate and self pity that all the traits and restraints that should define man as the civilized animal were obliterated. Possible consequences ensuing from what he was doing would not restrain him. If anyone tried to stop him he would do whatever was necessary to brush them to one side, kill them if necessary. Probable grief and despair that could be caused to others would be no deterrent. More than that, he somehow viewed his willing compatriots as mere tools to achieve his objectives. This was his revenge; his and his alone.

When the ransom was in hand, he would double cross them, take all the money and disappear from their view. Totally awake at two in the morning, Burnside got up quietly, opened a steel box he had kept under his bed and removed an automatic pistol which he checked to make sure it was loaded. He then placed the gun and a spare clip of seven rounds in a holster and put it under his pillow. In the morning he would clip it on to his belt and cover it with an old cotton jacket that he had been wearing for the past two weeks, regardless of whether the given day was warm or cool. Now, for several hours, he slept.

CHAPTER 13

Early the next morning they prepared to leave the old farmhouse for the last time. Grunt prepared breakfast, but appetites were sluggish. As they climbed into the pick up, Bart was last getting behind the wheel; he had placed an incendiary device so that it would involve the whole house in flames before any volunteer fire department could possibly respond.

The men didn't care if the local investigator determined that the fire was arson, they wanted only to conceal possible finger print or writing evidence that might reveal any of their identities. Bart smiled in spite of his anxiety, "the Boss thinks of everything."

Titusville police chief Harold Miller and Marcus Comstock Jr. were on the golf course. Comstock was encouraged because on the sixth green he made par, and had a total stroke count of 30! Today was the best chance he had had in his first two years at golf to break one hundred.

Titusville police rookie officer Rodney Griswold was following a sports model Honda with wheel covers that rotate in conjunction with the wheels and a loud resonating muffler and tail pipe. Tolerant as he was, 55 miles an hour in a 25 zone up the west hill on Reynolds Road was too much. When the driver was finally convinced to stop, Griswold directed him off the road onto a wide driveway that led to a ramshackle garage. There were no other buildings around it, and the building was obviously locked. Issuing the citation for the civil infraction of speeding took about five minutes, and then both cars went their separate ways although Griswold noted that there were at least two sets of recent tire marks running toward the old building. With a padlocked door and nothing else disturbed, he had no right or desire to investigate it further, but he did conclude that although the old building looked abandoned, someone was using it.

Bonnie Gay Comstock had delivered daughter Cheryl to the school at 7:45. AM. A notice from the middle school principal informed parents that Wednesday morning classes would be in session as usual, but after lunch kids would be carrying their own locker content plus text books, P.E. equipment and miscellaneous school supplies to the temporary class room that they would use until renovations in their regular rooms was complete. Hence it again would be an extraordinary "dress down" day. Somehow, Cheryl seemed to be guarding her right pants pocket, but Bonnie had too much else on her mind to inquire. She was already late for the hair dresser. After that she would need to do some grocery shopping at Safeway. Then she thought she should be home by about 9:45 to 10:00 AM.

CHAPTER 14

Bart kept the truck at a moderate speed, 70, 60, 55, whatever the posted signs directed. Naturally he was being passed by 90 percent of the incoming commuter traffic. That's fine, nobody will remember the slow truck. Arriving at the garage, Rolf produced the key for the lock and in a minute the door was open and the bright red Ford Crown Victoria had been backed out and the pick up had been driven into its place. Not a single vehicle appeared on this road while the exchange was being accomplished. Burnside himself was now driving.

The Red Ford was driven directly into Titusville. Some people would remember it; so much the better. That was a purposeful part of the plan; that's why the argument with the auto rental company. The car had to be red.

Recess at the school would start at 9:45 and end at 10:00AM. The red Ford drove slowly down Pearl Street. Driver Burnside snarled at his passengers, "look at the school, look at the houses don't stare at <u>him</u>!" His concern now was the blue Ford prowl car coming by from the opposite direction. Rodney Griswold stared at the red car and the occupants were in an instant cold sweat, but it was only guilty conscience. Rodney was simply admiring the new Crown Victoria. It was three years newer than the prowler he was driving, and the city would be buying some new ones next year. Naturally he was interested.

Just to be safe, Rolf drove on past the school yard and around several blocks in a direction away from where he last saw Griswold turn off. There was time enough to be cautious.

But now, the plan! Execute!! The Ford came to a stop next to the five foot cyclone fence. Grunt exited the car and bounded over the fence with the grace of a deer. He had the sugar beet sack in his right hand.

Cheryl Comstock and friend Stella White had been chattering and giggling about today's dress down. All the girls were in jeans and old shirts ready to spend the afternoon carrying their school supplies and books to the high school. That would be fun. Flirting with the high school boys, that would be more fun. And this morning Cheryl had something else to share. She slipped her hand into her right pants pocket and produced the gold bracelet. Stella insisted she put it on and for the moment they were standing in the sunlight admiring the flashing reflections of the red and green precious stones.

Then the girls saw him. But the whole event was so unusual, so startling that they just froze in place. This large individual swooped in beside Cheryl, thrusting a sack over her head, upending her, and forcing her feet into the huge sugar beet bag. There was the blur of a tie string. With a jerking, twisting motion it was knotted tightly; and then the man was off on the run carrying Cheryl in his arms.

Grunt had no difficulty hoisting this 100 pound load up to where it was under his chin and then vaulting it over the fence toward Arnie and Bart. Arnie was near panic and he was leaning over the fence farther than he should have. Grunt launched the human load with unbelievable force and both men fell back. The sugar beet sack was writhing and kicking as its frightened but very agile content fought to free herself. She managed one good, healthy kick into Arnie's soft mid section and that plus his precarious lack of balance sent him spinning into a growth of blackberry brush that covered the fence some five feet away. The blackberry thorns penetrated the right hand glove drawing blood. When he pulled away in pain and panic, the berry bushes returned to their former shape leaving no sign of their temporary displacement. The glove fell to the ground under the car, but Bart saw and recovered it.

So intent were these players executing the plan that they had planned and practiced so hard and so long, they did not notice that another girl had followed Grunt almost to the fence and, standing there horrified. She was staring at the only face not covered by a mask. The view was oblique, but the features that she could see etched in her memory.

Arnie's fall and recovery was sort of comic opera, but the kidnapping would be admired begrudgingly by law enforcement in the weeks that followed. Gerald had lunged out of the car, jumped over the fence, grabbed Cheryl and returned climbing into the car, all in fourteen seconds. Arnie threw the sack into the open trunk and with his right hand he slammed it shut. Six gloves and three masks went into a sack and onto the front passenger side floor. None of that paraphernalia would be needed again, so the bag was to be carried to the camp and buried. Although tense with the danger and excitement of the caper, Rolf was immensely proud of himself and himself only. He had thought of everything. Muttering under his breath he queried, "what do you think of that, Comstock, you stuffed shirt."

Cheryl and her girl classmates had been counseled about the possible risk of sexual assault. When this smelly, dirty sack went over her whole body, she was momentarily frozen in fear, but for 13 going on 14 she was remarkably self sufficient, and presently her mind began to function. Assuming sexual violation was going to occur, she reacted the way she had been taught, kicking, screaming and doing everything she could think of to escape and to cause the world around her to notice. Nobody told her how you do all that in a burlap sack. Her struggle did accomplish something when she kicked Arnie,s solar plexus. The portion of the sack under her foot had spent too much time in a muddy sugar beet field and a small portion of the burlap was decayed. Now there was a hole in the sack more or less the size of a quarter. Unfortunately, the rest of the sack would not rip or tear and she realized she could not get away.

Cheryl was aware she was in an automobile and she was bumping and bouncing around on a hard floor. She could sense the vehicle climbing and descending, and she knew enough of Titusville that she was aware that they were going out of the main part of the city. She had spent enough time with her Uncle Harry Cottrell and his ranch hands to know that there were wires connected to tail lights. She remembered the profanity of the hands trying to get the old farm trailer's tail lights to work. The problem always was the wires. She had overcome her initial panic enough to squirm around within the confines of the sack so that she could push against the hole in the sack and finally force her hand through it. Maybe she could cause the wires to fail, maybe someone outside would notice, but then the vehicle had stopped and she could sense the men getting out.

The red Ford had retraced its route back to the garage. Several people saw and later reported that they saw a red car but that was all in the area at or close to downtown. Out at the remote garage location, no one saw what happened. The pick up came out and the rental Ford went in. The garage door was locked and they left. The bag was now inside the big tool box behind the truck cab. Grunt and Arnie were in the rear seat, and Bart was driving with Rolf in the right front seat.

Cheryl could not have been more bewildered. There was no light in the car trunk; there was no light in the truck's tool box. For now Cheryl's world was almost black with no sense of direction or location. The air was foul with the odors of burlap, mud and stale sugar beet remnants. It was so overwhelming she suffered periods of nearly vomiting. She had tried everything she could think of to end this horrid nightmare, but nothing worked. She didn't weep. She ultimately just curled up and remained motionless, silent, defeated. But then she began trying to imagine what might happen to her next. The stunning thought occurred to her: "What if these men were totally psychotic? What if they were going to throw her into a lake or river and watch her drown just for fun?" The thought triggered a sense of claustrophobia and in total panic she began again to jerk and tear struggling to free herself, trying to reach the tie string and trying to increase the size of the hole she had punched in the bag. She did manage to increase the size of the hole so she could force her whole forearm through, but struggle as she might, she could make the tear no larger. Nothing worked and finally she had to fall back, dirty, red faced and momentarily exhausted,

The occupants up front were now wearing white shirts and white caps. The sides and the rear of the truck now displayed prominent red and white signs proclaiming the vehicle to be equipment of the "Sylvester Brothers, Painting, Interior Design and Decorating." Below that was a whimsical byline, "Need Help? We Beautify What Your Husband Messed Up." Rolf looked at his white clad conspirators, contemplated what people might think about the signs and he smiled murmuring, "Rolf, you old fox you do think of everything, what do you think of that Bonnie Gay?"

Law enforcement vehicles were now out in force, and many passing cars got the once over. The truck didn't vaguely resemble the vehicle that had been described, and none of the several prowl cars that went by it in the opposite direction gave it any attention. Bart drove leisurely along the west bound balance of SR 18 to its connection with SR 169 and ultimately they drove into a perimeter area of Renton Airport.

The white truck made its way to the hangars just across the river from the Boeing assembly plant. A dingy old Norseman aircraft was rolled out, started and eventually left. Tower was told that the sole occupant was just going to spend the day at Easton Field some distance east. Tower was not told about the wriggling sack behind the pilot. The normal engine noises around the airport blotted out the sounds of a girl screaming.

When the Norseman's engine barked to life, Cheryl was bewildered all the more. Baffled at first, then she was angry and frightened again. "Where are you taking me she demanded and the response was a gruff voice saying, "just shut up and you will find out." Still confined and nearly blind in the sack, she now could sense that whatever she was in, it was going along some sort of road or whatnot and there was chatter going on between her captor and someone whose voice was obviously coming in by radio. Her captor talked several times referring to himself as a string of numbers followed by the word "Bravo."

Later she rebuked herself for missing an opportunity. Perhaps if she had screamed at the top of lungs, the voice on the radio would have heard her cries for help; but now the radio chatter ceased and the space she was in filled with a loud roar. In all of her 13 years of varied experiences she had never been close to an old fashioned radial engine before and she was baffled all the more. Only when the plane became airborne and jolted slightly in response to a cross wind did she finally realize she was flying. Her stomach knotted with fear again as she wondered how far they were going. One more time she made herself heard, "where are you taking me, what are you doing?" The response was meant to scare her into silence, but actually, it calmed her and gave her a feeling of understanding, "keep still or I will dump you out and let you fall. You are being kidnapped. Keep quiet and behave yourself and after I get all your daddy's money, I might even take you home." Cheryl relaxed and the fear abated. In her mind her daddy was a man of many talents. There was little he could not do or cause to be done, and he would fix all this somehow. She felt better now; this might work out well after all. Then she thought about both of her parents and felt badly that she could not tell them where she was and that she was alright.

There's no tower at Easton Airport. The Norseman landed and taxied to a remote location where there were no other aircraft and no people. It sat there for two hours. Then its engine started and it pulled onto the main landing strip just as an automobile drove up to get a better look at this antique aircraft. Rolf waived congenially, and then started his take off run. The little plane turned and flew to Ellensburg maintaining strict radio silence. Two hours was the estimated time for the pick up to drive from Renton to Ellensburg. If it were stopped on the way, it would appear to have no part in events that took place in Titusville.

Bart had driven slowly through Renton, onto I-405 continuing a diverse route that eluded any early roadblocks.

At I-90, they headed east crossing the mountain pass without incident. The conspirators rendezvoused at Ellensberg Airport and drove away, sack and all. Then the pick up traveled toward the mountains and up the forest service road toward the camp.

At the gate, Arnie got out and pulled the post loose and swung the entire gate assembly clear for the truck to pass through. Arnie got back in the truck and closed the door, but Bart did not start up immediately. He said he thought he felt and heard something from the rear. He listened carefully for a moment but then there was nothing more. Just to be sure, he got out from behind the wheel and looked into the truck bed. Finally he just shrugged, the beet sack seemed to be securely tied. Later he would remember that he did not check to make sure. Cheryl sensed his presence and kicked violently in his direction. Bart smiled, reported the kicking incident to his passengers and drove on until they arrived at the camp. The kidnapping itself was complete, but the setting sun was shinning on the gate and just beyond. Standing there one could see the glint of gold in the dirt.

Rolf smiled to himself. He had thought of everything. In addition to the execution of the kidnap, he had devised a diversion that would, steer attention away from himself as the possible suspect. As the big white pick up bumped and jounced along the road toward the camp, he remembered his trip to the post office some five days earlier. He had sent a letter to a confederate overseas together with cash money. As a result, in a few days from now there would be an envelope delivered to the panic stricken Comstock home post marked from some city in India. Inside there would be some sort of money order sending Bonnie the sum of $250.00; child support for a month, albeit 13 years late.

There also would be a letter hand written by Rolf conveying the most apologetic and cordial tone. Rolf would be declaring that he now could see his failings and he would lament his abuse of Bonnie and thank Harry Cottrell for bringing him to his senses as to what a real heel he had been. It would note the money enclosed, state that he had now found himself in India and was doing well financially. He would be promising regular monthly payments as contribution to Cheryl's support. Of course the purpose of letter was to post seemingly positive proof that Rolf Burnside had no part in the nefarious event now taking place, that he was thousands of miles away and could not be a suspect in the kidnapping. The letter inferred he was innocent of all involvement. Now he was somewhat in a ranting mood. He would show that bitch. He would show that stuffed shirt she married when she had a chance to live with Rolf. To himself he thought, "I'll show the whole damned world, nobody messes with Rolf Burnside. Ah Rolf, you are one smart son-of-a-bitch you are."

Telling all this to his helpers he laughed, "isn't that a gas?" Cheryl could hear it all and she was astonished. There was some connection between this guy and her mother! She knew her biological father had disappeared, but that was years ago. "Who is this guy?"

CHAPTER 15

"OK, so far so good men, we have our little lady here and she is going to make us rich," Rolf proclaimed.

"You're all a bunch of crooks. My dad and the police will catch all of you." All four men started a bit at the defiant and unexpected outburst emanating from the flushed, glaring, angry face of their captive as she now sat, handcuffed to an old tubular steel kitchen chair. Surprisingly, she revealed no sign of fear, no sign of being in any way submissive or afraid. Literally snarling now as their astonished looks gave her encouragement to continue, she charged, "I know what you have done. I am being kidnapped for money, well my dad won't pay you a penny."

If Cheryl had been a younger child her outburst might have provoked only laughter, but she was so spirited and for the moment looked so mature that at least two of the men visibly reeled back. For some reason, Grunt did not. He actually smiled uttering a barely audible chuckle.

Rolf on the other hand was neither shaken nor amused. He flushed with anger. For the several past months as he had painstakingly fashioned, brain washed and trained his minions, he had held them spell bound by his genius. They had come to believe that he was a rascal wizard without peer; and Rolf, who had never been so regarded by anyone in the world except his mother, was not about to dispel the illusion.

"Well little lady," he said, endeavoring to look as threatening as he might, "what if we just throw you out in the cold. This is mountain country, there are bears and cougars out there. What if we let you loose and you get eaten up?"

"Cougars won't eat people unless they are very hungry. It's too early in the year for that. Miss Hamilton told us that when we studied cougars in class. Bears are scaredy cats. My uncle tried to show me a bear once in Texas, but the bear ran away so fast and we never saw him again."

"Oh really and just what do your lippy teacher and your big loud Uncle Harry know about it?" Ah! Rolf thought, that stopped her cold. Now she was just staring at him somewhat incredulous and actually shaken, she but did not retreat, she held her ground in the give and take, "How did you know that my uncle is big and that his name is Harry? Just who are you anyway?" Now Rolf was a bit shaken, revealing his awareness of Uncle Harry he had clearly said too much.

Grunt, in his simple good nature did not sense the tension growing between captor and captive, and now he attempted to join in the conversation exclaiming in a happy tone, "Missy Comstock, don't you know, this is your real." "SHUT UP GRUNT! NOBODY ASKE D YOU, STAY OUT OF IT!" Rolf's anger of course was born of frustration. He had long since decided that he would reveal his relationship to Cheryl only after he had the ransom in hand and just before he either took her back or killed her as the climax to the total agony and despair that he was going to rent on that bitch and the scummy Cottrell family.

Rolf quickly recovered; he tempered his mood and continued. "Well, well, men Miss Lippy here should keep us entertained. She knows all about cougars and bears, did you hear that men?" The sarcasm bolstered the conspirators and with confidence restored, they all laughed, even Grunt.

"I'll say this Miss Lippy you've got a brave mouth, but you better be careful how you use it. I'm not against cutting me a stick and thrashing you 'till all the smart ass talk is out of you is that clear?"

She dutifully nodded her head, but shot back "Miss Hamilton told us in sex-ed class that there are men like you to look out for." The ongoing resistance was something Rolf couldn't deal with and now he lost his temper again. Raising his hand as though he was going to strike her, he roared back, "Do you want me to thrash your little butt right now?" Cheryl closed her mouth tightly preparing to take the blow she knew was coming, but in a rare show of initiative, Grunt responded, "oh come on, boss, she's just a girl. Girls always talk too much. Why don't you all sit down while I make us something good to eat."

Well, that finally broke the veil of hostility, and the men began to converse about the adventure of today. It was brilliantly executed and they knew it.

When the snack was ready, the men gathered around the battered old kitchen table and Grunt served them all. Then he prepared another plate for Cheryl and set it on an overturned paper box where she could reach with her right hand while her left was cuffed to the chair arm.

Boomer and Yelper sat attentively ready to accept any morsels that might be offered by the feasting humans. Only Arnie responded giving each of them a tidbit of his hamburger sandwich. But Rolf objected even to that, "Arnie, how many times do I have to tell you that feeding those mutts at the table bothers me. Just wait and feed them outside, OK?" "Sorry, Boss, it's just a habit." And Arnie did abstain from further table treats for the two animals, but

Cheryl took it all in. On one summer visit to the ranch, she had come across a well-soiled old publication some forty pages in length explaining the basics of sleight of hand. She read it carefully and practiced the lessons. Uncle Harry was delighted with her success. Now she deftly sneaked morsels of food from serving plates. Eventually the two animals would begin slowly changing their allegiance from the men to the young captive.

As Grunt was clearing the table and making ready to wash dishes, the boss began to review the next step in the operation. "Make yourselves comfortable, boys, it's going to be a long process. For the first seven days we're going to stay holed up here and not make a peep, and not move a muscle."

Bart knew more about the country than did Rolf or Arnie and the delay bothered him. "Does it have to be so long? You know in a couple of weeks it's going to start getting cold up here and the snow's comin' soon after."

"Yes it has to be that long," Rolf responded. "I would prefer thirty days of delay, but then the risks of getting' discovered get too high. But we are pretty well hidden, and I don't think there's much chance being seen if we are careful. There may be some hikers going back and forth to Gallagher Lake or what not, but they will stick to the easier going along the trail and nobody can see this place from there. Seven days will be time enough for anxious parents to get down right hysterical and be ready to dump money wherever I tell them to without daring to ask too many questions." Cheryl sat thinking she had a lot to say in rebuttal, and even though she could converse at a level far more mature than her 13 years, she felt she needed to know what her captors were up to so she remained silent as the plan was being verbalized, and she was determined to remember everything being said.

Rolf was obviously the leader and he spoke first. "A week from today, Bart and I will drive out. If anybody asks us we are cabin owners closing up for the year. Grunt and Arnie, of course stay here with the kid. It's going to take a week maybe a bit more after that to execute the snatch & grab plan for picking up the money then dropping it and then letting the plane fly off while Bart and I pick up the money and head back here.

Cheryl was visibly frightened by events of the past several hours, but that fear engendered a surprisingly feisty mood. "You'll get caught, just wait and see," Cheryl commented and then cringed fully expecting Rolf to strike her, but with a good meal and time to reflect on the brilliant success of the plan execution so far, he was in a much more expansive mood. Turning to her he grinned, "I'm gonna get all your daddy's money and then I'm gonna throw you out to the bears just you wait and see," he mocked, and that was followed by a prolonged laugh in which Bart and Arnie joined. Grunt, by contrast was strangely silent although that went unnoticed. Grunt was beginning to develop feelings about all this that he did not quite understand and which he kept to himself for now.

CHAPTER 16

The senior Marcus Comstock had a good first nine holes and Chief Miller noted that somehow today his partner had finally overcome the gremlins that had stunted Comstock's golf swing for so long. Marcus Jr. was a man used to achieving what he went after. He was content that some things in his life had been difficult and he had made mistakes from time to time, but defeat was not in his vocabulary except, however, for mastering this vexatious game. He was puzzled now hearing his name on the loudspeaker outside the clubhouse, and even before he could respond, Miller's cell phone rang. "We're on our way," Miller said, speaking into the telephone and then he blurted out the content of the message. Comstock's face flushed red and then turned ashen white. Abandoning golf clubs and cart they sped off to the Comstock office building to notify Marcus III

The Comstock father and son team were can-do type American guys albeit without much John Wayne swagger. They had faced a lot of troublesome times in past years and most observers thought they made their successes all look easy. But now they were faced with the likes of what they had never encountered in their combined lives before. Racing toward the Hellgraves mansion hoping to beat any telephone calls by well intended acquaintances or worse yet by some aggressive newsman, Marcus Jr. held the Explorer at a pace near double the speed limit. His son said nothing and seemed to urge even faster speeds.

In fact, Bonnie Gay was not home when they arrived and they were breaking the awful news to Hazel when Bonnie Gay drove in behind Marcus Jr.'s Explorer.

"Well, my two handsome men; which one of you is going to take me to lunch today . . . ?" But then she stopped short and stood shocked and silent. The gray, grief stricken looks on the faces before her were enough to say that something was terribly wrong. When her husband said the words, "Cheryl's been kidnapped," the effect was so great that the internal workings of her brain commanded that conscious function shut down. She collapsed as the men rushed to catch her.

With breathing irregular and pulse racing and then getting so light it could not be felt for moments at a time, Hazel took the initiative to dial 911. By time the men had carried her upstairs and laid her on a bed, the medical crew had arrived. Bonnie Gay did respond to the stimulus treatment administered by the EMT team and she was conscious, but so grief stricken that communication was reduced to one and two word sentence fragments. By now police were at the door, but on the advice of the medical response team, they took informational statements from Hazel and the two men and deferred questioning Bonnie Gay to a later time. Meanwhile, Marcus Jr. began the most difficult sequence of telephone calls he had ever made. Comstock, Burnside and Cottrell families had to be informed so they would be ready to face inevitable media inquiries and some times outrageously cruel questions.

Years later Sue Cottrell would tell the Comstocks that when husband Harry heard the description of the kidnap and that the men wore hoods, he roared like a lion yelling

"Rolf you son-of-a-bitch," and repeating the same oath no less than three times, he then continued, "when they catch you I am going to cut you up in little pieces and feed you to the pigs." At that point in telling the story, Sue would laugh adding that Harry paused and as an afterthought said, "I apologize, pigs, you have far too much class to stoop to eating that useless pile of human waste."

Chief Harold Miller called the King County Sheriff and the Seattle office of the FBI from the Hellgraves mansion.

By the eleven o'clock evening news, every TV station in Washington State and many more throughout the nation were broadcasting what little information the police would reveal. Cheryl's picture was on every screen, not once but over and over again; and the whole nation was on the lookout for a late model, Candy Apple Red Ford Crown Victoria. The whole nation of law enforcement officers was ready to locate everyone of the Candy Apple Red Fords in their respective jurisdictions that might in any way seem suspicious, and to make every owner explain their whereabouts on October 8. But within hours, a member of the sheriff's office had an inspirational hunch: Perhaps the red car was chosen because it *would* be noticed as a part of a diversionary plan. Why not check with the local rental agents first, and sure enough a Seatac Airport agent had rented out such a unit and it was now overdue for return.

Detectives and investigators of the City force, the King County Sheriff and the State patrol were opening files on the Cheryl Comstock kidnapping. Since Lindberg, the act had become a federal offense as well as state. Department of Justice would be fully involved. The FBI would lead the hunt.

Special Agent Roger Caldwell had been designated by the Agent in Charge of Seattle Office. He was on the scene by noon. The day flew by for officers on the scene; there was so much to learn, so many details to be noted and catalogued. Nothing was unimportant, at least not for now.

In the wee hours of the following day, Caldwell made a couple of calls as he finally left the Comstock residence. Dawn was just a promise now and the several recipients were awakened out of a sound sleep, but there were things he wanted done before he finally climbed into his own bed and tried to calm down enough to sleep. Bonnie Gay's obviously serious mental damage had gotten under his skin. His determination that this case be solved and the perpetrators apprehended was, perhaps, even more intense than it usually was. It was rare for an agent, but he was consumed and unaware that he was being watched. Clearly his lips were moving; he was talking to himself. Stopped at a red light some blocks from his home, a late night pair of revelers watched and smiled.

Within three days of interagency communication, the ground rules were laid. All officers were at liberty to pursue anything that might seem fruitful, but for the most part, local agencies would be the lookouts and would receive, log and forward all incoming calls from citizens about any sightings of persons who might be involved. The federals would bear the laboring oar on interviews and follow-up work. What was agreed upon during those meetings was already in motion. Caldwell and agents working with him had interviewed every teacher, principal and school child in the Maude Hellgraves population. Every telephone line serving the Marcus III family home and the Comstock enterprise was tapped and monitored all day every day from then on.

An agent interviewed Stella White, daughter of Judge Nancy Burser White. The agent sensed that Stella was suspiciously tight-lipped. She seemed to be uncomfortable and fidgety. Later he was told by a teacher that she was Cheryl's closest friend in school. The agent was certain that young Stella was holding something back. She fidgeted during the entire interview although the agent kept reassuring her that she had done nothing to be ashamed of and that telling everything she knew or even suspected was the best way to help get Cheryl back, alive. Nonetheless she avoided eye contact and she twice asked to be excused to go to the restroom. Three times she asked when the interview would be done. Caldwell was advised and he was not sure what to do either, but he ultimately decided to ask a clinical psychologist, Judy Myerson to talk with Stella. Myerson and Caldwell had worked together before. They were sufficiently well acquainted to tease and josh back and forth on such subjects as women in the workplace, over zealous cops, and social prejudices generally. The Myersons and the Caldwells socialized and enjoyed each other's company.

Judy Myerson spent less than an hour with Stella and was ready to guess the probable diagnosis. "Her parents have told her to shut up, even though Mommy as a judge should know better. My guess is they are totally scared for fear of retribution against this kid."

"Are you sure?" Caldwell inquired. "I'm never sure, Roger, but I would bet on it. Conceivably she knows who the kidnappers are especially if this thing has local perpetrators, but that's not likely. Somehow, I think more that she ran after the guy with the bag and got a look at them."

"Not likely," Caldwell responded. "All witnesses including Stella says these guys were wearing ski masks."

"Well," Myerson countered, "nobody could tell us anything about the driver. According to the playground-duty teacher, Stella ran right up to the car as it drove away. Let me talk to both her and mommy. There may be a loose end here. Assuming that Stella told her mother that she got a good look at the driver and maybe could identify that person, then mother could conceivably be trying to shield the kid against appearance at a line up, police interrogation, defense counsel grilling, the whole nine yards. As a judge, all this stuff had to go through mother's mind and hence she ends up advising the kid to lapse her memory. It's no surprise if motherhood trumps the judicial. role. So, again, let me have a go at it." Reluctantly, Caldwell agreed.

It developed that the White family trusted Dr. Myerson and ultimately Stella told what she really had seen. That was not much and the time was only a few seconds, but she had seen the face of the driver.

Agent Thomas Burns was also a sketch artist. In response to his questions, Stella responded with remarkably descriptive detail.

The bureau refused all media questions as to the source of the sketch, but by 11:00 PM it was broadcast on many TV networks.

Unfortunately, Marcus Comstock III had never actually seen Rolf. He had seen pictures taken years before that did not reflect the puffiness resulting from excessive eating and drinking together with more than a decade of time. Bonnie Gay was not yet really recovered and somehow none of the Cottrell's saw the picture. If any of the Burnsides saw it, they said nothing.

As another day passed an early morning conference convened at the Titusville Police Department Headquarters. Marcus Comstock, Chief Harold Miller and Roger Caldwell together with numerous city detectives and a task force of King County deputies crowded around a conference table.

93

Caldwell had made written notes about his analysis so far and he addressed the group. "If this abduction had only one perpetrator, I would really fear the worst by now knowing that we were probably dealing with a sexual psychopath. Psycho victims have a very low rate of survival, but I can't seriously believe you would ever have four men working as a team to achieve sexual gratification. This has to be either a taking for ransom or else it has to be a hate crime against parents or perhaps the Comstock family at large. However if the motive is ether money or hate, we should have heard something by now either that the plan has been aborted and Cheryl is calling home or else a demand for a large amount of money or some similar concession from Comstocks. The silence for three whole days or more is unique. Kidnappings for money have not been a crime of choice for some time. This case is developing a profile that doesn't compare with any case that the bureau has dealt with in recent years."

Marcus felt a cold chill cut though his stomach. Caldwell had come on the scene radiating strength, competence and control, but now he was downcast. and the rest of the lawmen were not more encouraging. Local law enforcement had thrown its full support toward this vexatious case. Cooperation had been unrestrained. Everyone knew what everyone else knew even if that was not much.

Marcus Comstock had retained his composure throughout the ordeal. He had shed not a tear and showed little outward emotion other than for a gray facial complexion that made him appear older than he was. Somehow Bonnie's breakdown and her frequent periods of hysteria forced Marcus to maintain a stoic appearance of strength, and Bonnie, now in her warped view began to interpret that as indifference. With irrational rage she now refused him entrance to the bedroom. Caldwell's admission that the case was beginning to take on a character that was new and baffling simply broke his defensive shell. Tears welled up and without saying anything he abruptly exited the room.

Getting into his car, Marcus drove out of the city hall parking lot and onto the street. Good fortune had the driver of the big garbage truck awake and attentive. When a vehicle came out of the city driveway violating his right-of-way, he locked up all eight wheels and the truck responded well. The long, loud blast of the air horn brought Marcus back to reality, but he wept all the way home. The strain of the Titusville kidnapping was taking its toll. The "boss" was achieving his desired effect even more than he knew.

Throughout the rest of the day and for four days thereafter, there were no other significant developments. No ransom demands were received. The investigation was stymied. Bonnie Gay slowly lapsed into mourning becoming steadily more convinced that her daughter was gone. Her expression was one of morbidity and grieving. She slept only moments at a time, would not shower or bestir herself to dress her hair or do anything else to make herself look presentable. She did nothing physical becoming more and more lethargic. She wept uncontrollably. Doctors were now reluctantly guessing that her condition would not change until Cheryl was recovered or remains found.

As the planned seven days passed, it was not only agonizing for the families and friends of Cheryl Comstock, it also wore abrasively on the nerves of the conspirators.

CHAPTER 17

Up until now, execution of Rolf Burnside's complex scheme kept Burnside and his minions unceasingly busy. The plan was reduced to writing and he made Arnie and Bart read it over and over again. With Grunt, he explained over and over how these Comstock people were wicked and how this girl was the means to bring them to their knees and make them disgorge what they had savagely taken from Rolf and other innocents. Arnie and Bart sat amused as Rolf spun wonderful tales of the wealth and pleasure Grunt would experience once this ugly caper was completed. No one had ever made such promises to this handicapped youngster before. Rolf had maintained a mental superiority over all three of his companions and he had kept them busy with planning and conferencing and even rehearsals. Time and again he would order the men to assume their positions inside the old Oldsmobile Firenza or the truck. They would drive to a remote location on the old North Bend road and stop. Grunt would jump out and leap over a barb wire fence and run to where a hundred pound sack of sand had been placed. He would throw the big sugar beet sack over the sand sack and lift the whole package up and run to the fence.

Throwing the sack across the fence created enough force that it was decided both Arnie and Bart had to stand there and catch it together. Sometimes they would do this practice run four or five times. Arnie and Bart got a little beat up by the sack, but Grunt got faster and faster with his execution. For him it was an exciting game and he would gleefully agree to do it over and over again as many times as he was asked. Time was spent acting out how to rent cars from the agencies at the airport pretending to be businessmen in town for a brief time. More time was consumed contacting the shady characters Rolf had met during his bank robbing episode. From them came fake driver's licenses, insurance cards and even credit cards so as to create rather complete false identities for all of them. Time and again each of the men would sit behind the wheel of the old car and calmly answer stern questions and display phony drivers licenses and insurance cards in the manner that might occur if they were involved in any sort of routine police inquiry. Rolf, of course, played the role of the inquiring police officer.

In all it had been a full time occupation right up until the kidnap itself. But now, by the fourth day, the small ancient motor home was getting more and more confining. The men began to get on each other's nerves. Rolf realized he should have spent time warning the crew about how boredom had to set in and to be prepared to deal with it. And there were times when Rolf Burnside did not deal with the confinement any better than the others. He was grumpy and given to more and more outbursts of temper over what were minor things.

Yelper and Boomer were no help. Yelper would bark louder and louder as Rolf's voice got louder. Rolf would yell at Yelper and Bart would defend his pets even though he was otherwise subservient to Rolf. On the whole however, Yelper and Boomer were the happiest occupants of the camp. The woods were full of mice, rabbits and birds which

Yelper would chase and which Boomer would kill if he got the chance. Once they forgot to let Boomer out for his early morning run and in protest he sprayed urine all over Rolf's shoes, even inside. Bart agreed to clean the shoes in order to save Boomer from the death sentence. Boomer himself was unimpressed with the whole shouting match that had ensued

And then there were the problems of Cheryl's confinement. The little bathroom did not work very well. The toilet was nonfunctional for the lack of running water. Bart had rightly insisted on renting a portable privy from a rental company. It was cold but better than the last alternative. Washing hands and faces was limited to cold water in a basin. There would be no changing to fresh clothing; there was no shower or bath tub. Grunt was assigned most of the tasks connected with her needs, although Rolf grew uneasy about that arrangement. Cheryl and Grunt were getting to know one another, and the hostility Rolf had inculcated in Grunt was visibly fading. It seemed whatever Cheryl asked for, Grunt would accommodate her. A comb, a washcloth and a toothbrush for her all appeared out of Grunt's personal toilet articles. Sitting all day everyday was tortuous and Grunt came to see that. Holding her chain firmly, Grunt walked her around the area during restroom trips. Rolf cautioned Grunt to keep these walks under the cover of trees and brush.

If the ugly three knew as much about Grunt as they thought they did, they would never have let him get close to Cheryl in any way. Bart did admonish him about becoming too friendly with this little witch and Grunt nodded and said he understood, but in fact questions began to form in his mind. Grunt found himself having difficulty sleeping for the first time in his life as he lay awake those nights pondering and wondering. How could a witch be so kindly and considerate not to mention being rather pretty?

For each favor Grunt did for her, Cheryl would smile and thank him. Grunt would blush and grin in response. Whether his limited cognizance still recognized her as an epitome of evil was becoming very doubtful. But Rolf finally concluded that he really should not be concerned. The only time he really needed Grunt was for that critical 14 seconds on the school grounds. He didn't care what Grunt thought about anything. Grunt was not a person, he was a thing, a tool. Never once did Rolf visualize Grunt as getting any of the ransom money.

Somehow Rolf was also bothered by the increasing attention the animals were giving Cheryl. That should not bother him he knew but somehow it reflected ominously. Why was it happening?

Eventually the press of the togetherness began to cry out for solution. Deciding that the risks of being discovered were really quite remote, Rolf ordered that the door be opened during daylight and that the men get out and move about a bit, cautioning them to conceal themselves if they saw or heard anyone approaching.

Relief from the confinement was a tonic. There were several times when hikers were to be seen walking the trail, but none of them so much as glanced at this hideaway a hundred yards back in the brush. Walks into the deeper woods relieved tensions and humor began to replace acrimony. The friendly banter that had prevailed for so long now returned. The presence of body odor was abated by baths in the open air with water heated on the propane stove.

Grunt now volunteered to do some laundry, and the men expressed their appreciation. Not surprisingly such praise increased Grunt's loyalty to the older men and their mission, but it also made his feelings about Cheryl all the more troubling. What was being done to Grunt was despicable. He was truly a victim of cultist-like brain washing with tales of what a hero he would be and what riches he would enjoy when the ransom was paid. Grunt yearned to discuss this problem with Bart, but he had been rebuffed when he tried to initiate any conversation in the presence of the other men, so he chose to continue pondering in silence.

Yelper and Boomer soon decided to adopt Cheryl as she continued to ply her amateur sleight of hand skills. So, in spite of Rolf's strict orders that no one "feed those damned mutts at my table," Yelper and Boomer strangely stayed in between the menacing shoes and boots under the table and later came away showing only casual interest in the dry pet food placed in their feeding plates. Their allegiance began to shift and arguably they were no longer Arnie or Bart's pets.

None of these events was reassuring to Cheryl. At night and with all the men sleeping she would weep silently. How she missed her comfortable life. How she would now even welcome her mother's chastisement in dubbing her bedroom as the trash dump of the house. How she missed a warm shower and clean clothes. How she would love to have her mother comb her hair complaining that she could do nothing with it. How she cared for her parents, her school friends and even Miss Hamilton. Oh for the chance to sit on a bed with Stella and once more pan the clumsiness of the boys at school She would never again forget the warmth and comfort that familiar things and circumstances bring to the human soul. She would never again proclaim the popular teen refrain that life was "boring."

CHAPTER 18

On October 14, things would begin to happen.

Bart and the Boss finished their breakfast, checked to make sure they had plenty of cash and then they drove out and away from the area. However Bart made one last trip to the outhouse, and as he came out, Grunt was at the doorway waiting his turn. Bart was a criminal. As to anyone who had money and Bart could get it by theft or fraud, that citizen was fair game in his mind, but as penitentiary wardens will tell us, many of their most hardened and incorrigible anti-social types nonetheless have a sense of honor about other forms of criminal conduct. A child molester has little chance of survival in a lockup composed of bank robbers. Bart remembered Arnie's lecherous comments during their first meetings and he had noticed Arnie's intense interest in Cheryl. He watched Arnie stare at her literally undressing her with his leer. To Bart, Cheryl was a legitimate pawn, but she was also a little girl who deserved to be treated accordingly.

Now Bart was whispering to Grunt, "look, Grunt you are going to have to stay here with Arnie for a while. Keep an eye on him and don't let him do anything to her. Don't let him have her out of your sight OK?" Grunt's expression grew very serious. Although his intelligence level might be in question, his own manly instincts and the training he received in the parochial school were enough that he clearly understood Bart's order, and he would do whatever it took to comply.

Now the rest of the plan would begin to unfold.

The agent monitoring the telephone tap on the Comstock residence was staring idly out the window when the bell sounded and he remained in a state of relaxed inattention. He had listened in on what was possibly the busiest residential telephone in King County for some six days. All of the calls so far were of no consequence to him and as soon as some familiar voice began speaking, he would yield to Hazel Phong who had now been retained by the Comstock family to nurse Bonnie Gay on a full time basis. She was now sleeping and eating as a resident of the mansion. But this time the male voice coming in was unlike any that he had heard before; this was not routine. Further, the voice faded and then returned to full volume. Prompting him to yell to others in the room, "cell call coming in," and they in turn became tense with anticipation.

"Get that God damned, money grabbin', thievin' scum Comstock on the line."

Responding with an anxious and obedient tone, the agent glanced quickly to make sure the recorder light was on and recording and then replied, "Just a minute man, he's not here but I will get him, hold on."

"No hold, cop, you aren't going to trace this call, I'll be on the horn at 2:00 PM tomorrow. If Midas wants his kid to stay alive, he'll answer." And then there was silence. While the brief contact lasted, the agent strained to hear anything else that might give away the caller's location. He said he could hear nothing of interest. However, Marcus Comstock and the agents were all encouraged. The criminal scheme had not derailed. Experienced officers, even those who were previously skeptical now agreed. Dr. Myerson spoke first, "this guy is good, and he has complete self control and control of his situation. He's playing us like a fiddle, and he knows it."

Marcus bounded upstairs and for the first time in days asked if he could come in. The answer was mumbled but affirmative, and Marcus opened the door allowing the first flood of natural light enter the room in the past week. Bonnie Gay, looked so haggard that Marcus was visibly shocked. She searched her husband's face for any sign of encouragement as she mumbled, "you think there is any hope?" Marcus thought that is an improvement. Up until now she kept telling Hazel that Cheryl was dead and that was the end of it. "Bonnie, there has to be hope. They wouldn't call if Cheryl was not alive. Don't you see, unless she lives they have nothing to bargain with. The psychologist here has said that with more than one kidnapper, this is not a sex crime, she wasn't taken for sexual gratification." Bonnie now forced a half smile, but then doubts and fear overwhelmed her and she turned and returned to the bed. Marcus ached to hold and reassure her, but he was still stung by the fury of her response the last time he tried to hold or hug her. The Drs. had been consulted and both of them advised that although Bonnie should get up and around for her own physical and mental good, that for now less damage would be done if Marcus refrained from trying to help.

The following day all was tension in the Comstock living room as the afternoon wore on. Waiting was nerve racking. 2:00 came and went with total silence. Myerson restated her analysis, "This bastard is playing with us like a cat plays with a wounded mouse. He's no dummy, and he is very sure of himself and he is skillful in using people. He's trying to make Marcus putty in his hands so as to justify his own revenge. He'll call sometime today and when he does, let me talk. He thinks he is a woman killer of legendary proportions. Who knows I might be so fortunate as to get a proposition," she grinned and winked at the men. It was a great tension reliever. "How can you tell so much by what little we know so far?" Caldwell asked. She shot back, "'cause I went to school, didn't you?" Caldwell grinned in response; they had bantered back and forth many times before in the manner that friends can without any fear of hurt feelings.

At 2:30 the phone rang and everyone tensed. "Hello, this is United Glass Associates, and how are you fine folks today. We will be in your area this week, offering great discount prices. Do you have any automobile windshields or windows that need replacement?" ":Nooooo, thank you we do not." "Click." With emphasis.

It was almost as if re-cradling the receiver caused it to ring again. Everyone jumped but with more deliberation this time.

"Is that you asshole?" "Wow" the sultry female voice answered. "I'm hungry and I sent him into the kitchen to make me a sandwich, he'll be a couple of minutes." "No minutes," the voice exploded, obviously frustrated (and that was what Myerson hoped for). Now she quietly handed Marcus the receiver and nodded yes for him to begin answering however he chose.

"Yes," Marcus quavered, "yes, how do I help you?"

Now the voice was loud enough for others to hear as he roared triumphantly, "well, would you listen up now, almighty emperor Comstock wants to help me. Comstock, the ruler of all he surveys is down on his freaky knees to somebody he has treated like scum of the earth. Now listen, asshole, and listen good. Twelve million, that's my demand, hundred dollar bills, unmarked. Twelve million and you get the kid back as long as the cops stay out of it. If I see one person other than you, I signal my men and they will kill her then and there, and so help me I'll give her back to you all cut up neat and in a sack. If it's just you, fine, you put the money in heavy, waterproof canvas bags and deliver it to this location and don't substitute. Heavy canvass equal to a military duffel bag and waterproof. Nothing less than that. Anything else and the deals off, the kid's dead!" "Couldn't you settle for ten million?" Marcus countered. His voice quavered as he posed that question and he was amazed at himself for trying to bargain with Cheryl's life in the balance, but later the FBI would assure him that the question would be helpful in tracking the caller down if there was a pay-off. Indeed the response was revealing. "Ten is fine for me, asshole, but that FBI, fat boys institute, is gonna have every damn serial number and you bastards are not gonna trace it to me after I get it. It goes overseas and is traded for currency that can't be traced. My friends in Africa and the Near East will need to be paid the remaining two mil as a commission.

"Now there is a 640 acre field of flat wheat stubble at the corner of Tokio Road and Lauer Road near Odessa in Adams County. Those cops listening to all this can tell you exactly how to get there. There will be a red flag on a pole right in the middle on October 20.

"Drive your fancy Explorer out there and leave the bags and take off down the road. No cops nowhere, no how. One movement out there and I send the radio message and bang, one dead kid. I gotta have time to check the bags. I have figured how much they will weigh with that much currency and they better weigh up right or again, bang, one dead kid, YOU LISTENING ASSHOLE?" "Yes," Marcus answered again with a voice literally quavering with dread.

"You make the drop at exactly 7:45 PM. If you are either early or late, the deal is off and the kid's gone." Marcus Comstock's dread and desperation now prompted another question with the hope it would not agitate the caller more, "will you harm her if you get the money?" In response, the receiver blared a long and raucous laugh, "you can quit your whimpering, mighty emperor, you play fair with me and that kid will be turned loose on a public road somewhere in the state with enough money to call home." I am just going to get the money, because I know the coppers will lose enthusiasm if the kid comes home but if I bump her off, they will try to find me for the next twenty years. There was a moment of silence and then the voice laughed again and added, "oh, by the way, she'll need a bath."

Marcus continued to pursue the details. "You know nobody keeps twelve mil on hand. It's going to take few days to arrange it." The voice responded and it revealed the caller had been doing some calculating, "yeah, asshole, it's a big order, it's a hundred and twenty thousand one hundred dollar bills." Marcus was now gaining more composure as he asked "how about the 24th as the date?" The line was silent for a moment more. Yes, Rolf knew from the various takes he had garnered from local banks that likely was true. In fact he had never seen that much money at one location. He could guess that it would take time and perhaps help from a number of banks, and he responded, "OK, you got it."

There was yet more laughter and then in a mock conciliatory voice the words "oh never let it be said that I'm not a patient, generous man. You have until the 24th just like you ask, isn't that good of me?" Prolonged laughter followed and then "deliver the money on the 24th, 7:45 PM, and if you are one minute early or late, the kid's dead.

Oh, and one more thing, Fat Boy's Institute, you or any of your cop cronies show any sign of following me out after I make the pick up and it's the same result, dead, kid cut up in little pieces, remember that!" And with that the line went to dial tone.

Caldwell now looked at Marcus thinking he looked like he had aged ten years in ten minutes. Protocol possibly would direct that he ask this victim if he wished to pay the ransom at all, but Marcus, both by a light affirmative nod and the expression of hope, answered the question. He would take the risk; it was only money. Marcus had already explored the matter of a large demand with his own bank and with most of the local Comstock family. Burnsides and Cottrells weighed in that they were ready to help if needed. Actually more in the neighborhood of thirty million could be raised but no need to let on to that.

Caldwell turned to agent Barnett and asked, "we got all that?" "Every word and good quality sound record, but I'm afraid we won't learn much. The call was a cell transmission, and this guy is obviously mobile. I think forensics will pick up a lot of automobiles and a number of trucks in the background, so it came from a main highway somewhere, but that's about it until we find out what towers carried the repeat; and that won't tell us much because this guy is obviously on the move at freeway speeds."

Roger Caldwell thought for a moment and then, smacking his right fist into the palm of his left hand he exclaimed, "the bastard is going to come in by airplane. That has to be it. It would be the only way to get out of that farm area without having to expose himself to apprehension somewhere over at least fifty miles of open road. He's going to land just as it's getting dark, probably flying something that can land pretty slow and can carry off a lot of weight."

At that point Barnett, a licensed pilot, joined saying "He knows he can't shut down the likes of Auburn Center and Seatac tower, but he can coerce us into not putting a following aircraft on his tail. He knows we will probably know where the airplane goes. He lands, load the bags, takes off, and flies until it is too dark to see him clearly and then drops the bags from mid air, probably flying pretty low."

Whereupon Caldwell broke in. "that's why he wants it in stout canvass bags, so it will take the drop without splitting open and spreading the bills out to the four winds like they showed in that Butch Cassidy-Sundance Kid movie when they dynamited the box car." Then Barnett continued, "He will bail out near the drop D.B. Cooper style planning to disappear into the woods."

Caldwell now turned to Dr. Myerson, "Judy, what do you make of him now?"

She finished scribbling a note on her yellow pad and, looking up, she answered, "psychotic, legally sane, a narcissist, totally obsessed with hate, primarily for Mr. Comstock and secondarily for society as a whole, strongly convinced of his own infallible brilliance; and there is more, maybe you noticed it. Throughout the whole conversation he never once used the pronoun 'we' and yet we know that there are at least three other people somehow involved. It could be that that is only because he has obviously masterminded this whole caper and that he regards his companions as mere helpers, but also may reveal an intent to liquidate all of them to raise his share to the whole ten million. Of the two alternatives, somehow I am more persuaded by the second. I don't think his concern about the consequences of killing his hostage translates into the same concern for killing off his fellow criminals. We know he wants to leave the U.S., it's the only way he can effectively deal with the types that will launder the money for him in the third world. But if he knocks off his conspirators in the wilds of Afghanistan, who is to know?"

Caldwell thought for a moment and then got out of his chair saying to Marcus, "Well there's a lot to do. Again, the Government usually will not suggest that you actually make a money drop, but you say you are willing to risk it so you better get the money ready. Federal Reserve and Treasury can supply these amounts in hundreds, it's a bulky package, but they can handle it if they know it's urgent, but the risk of loss is yours if you choose to do it."

There was no doubt in Marcus's mind, the risk had to be taken and the issue of how was perhaps still open but the risk of whether was an issue now firmly resolved. He answered with a calm that surprised even himself, "between them, my broker and my banker say they can liquidate enough of our holdings to raise the money. With good luck we can make it back in three years. The whole family has weighed in. My dad and uncles want to raise the whole thing. They said it's like the fire they had some thirty years ago that wiped out our plant. They were stunned for one or two days and then they came roaring back and determined as Hell to rebuild and recover. They did then and they are together and determined this time too. They will do what they must to get Cheryl back."

Caldwell smiled, he was always a bit skeptical of the character of third generation well to do who had known wealth all their lives, but this Marcus III was a scrapper. He was growing to admire the Comstock character.

The stranger had admittedly created his plan skillfully, but he really knew little of big money and securities trading. The plea for a delay in the ransom date was Marcus Comstock's brain child. For all that he would abhor taking any risk that put his daughter in further jeopardy, he was willing to bargain for four more days during which Caldwell's team could pursue the kidnappers before the pay-off occurred. FBI and all local law enforcement groups had been swarming this case from the beginning and the exchange of all incoming information had been going on continuously. It was an integrated team, Marcus had become impressed with Caldwell's energy and determination in directing the investigation. He sensed that Caldwell listened sincerely as other police shared what evidence they had. So, as he endured and suffered the sarcasm and insults of the caller he was also thinking. Every day of delay he could arrange would be helpful and possibly bring about the miracle of finding where Cheryl was held and who were her captors.

In fact, the Comstock family broker would not go into the market for a day or so. Ten million in sales would take no more than an hour on the trading floor. Cash would be in the brokerage account in three to four days and be delivered to a location by Federal Reserve's direction. Early on the fourth day government employees under watchful management would place neatly banded bundles of new $100.00 bills in bags, 100 bills to the bundle, 120 bundles per military type heavy canvass duffel bags. Ultimately there are ten bags that gross 44 pounds each. These are flown to Renton Airport and transferred by armored car to a Titusville bank for storage in its vault until called for.

But while all that was going on other things were happening.

CHAPTER 19

Rodney Griswold was not part of the Titusville detective squad working the Comstock case. He was on day shift, scheduled to begin routine patrol, but something had been nagging at him for days. His recent lecture from the chief and that old retired cop, Frank Hart, had him thinking and now, before going downstairs to his assigned patrol car, he was reading through several pages of the Comstock files. Many things had come to light from numerous contacts with citizens who were in the area where the red Ford was known to be before it disappeared from view. Some statements had value, some did not. As Hart had lectured, which ones are valuable does not always just jump out at you, so, think, imagine and then think again.

Now here was something. It was fairly certain that the Ford did not attempt to cross Titusville and escape to the east, and yet to the west a vehicle would soon run into a police substation and later a satellite sheriffs vehicle yard and dispatch office. Guys as crafty as these kidnapers, would they take the risk posed by the western route knowing that their crime would almost immediately be reported? Not likely. But then, where did they go? Think, imagine and then think again.

Oh, and here on the next page, the statement of one Leroy Smathers, who was working at the 7-11 convenience store at the corner of Pearl Street and an east—west street called Reynolds Road. This bright red, or orange car had come hell-bent down the hill on Pearl and then did a sliding, squealing turn onto Reynolds Road. "Witnesses were unable to identify the brand of vehicle or describe its occupants. One witness did watch the car up Reynolds Road about two blocks where it disappeared from view. It was a statement that did not render much value in and of itself, and yet, look here, several pages away, a seemingly unrelated witness statement. Grumpy old widow, Geraldine McConkey lives on Reynolds Road about two miles west of the Pearl Street intersection. No, she didn't want to talk to police at all. She would give no statement. However, she admitted she was outside at the time of the kidnap using her Rototiller to plow up a portion of her garden patch. No, she didn't see any red cars. Any other cars? She didn't notice, "Damn Rototiller jumps and kicks as it hits rocks and roots, didn't have time to look for no cars although, hmm, yeah there was some sort of truck, pick up, went by . . . no I didn't notice what color, no I didn't notice who was in it."

Rodney closed the file and placed it back in the cabinet and went downstairs to start the day's routine. But his mind kept returning to what he had read. One couldn't really expect to glean much from those two statements and yet, he had the odd feeling he was missing something and so he departed from his usual route of patrol and drove to where he could intersect Reynolds Road and then he turned and drove west. He was half a mile from McConkey's place. Think, imagine and then think again.

He remembered the speeder and the citation he wrote while this discontented young motorist waited. And then it hit him. The tracks into the old garage! What if the culprits had another vehicle at the garage and switched before they left town? Griswold stopped at the garage building and approached it on foot. It was an unpainted affair giving the appearance of being about ready to fall down, but the double doors were securely locked with a hasp and padlock, and they were shiny new! Why would that be?. Years of use had racked the once solid home-built doors and one could slide a hand between them. By pulling or pushing one could separate then just enough to peek inside, and Rodney did that. With the sun still low in the sky the light was poor, and with broken clouds it was darker yet for moments at a time. Going back to the prowler, he secured his flashlight and peeked again spreading the doors an inch or so first one way and then the other. He couldn't see much, but there was something in there!

Finally he decided to muddy his blue uniform trousers by kneeling down and then taking hold of the door edges farther away from the secure hold of the lock he could spread the doors about four inches. With his chin against the ground and his derriere high in the air, he looked ridiculous, but his discovery was most important. Now he could force the flashlight into the space above his head and although nearly falling over in this unbalanced position, he could see that the object was red and written across the back were the words "Crown Victoria." Forcing the flashlight to the right and tilted somewhat lower, he could read a license number.

Griswold called in revealing his find. He was ordered to stay put. Other officers and one FBI agent were soon on the scene and Rodney was relieved to telephone the details of what he had found and how he found it to the district attorney's office in Seattle. Witness statements about a red car going onto Reynolds Road at high speed, Griswold's traffic stop four miles away and his description of the fresh tracks into the garage, and that the license number was that of the rental car still missing all taken together was enough to justify further search. A warrant to search the garage issued.

Rolf had chosen his lock well. The bolt cutters would not cut it, so the hinges on one side fell victim to the crow bar and the doors were pulled away together and left hanging by the other set of hinges. The car was locked and could have been broken into but anticipating the need, the rental agency had volunteered to bring a spare key for the Ford. Finding the get-away car by itself was of little value except to call off the regional scrutiny of red, late model Ford sedans.

Within minutes the vehicle was backed out into the late afternoon light. The car was impounded and tested for finger prints. Arnie did not remember that when the blackberry vines and cyclone fence viciously ripped the glove and painfully cut his left palm, he had pulled the glove clear off and then had slammed the trunk lid shut, leaving his palm and finger prints. The plan had been perfect; blackberry vines interjected a minor flaw in execution.

The ensuing process did not take long. Arnie's prints, taken years earlier by Idaho authorities, were soon matched with the national data base entry bearing his name and description. Other records were checked and by next morning every agency working the case had a copy of the necessary information including mug shot type picture and a data sheet listing descriptive characteristics.

Name: Arnold Robert Sorenson

Height: 5'-11"

Blonde, Blue, small scar over right eye

Various types of employment, welder, machinist

DOB: 8-7-70

POB: Billings, Montana.

Convictions for theft, fraud, assault

Investigated for child molestation. No charges filed.

CHAPTER 20

To Cheryl her time in custody seemed like forever. The first night she quietly wept in despair sleeping little A general feeling of fear kept her listless at first but as day after day had passed without her knowing what her ultimate fate would be, she began to notice that her captors had their emotional problems with this adventure too. She began to see that they tended to get on each other's nerves and that the narrow confines of the old RV were taking their toll. The men laughed less and less.

She was held captive by her wrist held in one shackle of a set of handcuffs connected to a length of chain looped around a chair rung and long enough for her to sit up at the table, but not so long as to allow her to reach the door to the outside. At bedtime she was allowed to stretch out on a musty old mattress down on the floor, but the handcuff remained in place on her wrist. On the third day Bart had suggested that the handcuff be shifted from one wrist to the other every other day or so. After all, they were just holding the kid for ransom. Torture was not their intention.

Bart and "Boss" had been gone for some time now, but she was still bothered. He must have a name other than "Boss" but none of the men ever used it. Somehow she knew something about him but what was it? She just had the feeling that he was somehow part of her life, and by the way, how did he know she had an Uncle Harry? And, where were he and Bart off to now?

She closely studied her two remaining captors. Arnie frightened her. He would stare at her from head to toe for long periods of time, and she was mature enough to sense that he might physically victimize her. Several times Arnie had playfully touched her along the top of her blouse commenting that for such a tall girl some of her essential growth was falling behind. Girls in her class had been warned about men who acted this way Her face would reflect the terror she had of him and then Grunt, the gentle giant, would somehow move in close, there would be snarls and scowls exchanged by the men and that incident would be over. Meanwhile, there was nothing for her to do; there was nothing she could do. Maybe she would be abandoned here to starve. A multitude of other dreadful prospects fleeted through her mind. Her anguish was accentuated by her total isolation from the rest of the world. She had never been so alone before. It was more than a 13 year old should have to deal with, and there were times when she simply stared, shivered and thought very little.

There was nothing to read, and her requests to go outside and stretch a bit were met by Arnie's blunt refusal. Grunt, on the other hand would violate Arnie's orders and he would undo her chain from the chair and lead her in a walking-the-dog fashion around the camp area. That would lead to harsh words between Arnie and Grunt, but more and more Grunt was becoming protective of Cheryl, and there were more thank yous which clearly trumped Arnie's veiled threats. She grew more and more afraid of Arnie and less and less afraid of Grunt. She was not quite sure of what to make of him and surely he must have a name other than Grunt. It all struck her as mysterious; "Grunt" must have some other name and "Boss" must have some other name and yet Arnie was Arnie. It just didn't make sense. Cheryl did come to understand that the giant one had a limited mentality even though she had never talked to such a disabled person in her life before. He was kind to her and in nowise threatening. She felt secure when he was in the building and very insecure when he was not. He would couple some liberty time with her trips to the outhouse on her promise that she would not run. She kept the promise faithfully because she was terrified of the thought of Arnie catching her alone in the deep woods. Walking about with Grunt for a few minutes several times a day was refreshing. It was obvious that this mental ten to twelve year old was becoming fondly attached to a thirteen year old with what appeared to him to be a normal grown up mentality.

In addition to a faint friendship with Grunt, she experienced hours of pleasant diversion with Yelper and Boomer. She kept up her constant sleight of hand feedings of choice table morsels and they in turn grew closer to her. They took to sleeping at her feet. Many times when Cheryl asked for Grunt to lead her to the outhouse, Yelper and Boomer would follow along both going and coming. Her wrists were sore and sensitive to the constant pressing of the handcuffs, but it was not overly painful. Grunt had found clothing she could wear temporarily as he washed and dried her clothes. He curiously studied her underwear but something in his limited mentality prompted him to keep it out of Arnie's reach. Cheryl Comstock was surviving so far.

CHAPTER 21

On October 19, David Julliard led his scout troop south down past Lake Hyas and thence along the next portion of the trail finally to the parking lot which marks the northern terminus of Forest Service Road 4330. It was Sunday, 3:00 PM. He urged the boys to load their packs and then climb into the seats of his carry-all quickly. Several mothers had voiced concerns about this fifteen mile hike because TV weather forecasters had predicted that there would be heavy rains in the mountains. He wanted to get the boys to their homes by 6:00 as he had promised, and it was a three hour drive to North Seattle. Driving the rough dirt course of the road, the boys were laughing and making exaggerated noises about how they were being bounced around as Julliard held the speedometer well above the posted 25MPH speed limit.

Robert Wellington, sometimes referred to by his fellow scouts as Porky, was now calling that he needed to stop by the side of the road to relieve himself. Julliard could not hear what he wanted and called back for Robert to repeat his request. Before he could do so another boy called out, "he wants to have a draining experience." The carryall exploded with twelve year old laughter. Nonetheless Julliard got the message and now the Fortune Creek side road offered

Robert a bit of privacy from any vehicles that might drive by. He turned in and drove to a locked Forest Service gate.

By this time, Robert was desperate and he bolted from the door and ran up the side road until he was sure he was far enough off the main road to be concealed from any passing vehicles. As he stood in that rather awkward manly position the fading sun, nearly down behind the ridge, caused something to glint. Although the scoutmaster was sounding the horn trying to hurry Robert along, young Wellington bent over and picked the up the object. It bore the marks of having been run over several times, but there were some pretty green and red stones that flashed in the sun with more brilliance than the metal. He shrugged and put the thing in his pocket and began to run back down the incline.

A few days later Rosemary Wellington was doing her laundry. Robert's scout uniform was a mess. The woods had been wet, and boys camping out two nights seldom stay clean. With dirt in each pocket, she decided to take the whole outfit outside and turn all the pockets inside out. The left pants pocket yielded something that was dirty but it was not dirt. Not being just sure what this item was she rinsed it until most of the dirt fell away and then she soaped and washed her own hands. Wiping the object dry she noticed that the sets of red and green glass all of equal size and as big as her own ¼ carat wedding ring. She wondered what it was assuming that the red and green portions were colored glass.

Finally she moved toward the wastebasket to dispose of it but then, recognizing that it was probably intended for a girl, she put it up on a shelf above the washing machine intending to tease Robert at the dinner table about who was his new girlfriend. As she did so the telephone rang and she went into a half hour conversation with her favorite shopping partner making a date to prowl the local Nordstrom and Macy department stores that afternoon with plans to be home again by 4:00PM to watch a local talk show.

Meanwhile Caldwell was contacted by the newsroom of a Seattle TV station. An afternoon talk show host wanted the bureau to know that it was going to televise something that might be of importance in the Comstock kidnapping. This odd sounding crank type called saying she was a psychic, and she had vibrations about where Cheryl Comstock was. She would be on the air at 4:30, after the commercials of course. Caldwell had little faith in psychics, but he was hardly overwhelmed with more solid leads so he indicated he would be watching.

The talk show host was a bit ambivalent. The psychic showed up an hour before the broadcast dressed in a long rather garishly colored gown that was somewhere between a Hindu sari and Arab desert garb that was in need of laundry and festooned with small bells that tinkled as she walked. After the 4:30 commercials were complete and the director was calling for action, the talk show host gulped and decided to go ahead. More than half of the combined Comstock task force was watching, so was Rosemary Wellington. The studio audience tittered a bit when they first observed the self proclaimed psychic, but what she had to say was firm, possibly credible. "Oh yes, Cheryl is alive. When she was captured and being carried off, she dropped something, maybe some jewelry, my vision is not clear on that, but I see some red and some green jewels. She dropped this object on a dirt road. That road will lead to where she is."

"Oh great," Dr. Myerson grumped, all we have to do is check all the dirt roads in the western part of the U.S. and that will lead us to our hostage." "You are afraid your professional analysis will be outstripped by a mystic, a mystic who tinkles as she moves," Caldwell teased. "Oh, horse pucky," Myerson shot back. "Anybody could have made that story up."

CHAPTER 22

Late that same afternoon, Donald Robert Wellington came home from his office in downtown Seattle. Although this shift marked the end of the third seven day week in a row, he was simply full of himself. He was playful, and he spiced that play with a few suggestive squeezes and pinches here and there on Rosemary. Not only that, he was unusually warm toward the children. Wellington's work was long and hard, and it usually took him most of the dinner hour to reach a state of humor anywhere near what he was exhibiting tonight. Rosemary asked questions, but Donald was mum as to the source of his euphoria until dessert.

"My company is going to shut down operations for the holiday from December 15 until January 3; and we are getting bonuses. My share will be about ten thousand. So on a whim I called aunt Claudia, you know about what she proposed last year, and I asked her if that offer was still open and she said yes come ahead. So how would all of you like to spend Christmas and have a skiing vacation in Bavaria with Aunt Claudia and Uncle Carl." This was something the family had talked about before. Claudia had invited them three years in a row, but Donald's work schedule had not allowed for it all to the disappointment of Rosemary and the two children. Now they were going to go on an outing they had hoped for, and it was electrifying. Now the Wellington house rang with cheers and laughter.

In the levity Rosemary almost forgot something. "Robert, you don't happen to have a girl that you would like to go along do you?" Robert answered with a blank look, and a 12 year old boy's response. "No, why would I have a girl?" Then his mother produced the battered gold bracelet. Robert shrugged, "oh I found that up in the mountains when we went with Mr. Julliard and hiked up to a Lake."

Robert's father glanced at the trinket and then began to focus on it more seriously. "Dime store junk" Rosemary declared. But Donald was not so sure. He tuned it over and over and then he saw something neither Robert nor his mother had perceived. "Looks like this belonged to somebody, there is a name on the back. It's all scratched up apparently from being driven over or stepped on but those stones look like something better than imitation." Then he rubbed it some more and ultimately he got up from the dinner table, walked to a small desk and took a marking pen from the drawer. He rubbed the black ink over the back of the object and then rubbed it clean with his handkerchief as Rosemary groaned in disapproval, that ink would never come out of the white cotton cloth. But now Donald held it up to the light and mumbled, "I don't know if this is a name or not, at first I thought it was but who would have the name Cherry Blosso?"

Suddenly the content of the talk show came rushing back to Rosemary and now she grabbed the bracelet out of her astonished husband's hand and stared and then with great excitement exclaiming, "there is an 'M' missing at the end, the inscription is Cherry Blossom!" And then came words tumbling from her mouth so fast, Donald was not sure he heard it all but the long and the short of it was this might relate to the case of that kidnapped girl out in Titusville. She had been given the nick name Cherry Blossom. That crazy looking psychic on TV said the girl would drop something on a dirt road indicating where she was being held!

The night receptionist at Titusville police station had some difficulty gathering all of Rosemary's excited discourse. She asked to hear it a second time and then confessed she still was not sure she had heard it right. Then in frustration, Rosemary handed the telephone to Donald and he, in a bit calmer voice, told the whole story. The dispatcher took the Wellington's number, and indicated that this was all quite important and that they would receive a call back shortly. Soon the lines of communication among the members of the task force were buzzing with the news.

It was three o'clock in the morning when Marcus and Judy Myerson approached Bonnie Gay's locked bedroom door, and Judy used her best skills to induce Bonnie to respond. It was no great inconvenience for Bonnie; she was not asleep. Marcus was sure this bracelet was the one her aunt had given her, but due to Bonnie's severe limits on when Cheryl could wear it, he really seldom saw it and, as a man, he really didn't look very closely anyway. Caldwell and Miller agreed they needed to be sure before they mounted the pursuit they had in mind. A number of people and a variety of vehicles had to be assembled, and it would take some hours to do it. Then based on what Kittitas County sheriff deputies and a Forest Service ranger could tell them there would be two and a half hour traverse if the road Robert described was the one they thought it was. Robert and Scoutmaster Julliard agreed to go along and confirm the location.

And so Judy Myerson carefully unfolded a cloth wrapped around the bracelet, and the instant Bonnie Gay saw it she uttered a shriek that could be heard even outside the house. Bonnie's emotional reaction when she saw the battered piece of jewelry confirmed it. This was Cheryl's bracelet. Thank God she defied her mother's orders and wore it to school that day.

Orders went out to assemble the investigatory force. Allowing for a few hours of sleep they were ready by noon the following day And the tension grew because by coincidence, Rolf telephoned to confirm that the cash ransom was going to be ready and he demanded delivery to the agreed drop area warning that delivery must follow the protocol he has specified. The conversation concluded with Rolf's gleeful warning, "you mess up in anyway rich boy and "POP," I put a slug through that kid's head and then send her back to you by UPS."

Something had been bothering Dr. Myerson that morning. So far the assumption that Rolf was far away at least eliminated him as the prime suspect. He could not be one of the four men seen at the kidnap site. Nonetheless, experience and a persistently recurring hunch bode otherwise in her mind. That feeling gained additional plausibility in a telephone conversation with Cheryl's uncle, Harry Cottrell, who volunteered that Rolf was such a con artist that he was perfectly capable of creating the illusion of being out of the country. Cottrell was unable to furnish Myerson with any facts supporting his position, but he said that he was absolutely certain from the very beginning that Rolf Burnside was behind the whole thing. After talking with Cottrell, Myerson sat and thought about it. That letter bore post markings indicating it was mailed from Calcutta. So that says we are dealing with a total stranger, but this case doesn't suggest that. It suggests some domestic connection, and Rolf Burnside is the only conceivable person who would fit that profile. Now then, if Rolf is the twisted but creative con man, and uses people the way Cottrell says he does, he certainly could be paying an agent overseas to forward letters so that they bore the appearance of origination from far away. Rolf now became the prime suspect in her mind. She telephoned Roger Caldwell's office and left a detailed message explaining her theory.

Another agent in the office monitored her message and decided to make a telephone call to Austin, Texas. Their local Bureau office obligingly imposed on the State licensing authority, and ultimately a picture of Rolf Burnside, now sixteen years out of date, was dispatched to Seattle and quickly forwarded to all agencies working the case.

On its 24th day, October's weather was still mild; about as warm as would be expected in the Pacific Northwest. If the money drop was to be made as Rolf demanded everything was ready for it. Marcus would depart the house at high noon. Backed up to a rear door of the bank, bank employees would help Marcus load the canvass bags into the back of the Comstock van. Seated on jump seats in the rear would be two grim Treasury agents armed with heavy military type automatic weapons, and the van was to be followed out of town by a car full of FBI agents who would be no more jovial than their counterparts in the van. Twelve million is a heavy responsibility for such guards. The good guys were ready to comply with the demands of the bad guys.

CHAPTER 23

At 7:45, PM Marcus Comstock Jr. drove into the open field described in the ransom conversation days earlier. It was vast, open farm country. The pole flying a red flag was visible about in the middle of the large field of stubble as Burnside said it would be. Presently the antiquated but still air worthy Noorduyn Norseman appeared from the east gliding downward toward the stubble. To Marcus the aircraft was much quieter than he thought it would be, and when it touched down it was slowed to taxi speed in perhaps three hundred feet. Indeed the Canadian built craft was designed to land in undeveloped fields and dry river beds at slow speeds and yet lift heavy cargo loads to service the needs of towns and villages in the far north where no paved roads or airstrips exist.

The pilot was alone. Now, with the van and the aircraft separated by some 50 yards the pilot kept the engine running. The officers stayed discreetly hidden in both the van and the auto a quarter of a mile away. Now the pilot was pointing downward. Marcus understood and dragged the sacks out of the back of the van. When the last sack was on the ground, the pilot pointed directly at Marcus and then jerked his thumb in the direction from which Marcus had come. In other words, "leave." Marcus Comstock complied leaving a sizeable fortune lying loose on the ground. The airplane waddled over to where it was close to the money. Following instructions Marcus did not stop to watch the loading procedure. Headed south toward I-90, he ignored the federal officers as if they weren't there. There was naught for the agents to do but go home. The Norseman was now far off to the north and climbing away. The federal officers watched feeling almost unclean as they allowed twelve million good American dollars to disappear from view. One would almost think the money was theirs; but they followed their orders. No effort was made to pursue.

Rolf Burnside flew a disjointed course first to the east and then to the south, but never more than a hundred miles from where he left Marcus Comstock. The Norseman flew slow but gracefully and he kept in cloud cover as much as he could for the first hour, but as darkness began to descend on the landscape, he headed downward and flew along the ridges of the hillsides scarcely more than 300 feet above the ground.

It was dangerous, but he was deliberately leaving a bewildering trail that would frustrate surrounding aircraft controllers especially Auburn Center which tracks virtually all flights in the general area. Watching his fuel, now he decided it was time for his rendezvous with Bart. Taking the most serious risk of all, he dropped into the Canyon of the Yakima River upstream from Yakima City and followed the twisting course of this high ridged canyon. Depending on the headlights on State Route 821 as it winds through the canyon toward its joinder with I-82, and knowing that with the dark they would be subsiding somewhat, he defied the treacherous winds and downdrafts that prevail there. Then, with all lights off, he increased power and began to climb out of the canyon and over the top of the Ridge. Then from an altitude of 1200 feet, above the ground he followed the headlights on interstate 90 east for some distance. North of the freeway, there were few lights and mostly the view was black with the night, but Rolf knew the vacant fields were there. He continued and lowered his engine to scarce more than an idle and then raced it a bit and slacked it off again. Then he saw the light he was looking for. Bart was shining a spot light straight up from the bed of the pick up acknowledging his location. Bart had parked in the middle of a vacant field chosen weeks before.

Rolf dropped down to what he guessed would be fifty feet above the light. Weeks before, Bart had modified the Norseman equipping it with a drop door on its bottom side. Bracing himself and powering the Norseman engine to its maximum, he pulled the lever releasing this trap door and with that the aircraft jerked with the added drag, but he held it steady. The canvas bags obligingly fell out of the bottom and within fifty yards of where Bart was standing. Rolf now climbed back to 1500 feet as Bart's contrivance went up into its second phase pulling the door closed.

Swinging back over the spotlight again, he aimed the faithful Norseman almost due east and engaged the auto pilot. He hesitated a moment now with gripping fear and trepidation. He was about to do something he had never done in his life before, and he had never even talked to anyone who had. But the lure of twelve million kept him focused, and made the fear manageable. He rolled out of the seat onto the wing struts and then dropped himself away. Jerking his parachute ring, he floated down 250 yards from where Bart was gleefully locating and loading the canvas bags. The poor Norseman flew to the Idaho border and crashed into a hillside. Obligingly, it burned furiously. Laughing and cheering, Rolf and Bart drove away across the field, onto the road from the farmer's driveway soon accessing I-90 and then headed west. As they drove through the night, Rolf again explained to Bart that, although he was not sure how closely his flight could be tracked, he did know that his jump could not be identified and radar observers would only know that the dot on their screens would show his aircraft flying easterly for one last leg of traverse and then the little dot on the screen would simply disappear.

Northwest air traffic controllers reported they had lost a blip from their screens, but until the burning wreck was called in by an anonymous motorist, no one reported anything unusual. So far Rolf's plan was working beautifully and he was now elated. He and Bart had the sacks securely tied down and covered. The next step was to drive northward, off the main freeways and into very remote country where they would simply lay low in two different motels for two or three days to allow for those law enforcement clowns to ponder the wreck of the Norseman. By then they would begin to assume that Rolf had skipped out and it should be possible to drive back to the camp in broad daylight and proceed from there.

Bart and Rolf now relaxed somewhat knowing that they were past the point wherein they had thought things might go wrong. Nobody knew where they were. Nobody could have any idea where to look. Bart literally bubbled over, "what a man could do with a share of all that cash!" Rolf agreed outwardly, but his elation was a bit subdued. He was now contemplating how he could commit three murders in a foreign country and get away to the rest of his life in paradise. He had not thought this part out in full yet, but what the hell. Hadn't his plan been brilliant?

He would be true to his promise to turn Cheryl loose unharmed. She was, after all, his daughter even though she had no idea about her father's identity. He had disappeared even before she was born. Nonetheless she was his and somehow that now meant more than it ever had before. This was a part of him, not just a child support obligation. But the money! Yes the money and the success of the elaborate, complicated scheme he had engineered. Yes people would talk. Taverns and other watering holes would ring out across the nation toasting the brilliant success of Rolf Burnside. Would be Robin Hoods would pronounce him the greatest since D. B. Cooper. And Cooper only he made off with 1/48th as much loot!

Now that curr dog Marcus Comstock would suffer a terrible loss because he stole Rolf's wife. Serves the bastard right, yes sir! And now, turning to Bart, he gloated, "you know Bart, I could have pulled off this caper in five or six days and ended up with just as much money as we've got back there now. Comstock was a push over, but by God I was goin' to teach those people a lesson they never will forget. They've been scared out of their skulls for weeks. I'll bet that Bonnie Gay, that whore, and big ass Marcus, that curr, have been through the hell they deserve. Old Marcus now knows his high falutin' money doesn't mean crap when Rolf goes after him. No sir it doesn't! I'm tellin' you. I can't wait 'till I get overseas and then let them know who it was that pulled off this brilliant caper and reduced ol' Comstock to beggin' me on his knees when I talked to him. You'd a thought I was God Almighty when he asked me what he could do for me. Oh man that was a laugh! And I bet that big boss father of mine and those gold plated favorite brother and sister of mine will have some respect for me now. Yes sir. It'll be the first time they ever thought I could do crap, but now they know. There's goin' to be respect for Rolf Burnside now."

Bart had been elated and in a bravado mood contemplating what he believed was to be his share of great wealth, but now his feelings were mixed. Bart was no psychologist, but Rolf's crazed expression and his ranting were alarming. Although he now for the first time knew the name of his boss, he relied on Rolf's story that he had to remain anonymous because someone might guess who he was. Now Bart was not sure, was Rolf simply excited by their successes so far or was he a bit crazy? He did not want to think the worst, but he was also unsure as to Rolf's future plans.

For the first time in the duration of their partnership in crime, Bart noted that Rolf's references to the act were all in the first person singular as though nobody else was involved. For the first time he wondered if Rolf, now appearing like a raving lunatic really regarded his three companions as a team. Bart had assumed from his earliest meeting with Burnside that Rolf's warm recruitment meant that they would be the four musketeers, one for all and all for one. He suddenly found himself wondering, could he be wrong in that assumption? Bart was now uneasy both because of Rolf's unexpected raving and because of the now twisted, contorted look on his face. For months Bart felt more and more confident of the success of this adventure because no matter what developed, Rolf was firm in his dealings with the men, and he had a self assurance in dealing with people that would equal that quality in the day dreams related in the book, The Secret Life of Walter Mittey, "the old man will get us through hell.' Now he was not so sure what the "old man" could get us through.

CHAPTER 24

Arnie pondered the delayed return of his co-conspirators, trying to reassure himself that everything was going OK. He knew the boss's agenda and fully realized that he was not due back in camp for several days after the money drop even if that phase went perfectly. He also knew that if there was some good reason for it the return might even be later. But today he was anxious about it and it affected his mood. He fully expected to see Bart and the boss arrive in the truck with those canvas bags yesterday as they had so meticulously planned; and when the next two days came and went without any sign of them, he grew more and more edgy. And that reflected in his attitude toward the mild mannered, simple minded Grunt. To tone down his concern, he violated Burnside's primary rule as he dug a bourbon bottle out of the tool box and began nipping at it from time to time. Being cooped up in this hovel with its minimum comforts for more than two weeks without any contact with the outside world was talked about in the planning, but actually enduring it was more wearing than Arnie had anticipated. In fact doubts about the wisdom of having gotten involved in this caper began to bother him It was midnight before the need for a restless, broken sleep overcame this strange new feeling of dread.

Oh well, perhaps today was the day. The thought had him awake by 6:00AM. Surrounded by high peaks the camp would be in the dark for some time to come yet, but Grunt heard Arnie stir and obediently arose and soon was preparing breakfast. Cheryl was becoming very weary of her incarceration and slept until later, but as Grunt was setting aside a plate for her and then beginning clean up of the remaining dishes, Cheryl awoke to pain. She complained that her wrist hurt from the constant presence of the metal cuff. Grunt stopped and examined the area of her complaint, and it was apparent that the skin was raw and red. Grunt had grown to like their young prisoner because although she was feisty and defiant with the other men, she was cordially appreciative of him. His childlike mind was awash with doubts now about how such a sweet person could have intentionally caused grief the likes of which had been described by the boss.

After some whispered conversation between them while Arnie was outside, Grunt unlocked the shackle with a key. Cheryl had been watching how the men handled that key all the while she was in their custody. They were careful never to let it be within her reach.

Grunt tenderly massaged the sore area and the raw skin. She hurt some from the salt in his moist palm, but it was a kindly act and she voiced no complaint. Instead, she busied herself pushing a small wad of paper napkin into the slot where the locking tang would seat when the two halves of the cuff were pushed back together. Arnie was still outside and saw none of that. About the instant Grunt finished his massage effort, Arnie walked in and the first thing he saw was that there captive was loose although making no effort to run. With his mind clouded from a hang-over generated the evening before, he had taken a foolishly long drink of the bourbon on an empty stomach before breakfast. He exploded with an invective of tension release and alcohol clouded judgment. He was especially unnerved by the sight of Cheryl without the shackle since he, like all the others, had come to recognize that this teenager was very resourceful and once loose might try just about anything. Cheryl quickly took the initiative replacing the shackle and with apparently a strong thrust, pushed the tang into the slot. The clicking sound of the tang being secured in the locking mechanism was muffled, but Arnie did not notice that detail, and then he continued to rant against Grunt.

"Grunt you stupid son-of-a-bitch, what'd you let her loose for?" "Her arm hurt, Arnie, we don't have to be mean to her," but Grunt's efforts to placate the nervous and addle brained Arnie were of no avail. Arnie ranted on and Grunt hung his head in response, his mind was too slow to mount any significant defense about being decent to this child. He turned red and stammered but could say little of consequence. None of what he said came out audibly and now Arnie was yelling again, "get out of here you slope-headed moron. Go down to the creek and wash some clothes or something, just get out of here." Grunt retreated through the door and walked away weeping. Cheryl had never in her life seen a grown man cry and sympathy welled up in her heart. Now she was weeping some too.

For all that Arnie was furious, he was also being moved by deeper and more basal instincts. "Well, let's see how badly hurt you are girly," Arnie sneered and with that he jerked her jeans down. Cheryl now froze as Arnie fondled her and she was doubly terrified as she noted that he was now violating the boss's orders. He had his 22 revolver tucked in his waistband. Her terror was visible, but it subsided in an instant as she also realized that it was her life that was being bargained for and if he harmed her fatally, he would have to face the boss's immeasurable wrath. Now affecting a juvenile voice, Arnie continued, "Let's have a look under these cute little panties and see just how grown up you are." He grabbed the waistband of the underwear and began stretching the elastic. Cheryl was terrified but not frozen, she responded with a fist to his ear and another between his legs simultaneously letting loose a blood curdling scream sufficient that Yelper and Boomer bolted out the half open door.

For all that Grunt was a child in mind, he was a man in physique. He naturally enough felt normal urges around adult women, but somewhere in his lifetime some mentor or custodian had drilled a strong sense of right and wrong into his mind with reference to sexual conduct. Not only that, Bart's parting words whispered to him down at the outhouse now came to mind. Cheryl's scream told him that what Bart warned about was now happening. In ten steps he was at the door and spurred by a sense of urgency, he inadvertently pulled the door so hard he ripped the top hinge loose from its frame and left it hanging awkwardly. Filling the doorway with his massive size he literally bellowed out, "you leave her alone. If you touch her again I will do very mean things to you." Arnie had a good deal of respect for Grunt's cooking, but otherwise had no respect for him as a man. He had great difficulty bringing himself to realize that if Grunt was ever angered enough to be violent, the strength and agility he demonstrated in the school yard would lay out a lesser man cold or worse.

"Awe fer Christ sake Grunt this little bitch doesn't mean anything to us, and you could have her in bed with you after I finish with her; would you like that?" Once again, pre-breakfast booze had led Arnie down the wrong path.

Grunt swept past their cowering hostage and in a single movement heaved Arnie out the door and slammed him up against the side of the RV with feet clawing the air some three feet above the ground. "All right all right, I won't do anything to her Grunt, now put me down." Grunt slowly obliged but Arnie was, if anything, treacherous when he had been humiliated. Suddenly the revolver was out, but Grunt knocked it to one side and in the next few moments they struggled back and forth trying to get possession of the gun, but now Arnie had it again and he fired at Grunt. Lying on the ground, his effort was awkward and he missed.

With the sharp crack of that first shot, Grunt was panic stricken and he ran. Arnie's alcoholic humiliation momentarily turned to madness. Running after Grunt he fired again, and Grunt went down in a thick growth of yew wood brush. Angered more and determined to take it out on Cheryl he turned and ran to the RV some fifty feet away. She was gone! Now he ran back, "Grunt, get up, she got away, the boss will kill us if we don't catch her, Grunt, Grunt what the hell is the matter with you get up!" Grunt moaned but did not stir.

CHAPTER 25

Cheryl had only a moment's lead, but she made the most of it. The paper she had stuffed in the shackle locking mechanism had done its work. One fierce pull by a frightened teenager was enough and the shackle broke open. She ran toward Gallagher Lake although she did not know it was there. Instinct told her that Arnie would pursue and probably go the same way, so when she heard the second shot, she dove into the brush on the side of the mountain and moved upward as fast as she could with her head bent down trying to remain concealed. However, she had more time than she expected. Arnie was now standing over the apparently lifeless body of Bart's gentle servant.

His body froze with fear when he began to think what Bart would do to him when he found out he had murdered Grunt. Then he agonized over what the boss would do when he heard Cheryl had escaped. Arnie was terrified by the circumstances that he had inadvertently brought upon himself. He resolved that although he now felt terribly sorry for the helpless man at his feet he must leave him and try to recover their hostage and failing that the only safe way for his survival both from law enforcement as well as Rolf and Bart's wrath was to desert this crazy scheme and run.

It was now 8:45 AM and the sun was just now peaking over the ridge of the mountains east of the camp. The brush was still wet with dew and Cheryl was soaking, but she never noticed it. Now she was high above the camp and trying to pick a route that would keep her concealed as she put more and more distance between her and Arnie. She had heard the shots from the .22 revolver but had no idea Grunt was the target. Her sole fear was Arnie. All during the time of her confinement Arnie tended to stare at her and his expression was not reassuring. The longer she was held, the more he gazed at her staring up and down her frame for minutes at a time. She was as uncertain as Arnie himself as to when the boss would return and restore the strict order that he had held while in camp. Escape was her only choice, but "my God," she thought, "where in the world am I? I'm in the mountains, but what mountains? Where? Which way do I walk to get home?"

After gaining enough vertical distance so that she could look down on the canopy of trees that marked the camp site, she altered her course and began a level traverse, hoping to put the whole mountain between her and Arnie. Her good physical condition served her well. Soon she was more than half way around the mountain and facing south. She failed to notice a small hole hidden by the mountain blueberry brush directly in front of her.

Almost 8 decades before Cheryl's desperate effort to escape, two Irish brothers, Richard and Randall O'Brien and a twelve year old orphan, Donald Skokolich were living in a small log cabin two hundred yards to the south. With the nation locked in the worst depression ever, the men were trying to eke out a living mining the paltry deposits of gold dust locked in Hawkins Mountain. Their mine shaft yielded scarcely an ounce for every foot of excavating progress.

Then one day, fortune smiled as the men inadvertently tunneled up to the beginning of a small lava tube created by volcanic actions millions of years ago. In the time that passed from the formation of the hollow tube until its discovery, uncountable spring snow melts had sluiced muddy waters down through the tube ultimately filling it with a rich condensation of dust and nuggets. They had struck it! Problem was the tube was so small that although a man could crawl into it, that would leave him with his arms virtually immobile and without enough room to work a shovel or any other tool to extract the gold-rich mud.

The men had taken Donald in to keep him from starving. They teased his skinny frame calling him a runt. Now, his undernourished skinny frame was a blessing and a reward for their charity. Donald could work the narrow tube just fine extracting one bucket full at a time. By time snow flew that year, the men and boy had bored their way to where the tube came to an end on the surface of the mountain. They split $21,000, a respectable fortune for those times.

Nature began refilling the tube, but she was in no hurry and a skinny person could still crawl down its length if one did not mind getting muddy.

* * *

Suddenly the brush let go and Cheryl was waist high in a strange depression. For the moment, the mystery of the hole was less inviting than the freedom of being out in the open and she managed to pull back up out of the hole ready to run some more. But at that moment she heard a yell, "You may as well stop kid, I see you now. If you don't want to get hurt stop right where you are." It was Arnie yelling at her from 150 yards away. By good luck or by impulse or both, Cheryl pulled deeper into the hole and was now invisible.

The blueberry brush obligingly closed in over her head. The hole was uncomfortable, but it did seem to be a possible hiding place and so she managed to get herself turned around and began crawling.

Much of Donald Skokolich's excavation had been lost to silt and sand from annual spring snow melt. In places she could just barely squeeze through, but her mortal fear of Arnie kept her going despite a spate of claustrophobia She crawled for what seemed to be an interminable distance, but now having been blind as a mole for some thirty minutes and with her hands and knees thoroughly mud soaked, she thought she could see a faint light ahead. It wasn't enough to warn her and when she got to the place where the man made bore began, she could not perceive the drop from the lava tube down to the bottom of the intersecting, man made tunnel. Without warning the lava tube gave way and she grabbed desperately at the dirt overhead with both hands. It was not enough to cushion the fall but it did turn her from nearly upside down to a more or less upright position and her body fell to the tunnel floor.

Her right leg caught between two large rocks loosened by the last O'Brien dynamite blast causing her ankle to twist wretchedly and causing her to scream with a pain the likes of which she had never felt in her life before. She worked her way loose from the stones that had twisted her right knee shin and ankle and felt as though she had lost the use of her whole right leg. Nonetheless, she was determined to follow that faint light.

She began to bump along the rough passage, half walking, half falling and the pain increased. Then she passed out. When she came to the pain in her leg dominated her conscious awareness, but she had also hit her head harder than she knew. It was a concussion that bordered on being a life threatening fracture. When she could move, she made her way down to where she came out of the mine shaft and shortly came upon the ruins of the O'Brien cabin. The effort caused her to pass out again, and when she regained consciousness this time it was dark and raining. Cold and disoriented, she crawled under a remaining portion of the shake covered roof. There was a small area that was dry offering a cold refuge that at least was out of the rain. Still shivering in spite of her jacket and her heavy jeans, she slept off and on until dawn.

CHAPTER 26

Roger Caldwell and Harold Miller were starting another day. Now they were leading a caravan of vehicles east bound and then turning off the freeway onto Bullfrog Road. Coincidentally, a white pick up coming from the opposite direction, accessed the same exit about a minute later. Rolf and Bart had seen too many prowl cars on the roads everywhere they went, and, wisely decided to go into hiding at a dingy hotel for a few days. They knew Arnie would be anxious by now, but there was no sense getting careless now that they were so close to total success. A couple of days in hiding would cause the intensity of the post money drop response to cool

It was raining now, but the canvass bags were well covered and the load was shedding the water nicely. The plan was to sneak back into the camp and pick up Arnie, Grunt and the hostage. Then with Cheryl back in the beet sack and stowed in the tool box in the back of the truck, they would brazenly drive to Seattle arriving about 8:00 PM well after the rush hour. They would leave the beet sack and its human content out in the back yard of some one whose property was close to the freeway.

Cheryl could kick and scream and sooner or later someone would find her. Meantime, they would drive on into and out of Seattle following the freeway north to Marysville and then the men would hole up in a house

144

Rolf had rented weeks before. They would stay there until they could repackage and crate the currency marked as "Clothing Donations for Tsunami Relief," get it loaded on a freighter the master of which would transport them and the money to an India location where underground agents were waiting to do business. The devious merchant mariner would provide these services for $100,000.00.

But now Rolf was seized with panic. Bart's speed was faster than Caldwell's caravan and now as they all motored out of Roslyn, they were overtaking it! As Rolf stared wide-eyed at the vehicles ahead, he knew in an instant that this many police type vehicles all traveling together were either on a rescue mission or they were after someone. Suddenly he felt crushed. His voice surprised Bart. It was weak and quavering as he ordered, "Bart, turn around we gotta get out of here." The big Dodge turned around and disappeared from the area.

Based on what Robert told his parents and what David Julliard had described of the road branching off from Forest Service Road 4330, the Cle Elum office of the Forrest Service guessed that it had to be one of two possible side roads and that the probable condition of any side road would be passable, but barely so, and perhaps not very far in from 4330. Based on that, four of the six vehicles of the caravan now crossing Boulder Creek were four wheel drive. The rain was heavy.

Caldwell was intrigued. Just how accurate was this strange appearing psychic when she ventured to say "Cheryl has dropped something that will be found and identified as hers, and this will be on a dirt road. She will be found somewhere on that road."

The caravan crossed the Fortune Creek bridge and continued. Suddenly both Julliard and young Robert broke the silence almost simultaneously. "It's back there!" "Yeah we went past it." Caldwell stopped his car and the rest of the caravan stopped behind him. With all eyes on them, Robert and Julliard pointed back down the road; and, indeed, from this uphill position an intersecting road could be seen so the caravan awkwardly blocked the entire main road getting turned around.

With their course reversed, the six vehicles turned off at the intersecting road. Some distance eastward they encountered a yellow guard gate. The gate was chained to an upright steel post and the chain secured by a substantial padlock.

Now the men in the front rig were out and looking at the gate as Robert showed the approximate location where he stood relieving himself when he noticed the bracelet. Caldwell was about to try a C.B. radio call to the Forest Ranger office hoping to secure a key, but he inadvertently leaned against the locking post as he pushed the "talk" button on his microphone and noticed that it moved more than it could have if it was buried as deep in the ground as it appeared to be. Now he lifted on the gate post and it obligingly came up out of the ground. With a bit more effort it cleared the inner pipe the kidnappers had put there weeks before. As Miller and Caldwell looked at the altered gate, they could understand how the conspirators could be hidden out behind this gate for weeks without detection. The gate had looked securely locked.

They recognized now that it was a very clever subterfuge and Miller whistled softly, "boy these guys are something else." He had to have some admiration for the thoroughness manifested by these culprits so far. One way or another most criminals will make some mistake that hastens their apprehension, but if this crew had made a mistake, the law hadn't uncovered it yet. However both men and the supporting officers were encouraged because the bracelet was most certainly dropped by the victim, and young Wellington knew exactly where he first saw it.

Now they were on their way up the road in a vehicle that was a little less crowded. Julliard and Robert Wellington were left waiting in one of the two-wheeled cars where they should be safe from whatever developed and further where another car could meet them and drive them out of the woods and thence home later in the day. For now both of them indicated they would like to stay and see what developed.

The four wheel drive police vehicles made their way along the drainage of Fortune Creek for several miles when the lead vehicle crested a rise and then dipped down where the road came closer to the creek. Caldwell was watching the road hoping not to get stuck or go off its narrow grade. It was slow going, but it had obviously been traversed before. At the top of that rise Harold Miller stiffened and raised up in his seat. "There's somebody walking down the road toward us." With that Caldwell signaled the caravan to stop and he shut down his engine and signaled the others to do so. Presently a figure came walking in a somewhat stumbling manner, rubbing first his eyes and then the back of his neck and mumbling. He was talking to himself appearing very distraught. He appeared to be oblivious to the presence of vehicles ahead of him. Miller voiced the opinion that this individual had drank his breakfast. After looking as closely as he could, Caldwell opened a file he was carrying and frantically leafed through it stopping at a photo and pointing at it so Miller would notice. "I think you're right" Chief Miller responded. The man kept coming toward them and was now within a few feet. His concentration on whatever was bothering him must have been almost hypnotic. He was now twenty feet away and still did not seem to notice the vehicles parked directly in front of him.

In fact, with the combination of inebriation and the agony of losing their hostage after so much effort coupled with a mortal fear of what Bart would do to him when he found out he had killed Grunt; Arnie was now drained of all initiative and all instincts of self preservation. When Roger Caldwell stepped in front of him, it broke his moribund spell. Caldwell spoke consolingly saying, "Arnold Robert Sorenson, you don't seem to be having a very good day." Sorenson looked up wearily, nodded his head yes and stopped with eyes downcast

"We know you were in on Cheryl Comstock's kidnapping Arnold, where is she?" Arnold answered in a monotone, "we had her up the road in a camp while we demanded a ransom, but she got away from me."

Puzzled, Caldwell continued, "*You* let her go, but Arnold we know there were four of you. Why isn't she with the others?" Without Rolf to coach him Arnold Sorenson felt all his defenses were gone. Further he was suddenly sick of the whole venture. He had shot that poor dummy and left him. He had lost the hostage and then spent hours looking for her without success. All the fight was gone out of him. He knew this was the end of the road for him, and somehow he was glad of it; it was a relief. Now the whole story tumbled out of him but in a disorganized narrative. Roger Caldwell felt more than a little amazement to learn that all of this brilliant yet grotesque scheme had been engineered by a father and ex husband that had had no other contact with the victim family for more than 13 years.

After listening long enough to know that Bartholomew and Burnside were picking up the ransom and would probably be arriving with it soon and that Cheryl had run away and into territory where she probably would get lost, Caldwell ordered the fourth vehicle to return to Salmon La Sac and begin to organize a search party. Hearing Arnie relate the facts of Grunts death, he and Miller quickly told the Kittitas County sheriff deputies that they probably had a homicide on their hands. Then with Arnie handcuffed in the back seat, Caldwell drove on at the highest speed he could attain with Arnie helpfully describing those portions of the road where he had best slow down to avoid tearing the undercarriage out of the vehicle.

Finally they came to what appeared to be nothing more than a stand of fir timber with underbrush, but under Arnie's direction they drove off the road, through concealing branches and broke out into a clearing with the ugly little house trailer and its several accompanying tents then plainly in view. Two of the deputies walked over to where Arnie pointed out Grunt's location and they made a cursory exam. In a moment or two one of them came running back to the vehicles. "Were going to have to get this Grunt down to the main road and have an ambulance there. He's in bad shape, but he's not dead." The deputy then went silent for a moment to catch his breath and then added, "we do have a blanket in our rig so we can fashion a stretcher, but it's going to take three or four of us to get him back up from the creek; boy he is one big dude."

CHAPTER 27

Cheryl had no watch and really didn't know how long she had slept, but she did know that she was now looking out of the collapsed roof and could hear the running waters of Boulder Creek some 50 feet away. She hurt worse than she ever had before, and she was as cold as she had ever been before. Arnie was no where to be seen, and hopefully, she had eluded him. She was frightened about that no more, but with the pain and the terrible emotional strain she had endured for the last several hours it simply drained her will. Now she sat down in the sunlight and put her head down between her hands.

Hungry, frightened and cold, she wept. But it didn't last. Suddenly a familiar panting bad breath caused her to look up and there was Yelper whimpering with alarm and licking her face. Although she still felt awful, and she knew she must look awful, Yelper was an unexpected tonic. She was not alone.

The search party Caldwell had called for was deep in the hills and quickly combing the wooded landscape. That should have yielded Cheryl's rescue before the day was out. Indeed much later it would be determined that the off-duty Cle Elum policeman would have walked right onto her location, but once again, things went wrong. He was making no effort to be quiet, in fact he had been calling her name farther down the Boulder Creek trail, but the climb was getting steeper and he decided to save his breath. The misfortune was that his civilian clothes were similar in color to what Arnie was wearing as he chased after Cheryl.

When she saw a figure working its way upstream from about 300 yards distance, she was terrified again. How did Arnie manage to get so close? She whispered to Yelper to be quiet and follow her. It was all she could do to walk but in her fright she was making better time than the volunteer looking for her. Her leg was awful and her gait was a hobble stimulated by the fear.

At the end of five hours she had done the unbelievable; she had hobbled and crawled easterly up to the headwaters of Boulder Creek. Doggedly she continued the trek and crested the ridge. Now she was going downhill and she felt better with that. Mercifully, her injured leg was more numb than painful especially if she could manage to keep the knee and ankle stiff and limiting the distance gained with right leg. Sooner or later she would get somewhere. For all of her pain, she was also hungry. Speaking to Yelper she murmured, "oh, how a triple sundae and a hamburger would taste right now." As it drew later into the day she felt she was no longer being followed. She descended more slowly down toward the De Roux Creek drainage, and felt some better as she intersected a trail going downhill that she felt must lead somewhere.

The autumn sun sets more quickly in the mountains as the ridges become the point where it slips from view. And daylight began to pale even more with the incoming clouds. She was beginning to be fearful of where she could get to today. The thought of staying overnight again without much shelter gave her a morbid and growing fear. But she found noting in the way of shelter, and so, taking short rest stops to nurse the injured leg, she hobbled on. In late October these mountains are almost never warm after dark. Walking had dried her clothing, but only continuing to walk kept her warm.

Now it was getting dark and the search was called off for the day. Knowing none of that, Cheryl was now alone with the hound and not sure what to do next. She was hungry, and oh how she longed for one of Grunt's meals. The rain was now mixed with wet snow and she was in the wet again. Walking was painful and now exhausting, but it kept her warm and mostly dry. The temperature dropped rapidly and even with her limited experience, she knew from girl scout training that her death by hypothermia was rapidly becoming a possibility. That frightened her but she had been frightened by so many experiences during this past few days that this new thought did not panic her. She was getting used to confronting frightening things. The rain became relentless and it peppered her with a scattering of large, wet snow flakes

Nonetheless, she kept going, she would have no idea how far behind her Arnie was, but if she never did anything else she was going to get away from his leering stare, his foul words and his roving hands. Earlier in the day it had been warmer and now the deluge of rain caused fog to form limiting her view in every direction. She was totally lost, totally disoriented as to which way might lead where. In fact she had gone a considerable distance for someone who could scarcely hobble Now, she could hear a rush of water that was more than a babbling creek, it was a river. The water was rising even this far upstream, but she thought she could see a trail on the other side of the river and decided to wade across. She stumbled twice and worried that if she fell on the slippery rocks of the bottom one more time, the water might pull her down and drown her.

Worse yet, Yelper had disappeared. She needed his company. She called and called again, but against the looming hills and the sounds of the rain, her voice was not audible over more than fifty yards distance. In one last effort to get somewhere, she crawled up away from the stream. She actually crossed a hiking trail but with the dark and the rain, she did not recognize it for what it was. As she crawled on she made another two hundred yards and then, in a thick grove of trees she dropped. She was done.

The temperature was now in the low forties. She was hungry, tired and her leg hurt so bad it made her vomit. Nothing came up except burning digestive acids, but that did not do much to add to the misery. She crawled up under the branches of a small tree, and when she endeavored to spread the branches so she could use them as cover, they cruelly dumped much of their accumulated water on her. She could not have been more drenched if she had been in a bath tub filled to the brim. She was frightened all the more because for the first time in her life she was so cold that she developed a violent shivering and as it descended on her she panicked by the realization that she could not control it, she could not make it stop. She rolled away from the sapling and then realized she could not get up again, and so she began crawling on her hands and knees. Mercifully now the leg was num. Now she was crawling on two hands and one knee while the other leg dragged behind her. She knew it now. She was going to die.

But again when all seemed lost, the young hound suddenly appeared out of the gloom, he licked her face as if to ask "why was she not on her feet standing above him and ready to pet his dripping head?" Getting no response, he bolted away again and disappeared in the night, and again in a moment he was back with an incessant yap-yap-yapping.

Her mind was dulled by the oncoming hypothermia, but Yelper was insistent, he would disappear in the dark and then in just a moment he was back. He kept at it. What was the matter with him?

And then she saw it. First she could make out the steps and the hand rail leading up to a deck and beyond that loomed a building. It was hard to get up the slippery wooden steps, but ultimately she reached the part of the deck that was covered by an overhang, and that shielded her from the pelting downpour. She rested a few moments and it helped. To Yelper she murmured through her shivers, "can we get in?" Yelper simply sat down and looked at her. He was no help. So she began to crawl around on the deck. It went around three sides of the cabin, and ultimately she located one door and four windows, all securely locked. She knew that she did not have the strength left to muck through the rain soaked yard, find a rock and break a window. Likewise, the door was far more than she could hope to break in, so what's the use?

And now she sat down against the wall where at least she didn't get the drenching the tree had dumped on her. Sitting there she closed her eyes. She was so tired, she hurt so bad, what's the use? The storm was getting worse. Winds were now singing through the trees. That's a pleasant sound as a hiker settles down in a warm sleeping bag after a day's hike and a good meal, but it wasn't very inviting now. The wind increased and then "clunk." Normally she would have been frightened at this unidentified sound, but now she no longer cared, and then "clunk' again; "clunk, clunk" Crawling in the direction of the sound, Cheryl bumped head against a large wooden box and then beyond that she could perceive motion. It was a small window shutter swinging in the breeze as it had done since August 15 last when Oxford Bowman and Harold Jacobs each left it that way each assuming the other would shut it and fasten the inside lock.

The window was chin high to Cheryl or it would have been if she could stand up straight. It was too high for her to crawl up and into the building. Then, remembering the box she crawled back until she felt it. It was heavy, full of something that had been stored there for the winter, but this youngster carried the blood of hardy fishermen. She was now functioning again. Somehow, she was mentally mastering the pain in her leg and she dragged the box to where it was under the window, and then she tipped it up on its narrow side, giving her the advantage of its length. She made several attempts to climb up on it and once she tipped it over and fell. Nonetheless, her determination prevailed and she finally got her good knee on top of the box and managed to grasp the sill with her hands. Fortunately, the window glass was not locked and with the shutter open she could raise the bottom half. It was a small opening, but it seemed big enough for her to crawl through. That is she could, if she could get her whole body up there. With a determined lift of her body, she managed to achieve a one leg stand on the box. Many 13 year olds and their parents could not have done it. But that was as far as she could go in that position. She could not raise her right leg enough to get it through the opening, and she could not hold her body weight with her hands enough to swing her good left leg through either.

In a second attempt, she assumed a position of holding on to the sides of the open window with her hands. Then she leaned back forcing her numb leg to hold her up for an instant and then, commanding all the strength she had, she heisted her good left leg through the opening. It was a narrow bathroom window. Resting for a moment she twisted her good leg back around, but this was not going to work. She eased herself back onto the box, grasped the bottom window sill with both hands and in a push up motion brought herself half way into the room with her head, shoulders and mid torso hanging in and suspended above the floor. The rest of her, hips and legs was still out in the weather. There was no way of knowing just where the floor was but she eased down, forcing herself to ignore the leg pain and finally getting to the point where her outstretched finger tips met the floor. Then she let go and fell the rest of the way.

It seemed like she was in a hopeless tangle of her own arms and legs, and she knew she was more or less wedged in between the wash basin and the toilet stool. Totally unannounced and uninvited, Yelper leaped through the window and landed, muddy feet and all on top of her. Now, mercifully, she was out of the wind, she was inside, but there was absolutely no light in the building, and she had no idea where the building was so, where in the world was she?

CHAPTER 28

The mixed rain and snow were falling at a furious rate. None of the people involved in the effort to find Cheryl Comstock were prepared to weather a storm. To continue the search would risk the lives of the many volunteers who had already arrived and who had scoured the drainage of both Boulder and Fortune Creeks clear to their origins. That was enough. The word went out to call it off even though the general feeling was that if this girl was not found before nightfall, her chances of surviving without proper gear would be next to none unless she found shelter; and for now, the faint possibility that she might find such refuge would keep hope alive.

The searchers regrouped where their vehicles were parked and drove out. Expressions were grim. They had been so close to success. They knew that much based on what Arnie told them about her escape. To fail now seemed to be the cruelest of ironic jokes. Marcus Comstock was the last to walk in. He had begged to stay out longer, but C.B. radio transmissions from down the valley told him he had to go, they had to get out. If this early season snow let up and perhaps even turned to rain, Forest Service personnel and local volunteers with their greater knowledge of the area would be on their way back. They would be equipped with their own personal flashlights, heavy clothing and their own survival gear as early as 3:30AM tomorrow.

For now the search party gathered for one last council at the Salmon La Sac campground. Nobody really wanted to talk to the TV news personnel, but Caldwell did manage to bravely face the glaring lights and cameras to express at least a fleeting hope that Cheryl could somehow survive until tomorrow. When the inevitable blizzard of follow-on questions assaulted them from the several reporters, Caldwell whispered to Marcus, "let's get out of here," and with that they walked through the crowd and to the government vehicle and headed for Cle Elum. On the way, Marcus managed to get through by cell phone to the mansion and briefed Hazel Phong on the terrible disappointment and prepared her for the very strong likelihood that the family had seen the last of Cheryl.

Hazel choked as she talked. She loved that girl like her own. Marcus suggested that Bonnie Gay not be made aware of the call. As a matter of caution, she was not told of today's expedition, and perhaps for now it would be best to avoid the roller coaster ride of hope and dismay. Bonnie's mental stability was not good, and nobody knew how much deeper she would sink into suicidal depression if she were informed. Hazel was at her side 24 hours a day not only because Bonnie Gay held her in complete, if sometimes contentious confidence, but also to maintain a suicide watch. Best for now to continue the subterfuge that "yes, the bracelet had been found and yes they could now narrow the search."

Marcus would go home tomorrow; there was little he could do to help the search party. Others knew the geography far better than him and the number of volunteers was more than sufficient to do the job. No use complicating their task by getting lost himself. However, for tonight, he would seek a Cle Elum motel room putting off the sad traverse home until daylight. He did not sleep well although his personal search efforts on the steep north slopes of the Hawkins Mountain area left him sore, exhausted and well aware of his own physical limits. His mind was pestered well into the wee hours by the concerns he felt about how Bonnie Gay would react when she was finally told of Cheryl's second disappearance.

CHAPTER 29

After falling through the bathroom window, Cheryl knew she must do something to resist the numbing cold. She felt that her shivering could be a precursor to death. Her right leg was a relentless source of discomfort. Every movement took its toll, but she was driven to begin a slow, blind, foot-dragging exploration of her surroundings. Up to this point, her fortunes had been all bad, but now pluck was rewarded. Exploring the doorway, looking for whatever she could discover, she became aware of a shelf just to the left of the door jam. Exploring it Braille style, she inadvertently caused something to drop off the shelf. It fell against her right foot but the foot was numb and it did not register any pain. Feeling around to locate the object took a moment or two, but once it was in hand, its round longitudinal shape could be nothing else. It was a flashlight, and, after some struggle to find a switch, she turned it on. It worked. Liberated from the dark, she began working herself around to examine the simple character of this rustic one room abode.

First, there was the wood stove. She knew what that was. Scout camps usually had a similar appliance although most of them dwarfed this one. There was a set of kitchen table and chairs, lots of cabinets, a battered old overstuffed couch and, of course, the bathroom with its shower, basin and stool. More important for the moment was a set of stairs leading to a loft. Shinning her light up the stairwell, she could see blankets lying askew on an unmade bed. Obviously the last person here had less than fastidious housekeeping standards. More importantly, warm sleeping accommodations, blankets, sleeping bags, and who knows what were clearly available.

Climbing the stairs was the next order of business. It had to be done; she knew she had to get warm. The merciless tumble in the old mine shaft had rendered her right leg usable only with pain and the trek to the cabin had increased the pain rendering the lower leg and foot hideously swollen. But Cheryl had the precious advantage of youth. Her left leg was strong, pain free and very flexible. An active youth had evolved her physique into excellent condition, and, she could think. After studying the stairwell for a few moments and realizing she could not address it facing forward, she reversed herself, sat on the second step and using her good left leg and her arms, she put her hands on the step above her backside and hoisted herself up one step. Her hands slipped and foiled the hoist effort once or twice, but by time she had raised herself to the loft level she had developed an awkward but practical method of negotiating the stairs that she would use thereafter. The ascent would get smoother and smoother and the descent was always bumpy but tolerable.

Indeed the loft was the sleeping area. From her scouting experience, she knew that the thickest of the rolled sleeping bags promised the most warmth, and she was ready for it. She unrolled the bag and climbed into it, clothing and all, and Yelper curled up next to her. Both of them were tired and hungry but for now fatigue deferred any search for food. It was 12:30 AM. For a long time Cheryl could not control her shivering. Curling up into a fetal ball helped some. The stamina of youth and Yelper's bodily warmth finally prevailed. She was still dreadfully cold, but she thought the shivering was subsiding. By 3:00 AM, she was warm enough to sleep, and it was long past dawn when she awoke.

Her ankle was now horridly discolored and swollen so much that she could not remove her jeans. They were still damp but much warmer, and finally hunger pangs forced her to leave the refuge of the warm, goose down bag. Getting downstairs was more difficult than getting up. She had to slide her bad leg ahead of her while moving by pushing her arms behind her being careful not to move the wounded limb in anyway that aggravated the pain. Downstairs it was still dark because shutters and curtains thwarted the natural light. Flashlight in hand, she began to explore the cupboards in a quest for food. A first discovery was a metal can with a painted label that indicated its original content was Fig Newton sandwich type cookies. They were long gone, but the sealed plastic sack of raisins was almost as welcome, at least for her. Yelper tried them but they were too far removed from his regular dog diet.

The owners had a passion for metal storage cans and self sealing plastic bags. Further exploration ensued punctuated by mouthfuls of raisins. Prying off the can lids revealed rice, flour and several types of dry cereal. Moving on to yet another storage cabinet, she found a canned ham and a goodly quantity of pork & beans packaged in 24 ounce size cans. Taking time to use the bathroom even though there was no water in the toilet, she then continued to search. Unbeknownst to her, this cabin's regular occupants were home made ice cream devotees. There was a whole 24 can case of canned milk that was labeled as being specifically for that purpose. It began to look more and more possible that Cheryl could survive here until her leg healed sufficiently to begin normal walking again.

Rustling about in the loft the night before, she had discovered several coats including a down jacket that promised all the warmth needed for this time of year. She had been wearing it ever since she crawled out of the down bag. Things were getting better. During her trip to the bathroom, she had noticed a medicine cabinet and another cabinet with drawers. A cursory search revealed bandages, aspirin, sun screen, soap, toothpaste and several ace bandages. From scout hiking trips, she knew the ace bandage well, and she stopped her general search and did a moderately firm wrap on the swollen leg. Aces are better on knees than on ankles, but it did help.

For now she lacked only one item; water. She was very thirsty and the raisins didn't help. Still guided by the flashlight, she found the door and determined how it unlocked from the inside without a key. So she interrupted her orientation search and began unbolting the shutters to take advantage of the daylight. Before opening the door she had discovered several hiking sticks. Taking one of them she could maneuver almost as well as she could have done with a pair of crutches; but the need for water was still crucial. There had to be a source of water somewhere. Far below she could hear water running loudly down a streambed, but the hillside was steep and it was obviously a long way down. She hoped there was something more accessible.

Walking both of the narrower decks areas located on each side the building, she could see a number of boxes closed up for the winter. She did not try to investigate all of them, but examining their closed lids did lead her to the end of first one side deck and then the other. There was some snow on the ground. She was about to go back and find a dishpan so she could melt snow but then she noticed the sound of another trickle of running water. It was noisy but obviously separate from the stream farther away. She went back in the house, and got a bucket that she had seen in the shower stall. She made her way with the hiking stick in one hand and the bucket in the other and limped out into the slushy snow in the direction of the running water. Even this part of the hillside was treacherous, and caution, born of her harsh fall at the mine, caused her to move very slowly testing each step by making a preliminary probe with the stick Forty feet down the hillside there it was.

Water was running out of a one inch plastic pipe and from the opening it had cut a small channel in the dirt clear to the creek now clearly visible ahead and way below where she was standing. A fall from here would see her tumble clear to the creek and then leave her facing an impossibly steep climb back to safety. She now moved with even more caution. Bending over and holding onto the cold pipe, she filled the bucket. It was too much so then she dumped out about one fourth of the clear cold water. The crouching position hurt her but she laughed to see Yelper slip and slide down the hill with his belly sledding on the snow and all four paws clawing frantically. When he finally stopped, he scampered back a ways and then began lapping water from the pipe. He did that for a long time. Cheryl was in an awkward, near falling position and though her thirst was compelling, she deferred having a drink until she could get back to the level surface of the cabin deck. She had been without water for some 36 hours and it felt as though getting back to level ground was taking forever.

As she stood on the level deck carefully balancing the bucket and the hiking stick, she suddenly noticed something else. It was a valve protruding from the edge of the deck. It was dry but emitting a hissing and bubbling sound. It was of a kind one raised in the city might not understand but she recognized it immediately as a water valve the likes of which could be found at every one of Uncle Harry's stock watering troughs. On a hunch, she hobbled over to where it was and turned it on. By time she had made her way through the slippery snow and started up the steps, she knew that she had both a blessing and a problem. She could hear water gushing from the shower head and the sink faucet. It was also splattering on the floor from an open valve on an old hot water tank located on the wood burning side of the stove.

Well, she could just as well dump out the water from the bucket now. Cheryl hobbled as fast as she could from place to place turning off each valve until at last the sound of water splattering on the floor had stopped. The plumbing was operational; the toilet filled itself and stopped hissing. Soon air in the lines cleared as she ran the faucets and then the water ran smooth and strong. The cabin had a gravity water system wherein they had tapped a spring high on the hill above the cabin and installed a one inch plastic waterline from there to the building. Although it was buried deep enough to resist freezing, it had been turned off as a part of winter closing. It was clear, cold, delicious water albeit with a grain or two of sand from time to time. She was in no condition to do it, but rigging a mop out of the hiking stick and a towel, she managed to mop up most of the water on the floor. The cabin was still cold and for several hours, the wet floor refused to dry.

Next she found sugar lumps and dry cereal which she put on the table along with a bowl of the condensed milk watered down about one to one, and this was breakfast.

Delicious! Yelper was devouring a dishful of canned salmon. The pain in her leg, aggravated by her determined exploration coupled with the comfort of food and warmth, soon rendered her totally exhausted. She crawled back into the big bag and slept for hours.

She awoke in daylight although she was not sure what time it was or even what day it was. She reluctantly crawled out of the bed and again endured the pain of crawling downstairs where she made additional discoveries including a small benzene lighter backed up by a full box of matches, and a coal scuttle full to the handles with red cedar kindling. She knew how to lay up kindling and light a fire. Cold, heavy air in the chimney caused the smoke to rise only sluggishly and some of it backed up into the cabin, but eventually the stove began burning brightly. All the wood was dry, the fire grew hot and within two hours the building was warm. Finally the floor was dry. Better yet, for the oncoming night, there was an oil stove hooked up to a fifty-five gallon oil barrel outside. Figuring out the outside shut-off valve and then the carburetor float valve lever took most of the rest of the day, but now she had heat and soon a tank full of hot water. Cheryl also examined the downstairs ceiling and finally discovered the Coleman gas lamps. They were just like the ones Uncle Harry's men used when they were working the outer range of the Cottrell grazing areas. For all that she was tall for her age, she had to stand on a kitchen chair to reach them. There were four of them and each had a Coleman type propane bottle attached. After a few experiments including one that left her with a singed eyebrow she finally netted success, and now she could have light after sunset. However for today, her right ankle had had enough. She fed Yelper and herself beans, boiled rice and a can of Del Monte peaches. Then she managed a sit down shower. It was her first full bathing since October 8. She found pajamas that apparently belonged to a boy her age. What a joy it was to be completely dry, warm and in sleeping clothes for the first time in 2 weeks. The Coleman lights were out and she was asleep by 7:00.

At 1:00 AM., snow was falling again and the wind was howling. Search personnel were dismayed. There would probably be no further search on this stormy day. But Cheryl Comstock didn't know it. She was sleeping soundly; the wood stove was now down to cooling wood ashes and the oil heater was performing well on a medium setting. The cabin had cooled but by no means as chilled as it had been.

Cheryl was snoring and Yelper watched this phenomenon with a questioning expression. Then suddenly he jerked fully awake hearing something no human could have detected. With a jump he shook Cheryl awake and clumsily he half ran, half tumbled down the steps yapping happily as he ran. Simultaneously the tranquility of the forest was split with a sound that could be heard down to the creek and beyond. "YEOOWW.," which, translated, means "let me in right now, how dare you keep me out here?"

How Boomer managed to track his newly adopted master to this remote location when extensive human searching could not locate her was an unexplainable but happy mystery.

Boomer was normally black and white, but he had been through freezing rain and wet snow which stuck to his fur. He was far more white than black, and his whiskers were dramatically highlighted with remarkable little icicles. He was a comical sight and he was in no good mood. Cheryl squealed with delight and now turned to get a towel to dry him off but before she could reach the towel, Yelper growled and attacked in an apparently violent assault, and Boomer rolled over kicking furiously, but it was the same old game and it lasted about a minute wetting down the floor and returning Boomer to his true color scheme.

Then both animals confronted Cheryl. It was time for their bed time snack. Cold canned salmon was the bill of fare and Boomer went at it ravenously. Then the flashlight went out and the animals bounded upstairs with Yelper leading Boomer to their new quarters. Cheryl followed slowly as her two charges waited impatiently at the head of the stairs. Boomer crawled into the bag, wet fur and all, but an hour later he squirmed to get back out. Then things settled down for the rest of the night and on into late morning with Yelper and Boomer curled up behind her.

What pets do for people is hard to describe, but the appearance of this quirky cat put a smile on Cheryl's face that remained until she dozed off again. She felt better than she had at anytime since she leaped up to spike the volley ball and then was thrust into darkness by a foul smelling burlap sack. But, understandably her feelings were sometimes gloomy. Once during the night she woke up and, she began to think about other things.

The events she had endured since October 8 were such a blur that now she really did not know what day of the month or of the week that it was. Counting the days as best she could she realized that in the midst of this nightmare of events, she must have turned 14, and it could now be November. Here she was. She was alone. Where, she knew not. How far the airplane had taken her she could scarcely guess. She fell into a spate of melancholia, and for some time she wept. Faced with a sequence of threats to her security and even her life, it was an awful burden to face at 14. Then another thought struck her. What must be going on with her family and her friends?

Being away for a month with Uncle Harry and Aunt Sue was a joy. Being out from under her mother's firm discipline was a tonic. The ranch hands treated her like a princess; a working princess to be sure, but nonetheless a princess. However after a month going home was always a joy too. She dearly loved her parents, and how she had missed her co-conspirator, Hazel Phong, and her closest schoolmate, Stella White. She realized they must be terrified about her absence, and now she wept again. She was so sorry for all the grief that she surely was causing them.

CHAPTER 30

The Comstocks were realists and as the dawn broke, they knew that although there was still a one-in-a-million chance that she found some sort of refuge, there was no rational reason to believe that a teenage youngster clothed in probably no more than jeans, a blouse and a light jacket could survive three nights outside at or above the three thousand foot level with wet snow falling much of the time. As time passed, grieving for her probable death began to quell any hope for a miracle. Reporters kept seeking predictions from the family members as to her survival. They wouldn't let up. Marcus gruffly ordered them off the Comstock Company premises, and company security guards took up positions at Comstock homes barring access by anyone not cleared for entry by the family. Hazel spotted a photographer trying to set up a video camera in the back yard. She burst through the back door of the mansion and took out after him with a broom. The agony was aggravated by a cruel twist as a morning mail delivery included another child support payment and letter from Rolf postmarked at some obscure location in India.

Gerald Graham was now out of surgery long enough that the physicians would allow some early interrogation. From Arnie, the FBI already knew that Graham was mentally handicapped. He viewed the world from a child's perception and the usual pressing and demanding style of police when questioning suspects might well drive him to simply "freeze up" and relapse into a staring, non responsive silence. Hence Dr. Myerson was called in to do the job. She started by telling him that Arnie had shot him with a pistol, that Arnie now realized he was terribly wrong and felt very badly about hurting Gerald. Then he was told that the surgeons had saved his life and that he would recover. Gerald seemed to understand most of that. Myerson was patient, understanding and reassuring. She fed him this information slowly in short, simple sentences and would then ask from time to time if he understood so far. Only when she got an affirmative answer would she then continue to another subject. Time after time during this session, Gerald expressed the wish that Bart was there. He volunteered numerous comments praising Bart for his humane treatment and understanding. Myerson worked about an hour and then agreed with the physicians, that was enough for today.

Caldwell sat behind a screen located between beds and said nothing. He made no attempt to whisper to Myerson or otherwise make his presence known. "Well, what do you think Judy?" As usual, she was still scribbling notes and it was a moment or two before she answered. "He is mentally about ten. Maybe twelve but I doubt it. This Bart rescued him from an environment where he knew nothing but abuse. Bart has been capitalizing on that ever since using this kid, especially his cooking and housekeeping. Gerald worships Bart and would be very resistant if someone told him that Bart was using him virtually as a slave. Bart can be credited for the decency he exhibited in looking to this kid's basic needs and for sheltering him from people like those in the warehouse. He also got a lot of domestic labor for free when he should have had him placed in special schooling.

"We can credit Bart for painting the correct picture about Arnie's probable move on the girl. I may have more detailed ideas later when Gerald is recovered enough for longer sessions, but my guess he is ultimately going to be a hero in the eyes of the Comstock family and in the view of the public at large for that matter. Good luck if you plan on prosecuting him. The whole world, me included, will be rooting for him." Caldwell grinned at Myerson's concluding remark and responded, "Oh I imagine the decision on that will be to subject him to something different than regular adult punishment. That's not up to me or wild eyed liberals like yourself." "Liberal, huh? Bite your tongue you overweight, backwoods sheriff." The exchange of such barbs was par for these two professionals. Their mutual respect had developed over a history of many cases.

Questioning of Arnie and Gerald revealed the whole bizarre plan that had been concocted by the "Boss." The identity of Bart was now known and a recent picture of him was in the files. A quick raid by FBI and Port police authorities made sure that neither Bart, "Boss" nor the money were on the freighter when it steamed out of the harbor.

Myerson and Harry Cottrell's unshakable suspicion that Rolf was the mystery man prompted a request from the federal office to the department of motor vehicle records for the State of Texas The driver's license picture of Rolf Burnside forwarded from Austin was enlarged and then a forensics specialist began altering it to add 16 years of fast food and heavy drinking. When Arnie was shown the altered photograph, there was no question. That was the Boss

The federal, state, county and city police team were discouraged by the probable loss of the victim, but they were re-energized in the pursuit. They knew they were looking for a John Parker Bartholomew, a Rolf Burnside, a white ¾ ton Dodge pickup with invalid license plates and a load of canvass bags. Clear likenesses of Bart and Rolf were on the screen and in the press.

But that is where it stalled again. Publicity elicited no tips of value. Highway patrol cars radioed in countless license plate numbers from white dodges seen on the road. All were legitimate albeit some were in need of renewal. It was discouraging, and Caldwell was uneasy. If one is determined to slip out of the United States, it is really not very difficult to do. Hopefully the heavy canvass bags would make it a bit harder. For what seemed like endless days progress on the Comstock case was frozen in time, and for law enforcement the case began to drift toward that discouraging status of a cold case file

Bonnie Gay continued to stay in her bedroom, locked in deep depression. She would talk to no one save Hazel Phong. She was a difficult person to nurse. She would not bathe, she would eat only the smallest portions, some days, none at all. She had not brushed her teeth in days and would let no one fix her hair. In a word she looked like a homeless hag living on the street. No one could have guessed what an attractive woman she was.

Marcus III resumed his work at the company headquarters mostly because he did not know what else to do. For all of the strain, worry and sadness, he was able to function and kept working toward the date set for demonstrating the Comstock sensor to the Navy. He was sad, and, melancholy speaking only when it was necessary. Employees were concerned and all of them wished there was something they could do. He seemed to age twenty years in a few weeks. The pastor of their church left a note on his desk saying that if and when they might want to plan a memorial, he would make time to talk with them.

CHAPTER 31

Cheryl had cleaned up her dishes after the evening meal. As a teenager at home she would have shied away from that chore, but here, with no mother and no Hazel, it seemed like the natural, enjoyable thing to do. The leg was still tender and discolored with ugly but slowly shrinking streaks of yellow and purple. She could now hobble twenty feet at a time without the hiking stick. Pain and swelling would return if she tried for more. Now she had her head down on the kitchen table and sat there sobbing. For the first week, it was something of an adventure. Learning how to use her unexpected refuge took up all her time. It kept her so busy that she had not given her family and friends much thought. But now, after scorching several pots and pans, she had developed a scheme of daily activity, heating, cooking and cleaning that took progressively less and less time. Concurrently she began to experience more and more daily leisure time which then began to be slow, boring time. The virtual imprisonment of her situation intruded on her thinking. The inescapable thought that her parents did not know where she was or even if she were alive slowly began to dawn on her. They must believe that she will never return to them. What an awful realization for a young teen to deal with, and understandably, tough as this youngster was, it brought on the tears. Yelper was uneasy. He had never seen a human weep before especially one to whom he was attached. He was frustrated; he didn't know what to do. First he would yap hesitantly and then he would run round and round whimpering. Boomer was unsure; something was wrong. Puzzled he ran from under her feet and half way up the stairs. And there he laid for some time looking down on girl and dog. Either he was trying to make sense of it all or else he just wanted to get out of the way. With cats it's impossible to tell.

Cheryl knew she was still woefully short of being ready to walk any distance. She thought it strange that she could not recover faster. She had sustained minor sprains before and they never lasted more than a few days. She was unaware that she had sustained an inline fracture. A bone was broken but it was not displaced. It would remain painful until the bone healed. In the meantime, the swelling was now rapidly receding. Natural color began working its way from the edges of the purple and yellow. Each day more normal coloring appeared. That made her all the more bewildered because the pain endured when weight was gingerly placed on the right leg would not lessen. Some days it even seemed worse. In any event she was stuck in the cabin. The early snow was now beginning to yield to pouring rains and the ground was peeking through here and there.

Meantime she was learning more and more about the place and its owners. There were many pictures displayed on the walls and many, many more stored in albums that she found on shelves. She managed to while away some time perusing the albums especially when Yelper and Boomer requested release to the outside. The pictures told a story of a middle aged black man and a hostile looking boy somewhat younger than her with a background of four naked walls and bare rafters. The story went on to show completion, painting and even later modifications of the building. They also depicted a shed being added behind the main cabin. As the building changed, so did the people. The boy got larger and somehow more happy in appearance and the man grew a bit older.

Throughout the pictorial history there was a smattering of photos of a black woman whom Cheryl guessed was the man's wife. Somehow, during more than 13 years in Titusville she had missed all contact with this slightly bent gentleman even though he lived within four miles of her home. There were delightful pictures of the man and boy and later man and man holding long strings of trout. Later still the changing young man quit changing so fast and an album or so later he is standing arm and arm with a smiling lady, and from thereon her face appeared often. Smaller young people began to appear. The covers of all these albums so far were older than the last one which she reviewed today. The older man now looked somewhat sad. The black lady has disappeared.

Her review of the last album did not take so long. It was only half full and could yet hold more new pictures. Placing the book back where she found it, she now turned to one of the intended projects for the day: to find something in the shed to twist open the fitting situated at the high side of the oil barrel's cylindrical end. She knew from what Uncle Harry had told her that the stove was not an efficient oil heater. It would probably exhaust the barrel in short order if left on all the time. So today, with that cap removed she would try to get a flexible branch down the opening to touch the bottom. Then pulling it up she could estimate the level of oil. It took her some time to hobble to the unlocked shed. Its principal content was dried firewood, but there were a few tools hung up along one wall. One of them looked to her like it could be a barrel wrench although she really had no idea what such a device should look like. Well, whether that was its intended purpose, it did, after several tries, fit snugly enough in the depression in the fitting that it would hold when she turned it.

Uncle Harry's words uttered during his repairs on the old utility truck now came back to her, "right to tight, left to loose." She turned, nothing happened, she turned harder yet, she thought this time maybe it budged, Then standing on her good leg, she held onto the bottom of the barrel with one hand and pulling on her wrench with all her strength, the fitting yielded and once it did then from there on it was finger loose and she spun it off. The twig test revealed that the level was down to about half. Regarding the slow healing of her wounded leg she resolved that from here on the oil stove went on for one hour in the morning to start heating the place; and then it was load after load of wood from the shed and keep the wood stove burning. Carrying wood the twenty feet or so to the cabin deck was pure torture and obviously was re-injuring the ankle. Then she remembered that among the few winter pictures in older the albums, the boy appears belly down on a sled. Later he is on skis.

Cheryl labored several armloads of wood and then the leg said "quit" so she searched the shed more carefully and this time she looked overhead, and there was the sled, rusty and with one slat broken, but it was still sturdy. Getting the sled down took some time, but once she had pulled it free and then just barely avoided having it crash down on her head, she got it on the floor and loaded it with wood. Then she pulled on the rope to start sliding the load to the cabin, but the shed floor was anything but slippery. The ancient rope broke. It took half a day of searching, but ultimately in one of the boxes on the deck yielded a 50 foot length of quarter inch nylon rope. Cutting a length of rope by literally sawing it in half with a butcher knife, she re-rigged the sled, placed it on the ground outside the shed door and pulled. It worked. And so it went. If Uncle Harry could have seen it all he would have repeated something he said to his wife, "good stuff that kid, and bright, I show her something once and by gosh, she can do it." Indeed, Cheryl was now surviving in part because she had become the tomboy her mother had feared.

During the prior summer Cheryl had ridden in Uncle Harry's jeep patrolling thousands of acres of range land, and she had sustained more than one initiation to the arts and crafts of cattle herding. One day, Harry had restrained the camp cook from his usual first chore of firing up the wood cook stove inviting Cheryl to try her luck at it. The bemused crew watched and grinned as Cheryl managed to bath herself in a lot of smoke creating an anemic fire The crew laughed and teased, but Cheryl learned more and more about the idiosyncrasies of wood burning stoves; and now she knew what to do to make this cabin's old iron woodstove burn smoke free. However, there was one quirk concealed by woodstoves that had not been revealed to her in her Texas adventures. This stove had a tall chimney that had already sustained several seasons of creosote buildup since its last cleaning.

The chimney fire was frightening. She could easily get away, but once she did, where was she and how far could she walk? She stood out in the snow and watched the flames reach some twenty feet above the chimney. Fortunately, Ox Bowman knew about chimney fires too. The chimney had been rebuilt during the latest expansion project. He used brick as the outside structure and lined it with the usual ceramic flues, but then he had an afterthought which was redundant but effective. Inside the flue he erected a stack of 8 inch stainless steel pellet stove pipe. The structure now successfully dissipated the heat without burning the surrounding wood or the steel roof. Cheryl imagined that the vigorous fire probably made the chimney safe for as long as she would be there.

She had discovered how to bank fires so that with one wake up call in the middle of the night, she could keep burning embers going until she got up in the morning. The presence of the oil stove was convenient but now she could get by without it, and she would remain comfortable.

Diet was another matter. Preserved meats eventually would be running low. The canned ham, canned tuna, and canned salmon, were not going to last forever. For one person, they would have lasted much longer, but Yelper and Boomer together were consuming more than Cheryl was. The dehydrated food which had been stored for future hikes was available too, but the pets did not like it much either. There still were copious quantities of canned milk, dry cereal, rice, raisins, coffee, oatmeal and beans. Her animal charges were eating but they did not relish the mostly vegetarian diet. On the night of November 4, Cheryl was boiling oatmeal and raisins; porridge would be bill of fare for the day, like it or not. Boomer did not and he sat and looked at the door until Cheryl let him out. Just as the oatmeal began to bubble, Cheryl was startled by a blood curdling scream. It was a noise she knew neither Yelper nor Boomer could utter. Rushing outside she finally illuminated Boomer's presence under the steps.

A beautiful snowshoe rabbit, now in full white winter fur was lying dead under Boomer's powerful right forepaw. Cheryl artfully induced Boomer to let go and she carried the animal into the house with Boomer and Yelper curiously following her. The rabbit didn't have an apparent mark on him. No sign of wounds, no blood staining the pure white fur. Apparently the sudden appearance of the cat caused his heart to seize with fear and he was gone. Cheryl knew what to do. The ranch hands had seen to it before she returned home late last August that she knew how to de-feather, skin and butcher pheasants and cotton tail rabbits. All in all, she had stood up well to the hazing she received from Uncle Harry and the ranch hands but she balked when invited to skin, fry and eat a rattlesnake.

Now she quickly bled, skinned and gutted the carcass and cut it into pieces for frying as the animals sat fascinated by whatever it was she was doing. Yelper once attempted to steal the fresh meat and was met by a threat of violent physical consequences. He retreated. Fried young rabbit was delicious, but Cheryl sensibly limited it to the six rations necessary to feed her and the animals for two days of special treat. Half of it could be held over in the ice box until tomorrow.

At the same time, meteorologists were carefully watching incoming satellite images and comparing what they showed with reports from commercial aviators that had been plying the Hawaii-Seattle and Hawaii-San Francisco routes. Heavy clouds had spawned in the north pacific area around Hawaii, and now they were rolling inexorably toward the Pacific Coast of North America. The so called Pineapple Express was sending another band of heavy precipitation eastward, and that was no news. What generated the interest this time was that a huge band of arctic air was lunging down across the Canadian Northwest Territory and thence across the southernmost provinces toward the U.S. Canadian line. Customarily the bulk of the coldest air would head south and then begin veering east so as to make its U.S. border crossing at least 800 miles east and hence blasting Montana, North Dakota and across the high plains from there. Why not? They expected it and were prepared. Such frigid winter episodes dropped some snow, but moisture was usually in short supply. Six inches would be a lot. This time the frigid blast obstinately veered west of the Great divide and bore down on the west coast as the pineapple express came surging the other way with perhaps a trillion gallons of water. Let there be no doubt, if the arctic cold and semi tropical wet collided, there was going to be a humungous snow storm.

CHAPTER 32

Not really knowing what might come of it, agents in Houston had fanned out over the state talking to every member of the family. Generally the Burnside family members were reluctant to talk about him. He was the black sheep. He was seldom employed in the family businesses and he messed up all the tasks that were given to him. He was a ceaseless braggart, a blow-hard, and the truth was not always in him. In fact it seldom was. Burnsides were proud movers and shakers in oil exploration. Rolf was an aberration and it was embarrassing for them to talk about him. Mother on the other hand extolled virtues of kindness and lovable demeanor that would never harm anyone, leave alone his own offspring. She did allow that Rolf suffered with problems of an ill-defined nature that impaired him, making it difficult for him to apply himself to work in the business world; difficult for him to apply himself to any other work for that matter.

Mrs. Burnside flushed when her husband commented that "there must be a lot of good work in Rolf because nobody had gotten much of that out of him." She exhibited a surprising shift in mood from willing advocate of Rolf's virtues to angered hostility when it was suggested that Rolf was in the Pacific Northwest and involved in the kidnapping. A tape of Rolf's ransom demand was played for her. She blushed uncontrollably and then recomposed herself and declared, "that doesn't sound like Rolf at all!" Mimicking an old popular song lyric, the interviewing agent wrote in his report, "her lips say no, no, but there is yes, yes in her eyes."

Later in the interview FBI agents asked her if she had heard from Rolf so that she could be sure he was in India. She made a mistake by enthusiastically saying "oh yes, I have called him several times at a New Dehli number," and with that she produced the number which Rolf had given her in case of an emergency. She volunteered that she had made the call right from where she was sitting now. It was in fact the number of his correspondent in India, but a search of Houston telephone records showed no overseas call to that number from the Burnside home. When confronted with the technical evidence, Mrs. Burnside stoutly stood her ground and firmly countered that she was no technician, and she neither could nor would try to explain why the FBI could not find any record of her call saying, "You just missed it that's all."

However, the seriousness of a kidnap case, the apparent falsehood about telephone calls taken together with affidavits from Seattle office agents that the ransom call was definitely a cell call probably from an Oregon location, when considered all together, was enough for the federal district judge. An order was issued authorizing a tap on the Burnside telephone. Mrs. Burnside's "Rolfy" was on the lam. In all probability, he was hiding literally under the nose of the Seattle office. He was now named to the press and media as a "person of interest," and the enhanced photograph which had first been shown to Arnie was being broadcast far and wide. Sooner or later, this suspect would see the broadcasts.

Meanwhile, there were other leads to follow: There were no bodies and no money bags in the charred remains of the

Norseman aircraft. However accident reconstruction people could demonstrate that it had been specially equipped with an auto pilot and a mysterious trapdoor and aerial drop system. Rolf and the money were somewhere else. Air traffic surveillance during Rolf's puzzling zig-zag flight across eastern Washington meant that the money was dropped and the pilot bailed out all somewhere within a hundred mile radius. Because it would be impossible to pin-point a money drop in total darkness, and because 10 bags of currency was more than any one man could carry, the pilot had to have an accomplice probably with a vehicle. But that was all they knew then. Now, with the interrogation of Arnie and Gerald, they knew Rolf had dropped the money bags in an open wheat field where Bart was waiting and then set the airplane on auto pilot. As he parachuted to the ground the hapless old antique flew into the side of a mountain and destroyed itself.

Assuming then that a motor vehicle met the pilot and picked up the money bags, that would mean that two men were somewhere on the roads of the area and they went somewhere else. The best guess was that the heavy money bags were now hidden or buried somewhere in the wilds. Since there was no radio transmitter in the old house trailer near Gallagher Lake, and with Arnie being in custody, it meant that Rolf had not communicated with his conspirators since the money drop, and he could not know exactly what happened unless he was somehow tipped off. So, what if two men were driving a vehicle into the Cle Elum area and began to notice numerous police vehicles, what would they do? They would turn off and maybe hide out or maybe just drive back toward CleElum and then Ellensburg or Leavenworth depending on the route they chose. That much was likely, but the scent of the trail went stone cold beyond that. The only reasonable conclusion was that after the money pickup the intended travel back into the camp area had been aborted. The Dodge pick up did not show up on the road to the camp. Obviously, Rolf had changed plans. Recreating the complex oceanic transport deal for the money bags would probably take more time than had elapsed: ergo, the money was probably still somewhere in the northwest. Now what?

CHAPTER 33

"Bart, let's go on back to the freeway and head towards Ellensburg. We can turn off on US 97 and then hole up in Leavenworth. The town should be full of hunters and tourists and we can probably blend in and not be noticed. We'll find a motel where we can just sit tight for a while and watch TV. If those cops we saw were after us, the news will be talking about it tonight for sure." By now Bart was by no means as sure of Rolf's judgment as he had been, but for now a retreat seemed to be the right move. "OK Boss, we're on our way."

It was late in the day when they arrived at their destination. Leavenworth is a small town snuggled into the foothills of the Cascade mountains on their eastern slope. It encompasses an area on either side of a picturesque river called the Wenatchee. Apple orchards abound along the river valley. According to its promotional advertising the fishing is good, the hunting is superb and good skiing is nearby. Years earlier town leaders had opted to work together remodeling the exterior of most of the commercial and motel buildings to a motif resembling an Austrian mountain village. Their duplicate Oktober Fest was a big annual celebration. People came from everywhere to take part and many were still in town. Rolf and Bart could move freely without being noticed.

But the first night in the warm motel room gave them a cold fright. The local TV station had a 6:00 PM news broadcast. Harley Miller was on the screen. They had found where Cheryl was being held, but she had escaped from her captors and was missing in the mountains. Arnie was in custody. Grunt was badly injured and being treated in a Seattle hospital. And, worst of the worst, the remaining suspects were last known to be driving a white ¾ ton pick up with the ransom money in the back of the truck. Obviously, Arnie had turned State's evidence and he had told every detail. Rolf was rabid with anger and Bart was mortified.

"We've gotta make some major moves right now." "Yeah Boss but what?" "Well, the truck is a liability, the cops will be lookin' for it anywhere we could go. We have to get rid of it." "Cripes, Boss that's the best rig I ever owned. But I guess we don't dare try to sell it if they are looking for it, we'll just have to ditch it and run, won't we?"

"Well, Bart, it's get rid of it or how do you like jail?"

"I gotcha Boss, what do we do?"

"The first thing we gotta do is get the money under cover. Right now with the truck parked right outside our window, we can watch it, but we gotta eat, we gotta sleep, we can't do sentry duty all the time. There's one of those public storage places where we came into town. I don't like letting go of it, but we gotta get it out of the Dodge and into another rig. Do you still have that telephone credit card I gave you?" Bart fumbled for a moment but finally recovered his wallet in a shirt pocket. Then he shuffled through various cards and folded papers in the wallet. The telephone card did not appear immediately and that made him nervous. He still did not want to cross the Boss in any way. "What's that under your social security card?"

"Yeah," Bart responded, "that's it." Rolf snatched the card saying, "it's too late tonight, but tomorrow I'm gonna make a call."

The agent manning the phone tap had indulged too much lunch His body was crying out for a ten minute nap, and he was nodding and then jerking awake, almost succumbing to the urge when the telephone intercept buzzed and jerked him awake, but not too awake. Mrs. Burnside spent much of her time chattering to her various friends exchanging gossip, scurrilous critiques, and all the delicious and well embellished rumors that ran rampant among her closest friends. This tap was dullsville!

Oh-Oh, not dullsville this time! To his companions in the van he was calling out, "let's get this!" In an instant he knew this was a call he was looking for. "Mother?" "Rolf is that you?" "Yes, Mother." "Well where are you?" There was a pause as the caller was obviously weighing the possible problems for him if he answers that question and then, "Mother I have been doing a lot of traveling, and right now I am in Chicago." As the caller said that, one of the technicians monitoring the call looked up at the others and shaking his head negative saying, "Northwest somewhere." With modern techniques, he already knew the area code.

"Mother, I have a great deal going, I am representing a big drug company and we have a multi million dollar deal to ship medicine to China. It's stuff they don't have and they are paying a good price for it. The company has me on a commission deal where I can clear $750,000.00 on this one shipment, and then there will be more to come, but I have got to pay some port fees to clear the cargo jet to fly this stuff from Seattle to Beijing. I had the money in cash to pay today, but I was mugged, mother, somebody knocked me down and stole the money." "Oh, you poor dear, are you hurt, are you all right?" "Oh, I'm kinda sore where my head is all black and blue, but I'll be OK, but I have to advance this money. I got the port fee from the company and they are holding me responsible for losing it."

Mother rose to her most angriest responding, "Oh, those terrible people, how can they do that, it wasn't your fault, you make sure you take care of yourself. Maybe you should stay in bed for a while. Do you want to come home and rest a few days?" The monitoring agent winked at his companions muttering, "Boy, don't we wish." "Can't do it mother, got to get back to Seattle, no sense staying here. I have talked myself blue in the face with the drug company president, but he won't budge. He just laughs and says you pay those fees or the deal is off." "That terrible man, how could he be so awful, but don't you worry, you just let mamma help out here, how much do you need?" "I need ten thousand, mother." "Whooee" Mrs. Burnside whistled, your daddy is gonna want to know how come I wrote a check like that, he's gonna fume, but that's OK, let him fume, I'll tell him I invested it, and that's what I am doing, isn't it? I'm investing in you, dear." "You bet you are, momma. Now momma, I don't want to carry money like that around, and I have to pay it to the port people in Seattle, so please send me a cashier's check payable to me and send it airmail Priority Mail to me at that last address I gave you."

Mrs. Burnside was silent for a moment as she tried to deduce what Rolf was talking about and then she remembered the address he had given her. Then remembering the Spokane, Washington, location she began to repeat it but Rolf cut her off curtly saying, "don't say the address mother, some competitors of the Drug company have been tapping my phone. So, just send the money there and don't tell anyone about it, OK?" "Gee it all sounds so exciting like you were in the CIA or something," she gushed.

Rolf smiled, he was working his magic again. "Can you do that right away?" "Oh yes for you, dear, I'll call a cab now and go down to our bank and get that check, I have to see that nice young Mr. Johnson, If I deal with that grumpy old Mr. Moore, he'll just call your father for an OK before he does it. But I sneak a little cash in Mr. Johnson's pocket and he does these things for me right away, isn't that good of him? Well, now that name it was, oh here, I wrote it down. It's Jack, Jack Hawthorne. You said send it to you under the name Jack Hawthorne?" Rolf flushed with fear, he hoped not to have even the name revealed over the telephone. "Yes, mother, that's correct but please don't say anything more. I have to be careful, Bonnie Gay has an arrest warrant out for me, she lies, she claims I am behind on Cheryl's child support, it's a lie mother." "Oh, I'm so sorry, dear."

Mrs. Burnside paused for a moment and then with a contemptuous laugh she continued, "You know I never did approve of that fisherman family of hers, no character, no character at all. Your father now, he thought they were just ducky, but I knew better. They have been in the fish so long they're, well they're smelly, and that Harry is just horrible, he smells like a fish in a cow barn," and then she laughed louder, pleased at her own assessment of the Cottrell family, and then continued to gush, because it was her favorite pastime.

"Rolfy, I am so proud that you are doing well. You should come home sometime and tell us all about your experiences in India, and I am sorry your work prevents you from coming home now. I would so like to have you lie down with your head in my lap so I could rub the hurt places and make them better just like I used to. Well, listen to me go on. It's two o'clock here, If I am going to do this for you today, I have got to get to the bank before 3:30 and then to the post office before 4:30, so I will just stop talking and get going. I will get it out today so you should have it in two days. Will that be all right?" "Yes mother, that will be fine, thank you mother I'll make this up to you soon." "Oh I know you will dear." "Goodbye mother and thanks again." Rolf had been scarcely listening to his mother during the last minute of the call. His face flushed and then turned pale.

The van came alive with jeers as each agent had a response, "Oh, thank you mommy dear," "Oh mommy, please rub my head and make it feel good all over," "Oh shit, excuse me while I go out and throw up!" Then the conversation continued as the first steps were under way to get the news of the call to the Seattle office. The agent making the call offered his assessment, "so this is the rich and famous social order, I am not impressed." Caldwell responded, "Uh . . . don't make the condemnation too fast, I was in Houston for ten years; you just got there. In past cases I have come to know a lot of the big money in that town, new and old. Donna Burnside is not unknown, in fact she could be called notorious for her drunken escapades and for her mindless antics in Houston society. As one of her acquaintances told me, with Donna Burnside, the wheel is turning but the hamster died.'

Mrs. Burnside effected the issuance of a cashier's check as promised and then mailed it. Since she had revealed no awareness of a crime or how she had aided it, she was not arrested, but the postmaster of the post office where she mailed it found himself confronted by FBI agents who wanted the address to which the money was going. The mailing then started its trek to a Spokane post office.

Roger Caldwell smiled for the first time in days. Since the lucky apprehension of Arnold Sorenson, nothing else in the Comstock case had gone right. The best efforts, the most diligent pursuit of leads, the utmost cooperation among all local law enforcement had led to nothing, but now the worm had turned! Weak, spineless Rolf would endeavor to use his witless mother one more time, get enough money to lay low until snow is out, scoop up the cache and beat it overseas. Now Caldwell mused out loud, "when he comes 'round the mountain,' we will all go down to meet him."

And that probably would have resulted in the apprehension of Rolf Burnside, but unfortunately the laws of chance gave Rolf one more break. His mother's voice had an ever so slight echo to it, and it did not have that quality the last time he called her. Because of the faint difference in voice quality, Rolf guessed correctly: "Bart, my mother's voice sounded just a little different, kind of hollow. I think somebody was listening to us." "We're not going to step into a trap in Spokane." Once mother's money got to Spokane, the cops would be watching. But Rolf was not going to show up. They could watch until Hell froze over. And with that Rolf's expression brightened with change once more.

Mumbling to himself about one of his banking heists, he blurted out, Honest to God I had forgotten that one, Bart" Bart smiled because Rolf was smiling but his expression was quizzical. "Forgot about what, Boss?" "one more key, one more key, one more box. It means more travel from here than I like, but it will take me right on out of the country." He had one more safety deposit box key in his coat pocket. He had to search the coat pockets for a minute or two, and then he had to study the key to make sure his memory was correct. Finally, he was certain. It was one of the last caches of robbery money and although he had now withdrawn all of the deposits in California, his post robbery travels never brought him very close to this one. Had things gone as per the original scheme, he might have just left this fund untapped and the State of Oregon would eventually seize the money as abandoned property. Now he was going to put it to good use.

"Bart, we're low on cash. I've got more but it's in a bank vault in Hermiston. The Dodge is too hot to use and we don't have anything else. We can buy something new in Hermiston when we have that money in hand, but there are pictures of us on TV and probably in papers and in post offices, so if we drive down there or even if we take a bus or train or something, we got a high risk of being spotted. So tell me, man, how are we gonna get there?"

Bart had been silently pondering the same problem. He had come up with a solution tailored to his own talents, and as a result, his response was so fast it actually startled Rolf. "Nothing to it Boss, at least if I saw what I thought I saw coming in to town. There's a lot of white Dodges out on the road. I don't think they are stopping all of them. What they're lookin' for is one with phony plates. I think there's a truck like ours in that car lot comin' in to town. His plates are probably good. If I can get lucky, I could sneak in after closing, steal those plates and get back here with them. We can change plates and drive out of town. If a cop sees us and radios our plates they will come back to a Dodge with a registered owner that's not us and that should do it." "It will if he doesn't start checking further, but that's a plan Bart. Let's go with it."

By 10:00 PM, things were quiet outside of Leavenworth's downtown area. Their motel unit had its own entry to the rear and Bart simply walked out making no effort to conceal himself. Toward the edge of town there were several joggers who passed him on the sidewalk and they exchanged greetings. The used car lot was farther away than he remembered, but keeping up a brisk pace, he was there by 10:45. Walking past the lot and its row of used autos, he deliberately kicked several of the exposed front bumpers and slapped several car hoods. If they had a guard dog, that should wake him up. There was no response. Then he cut into an adjacent vacant lot and disappeared for five minutes. Later he could be seen briskly walking back toward town but now holding something under cover of his jacket. Bart returned to the motel unit announcing that he had already switched plates. Bart was grinning. "I jimmied the window and I got the plates and the registration. Our truck now belongs to Billy Lambert, were just borrowing it for the day."

There was a brief discussion about the money. Neither man relished the idea of leaving those canvass bags in the storage unit, but for now, keeping them hidden was clearly the best plan. "My God," Bart mused, "if some kid decided to break into storage units and if he hit ours, wouldn't he think he hit a bonanza?" "He would until the cops grabbed him then he and us would all be in trouble," Rolf responded.

Banks in Hermiston, Oregon would not be open until 9:30 or so next morning. Personal belongings were left. They had paid for three nights so that they had a place to stay and a place to hide out in case the next phase of the new plan took longer than expected. Then Rolf suggested they at least cat nap until 4:00 AM. They would make the drive with one stop somewhere for breakfast at a fast food drive in. Once underway, Rolf congratulated Bart for his chicanery and his quick thinking in giving the truck renewed legitimacy, but even as he was showering his compatriot with these accolades, he was beginning to think that his need for Bart might soon expire, and a morbid plan began to form in his demented mind.

The trip was uneventful and they were in Hermiston by 9:45 AM

CHAPTER 34

Dr. Harold Jacobs and his family were coming home. After two nights in a Honolulu hotel on American mattresses they were refreshed and eager to continue their return journey. But first there had to be a detour to Spokane and then a commuter turbo prop from Spokane back to Seattle. The detour was a promise to Carla's parents in Spokane, who had threatened bodily harm if they didn't get a chance to see their grandkids. They had wanted the children with them during the whole sojourn, but Harold and Carla had located an American School for the children to attend during Jacobs' refugee service. Now, however they were back on Washington soil and the grandparents had a week in which to indulge the children and pooh-pooh the parents' worries about spoiling them.

The week in Spokane was helpful to Jacobs himself. The ceaseless dental work under terrible conditions had been very demanding, sometimes totally frustrating. But now the respite was over, and home beckoned. The flight was uneventful. The turbo-props operate at altitudes lower than the bigger jets so the window view of somewhat familiar territory was enjoyable.

But at one point, Dr. Jacobs raised himself up out of the seat, stared especially hard at something he saw in the snow covered hills. Then he sat down and fastened his seat belt again so as to be ready for the landing at Seatac terminal. As the aircraft taxied toward its assigned gate, Harold turned to Carla and asked, "when were Ox and Vivian due home?" Carla answered with a teasing smile, "you wrote it down, Harold, I saw you do it. They were scheduled to dock Halloween night and be home probably November 2." "So they should be home?" "I would think so," she replied as she was picking up her carry-on and moving into the line to exit the aircraft door. Jacobs paid the cab driver a goodly tip after he helped take the bags to the door. It was late and the house was cold from setting for so long, but soon they were in bed and the lights were out.

Warming up the house, unpacking, returning the calls on the answering device and responding to several crises at the clinic took all the first day and one half at home. Then, finally Jacobs started calling numbers for Ox and Vivian and their children. The kids had no idea where their parents were. Both these oldsters were adventuresome and the fact that the scheduled itinerary didn't see them home already was no surprise to the progeny of the traveling pair.

CHAPTER 35

As night drew on, the weather in the Cascades grew into a blizzard, wind, snow and all. The frigid arctic blast collided head on with the pineapple express and the howling wind gave notice that this was going to be a major storm. Cheryl decided to bring in an extra sled load of dry wood taking care to select it from the middle of the shed. That stuff she burned yesterday was wet because the roof was leaking next to the wall where she selected yesterday's supply.

The night's meal would be rice and beans and canned stew as it had been for several days. Nonetheless, she was happy with the day. This morning when she got up she was half way down the stairs when she realized she was walking normally with no hobble.

Having found old Forest Service maps of the area, and noting some red lines drawn in presumably by the usual occupant, she now knew, on the maps at least, where she was. She was a long way from a paved road where she could hope to hail someone, but the map told her the area was literally criss-crossed with hiking trails. However they were now hidden by snow and offered her no help anyway. More encouraging, there was a dirt road running down the North Teanaway River which should start just a few hundred yards to the south of where she believed the cabin was located. Even though the snow disguised it the map assured her it was there. Assuming the present wet snowfall would finally quit, then she would fill the old back pack, put on the young man's down coat, load the sled with Boomer and a supply of food and start the trek out.

The blizzard blew for a whole day and then the wind stopped but a persistent, day-long, slow falling snow continued to obliterate landmarks. Cheryl wisely decided to wait it out. The map indicated she had some 17 miles to go to the highway. The ankle seemed to be healing but even with a long day of good weather, the trip out was going to be a risk. If it got dark on her, where would she go? Snickering to herself she thought what a shame it would be to die after surviving all this time. Not all teen girls would think that was funny, but some of Uncle Harry's raucous humor had rubbed off on this tom boy.

For the next five days it snowed a little at a time and the wind blew a lot. Just passing the time seemed to go on endlessly and she was becoming bored, antsy to be doing something. She sensed her family would be having a terrible time. Nonetheless blessings come in disguises, the ankle could strengthen all the more making her decision to walk out all the more feasible.

Five days later, the sky was clear and the weather promised good visibility. By 6:00AM, Cheryl was up. She was moving freely and apparently fully recovered. The snow had settled and was fairly firm. It was time to try walking out. She put on the old down jacket and came downstairs to load and bank the wood stove. She noticed that it was not any colder than other nights according to the outside thermometer, After testing the snow depth, she thought if she were going to walk out, she better learn how to put on those snowshoes from the shed. Cheryl quickly discovered that one does not assume a normal stride when walking with snowshoes. It is more of a hitch and jerk motion getting each shoe up, out of the snow and forward in making forward progress without falling on ones nose. By time she had the shoes properly attached so they did not fall off with each step and by time she had whole process mastered, it was late morning, and she decided she would wait until dawn the next day to start her journey. Reluctantly she undid the most difficult job of preparing to march; she had to let Boomer back out of the box.

CHAPTER 36

Bart thought that it was strange. The Boss insisted that the Dodge be parked between two old abandoned Hermiston warehouses. That was a good place to hide the truck, Bart thought, but why bother? Within a couple of hours they could complete the purchase of a new rig and be on their way to recover the money out of Leavenworth and then be on their way out of the country. Nonetheless, the Boss was the boss and if he said park it here then that's where we do it. Rolf did say he didn't want anything else to go wrong and an early discovery and connection of the Dodge with the kidnapping was something they did not need.

Bart's second thoughts about the Boss's mental stability evaporated as he watched that con artist ply his talent. Rolf entered the savings bank and he strode up to the desk of a receptionist all smiles and full of warm greetings and wishes for everyone's good health. He correctly guessed that residents this far away from the Seattle area would not have paid close attention to the publications and broadcasts of his likeness. Producing his key and false identification, he was warmly guided to a bank officer who obligingly produced the bank's companion key to open the safety deposit box Burnside had rented earlier. The bank officer then invited him to use one of the small customer booths where he could be in complete isolation. Availing himself of the contents of the box, he now had the last $13,000.00 of his bank robbing spree. In the flurry of activity during the past several months he had actually forgotten this substantial treasure trove. Would his good luck never cease? Closing the box and stuffing its contents into a box he had purloined from the Leavenworth motel, he sat for a moment in the privacy of the booth thinking. Then he silently nodded his head approving his newest change of course.

With the money they purchased a very adequate 1990 Chevrolet Blazer. It could carry all the ransom money with room to spare. It was a veteran with an odometer reading of almost one hundred thousand miles, but Bart had inspected it carefully and had given it a rigorous road test. He assured the Boss that this truck, though by no means in prime shape, was capable of going anywhere the Boss might want to go. It had four wheel drive in case that might be needed.

There was another self storage facility in Hermiston, and though these men had nothing else to store, they did go there to purchase a goodly number of collapsed corrugated paper boxes which could be opened later and used to store 12 million dollars worth of hundred dollar bills. Rolf explained to Bart that with the remaining $9700.00 of the Hermiston cache still in hand, they could make it back to the coast and hook up with his shady contacts. They could arrange for passage on another freighter out of the country just as originally planned. The ransom money would be packed in shipping crates and marked as originally planned. What remained of the present $9700.00 would grease enough palms to get it done.

After going over all of this new plan and sounding altogether normal, Rolf temporarily lapsed into talking to himself again, "that scum, Marcus Comstock could kiss his money goodbye." God, Bart thought, there he goes again. But then, in an instant, Rolf was back in the real world. "Ok, Bart, let's head back to Leavenworth. We should get there about 9:00 at night. We can spend the night at the motel, pull the stash out of the storage unit tomorrow morning." "Sounds good, Boss," Bart responded cheerily, "we're on our way." "Uh Huh", Rolf, thought, at least I am.

As it worked out, the Chevy Blazer was parked behind the motel by 9:30 PM. Hunger and thirst had been addressed by drive in service where recognition of their faces was obscured; and by 11:00 PM they were snug in their unit and watching the 11:00 o'clock news. The announcer noted that the young kidnap victim whose picture he was displaying on the screen was still missing and hinted that hope of finding her alive was virtually lost. Search parties had been recalled days before because of an early November snowstorm covering much of the Cascade mountains. Both Bart and Rolf stared at the screen glumly but neither one expressed his reaction to the other. Rolf found himself truly sorry, almost grieving. The death of Cheryl had never been in his plan.

But, things were going well again. At day break they were back at the storage unit and no one paid any attention to them. On a cloudy day early morning light was not very revealing; and they drove out of town virtually unnoticed. Now they were heading west to intersect I-90 and hence on to the coast. However, the first leg of some 30 miles saw them turning off the highway and diverting onto an abandoned dirt driveway. This was national forest area, and the driveway led to a campground. The area would have been full of people in summer time, but with rain and snow mix pelting the ground, they were pleasantly alone. Now the two men set about an exciting task, actually laying hands on more money than either of them had seen before. The Federal Reserve bags were broken open and money spilled out crisp and new. They were ecstatic.

The collapsed boxes were unfolded and erected into their intended shape. There wasn't much organization to their activity. They would open and shape boxes in a frenzy for a while and then they would start stowing the packets of bills placing them this way and that trying to get the most packets per box that they could. Rolf had tried to figure the problem, but now he was not sure he had enough boxes. Unless it is in the form of a check, 12 million has considerable volume even when the bills are new and firmly packed. There just were enough boxes and they were all full. It took 2 hours of frenzied activity to complete the job.

All the original bags were stuffed into two of their own kind. Bart had stopped the Blazer in front of a 4 foot high bank of dirt that the Forest Service had dumped on the camp access to prevent vehicles from driving into the woods beyond that point. At Rolf's direction, Bart dutifully carried the bulging bags to the bank and threw them behind it. The road was muddy with mixed rain & snow so he was watching his steps as he moved away from the bank Looking down and concentrating on where his feet were going, he was unaware that Rolf was now in the driver's seat, and he really didn't take any warning from the roar of the vehicle engine until the last instant when he finally did glance up. His last ever vision was of a grinning madman behind a windshield and the grillwork of a Chevrolet Blazer enveloping him and mashing him into the bank. The bank partially collapsed revealing one of the money bags. Above the noise of the engine at 4000 RPM there was a crunching sound of yielding flesh and then the wet mud turned ugly steaming red. Then engine roared again as the Blazer rushed backwards, turned around and sped to the highway. "Damn you Marcus Comstock, I'll teach you to steal my woman, you son-of-a-bitch."

CHAPTER 37

Dr. Jacobs had waited a couple of days more before trying to call Ox Bowman. Now, he called again, and again there was no answer at the Bowman house or at the Turner house. Then he tried another number. Ox had a cell phone which he acquired only after months of loving elbow twisting by Jacobs and various members of the family. Oxford had a cell phone yes, but nine times out of ten he was not carrying it, or he forgot it, or the battery was run down. But Vivian was changing Ox's ways whether he liked it or not (the truth was he liked it). Now, Dr. Jacobs had the satisfaction of hearing the Bowman cell ring in answer to his signal. The response was intriguing. First there was the solid, if squeaky voice of Oxford, "Hello." Then there was a thump, then Ox's voice, loud, and upset from perhaps five feet away, "damn it! What do they make these things so small for?" Ox had dropped the phone and Vivian's laugh resonated across the room. Finally, order was restored and the conversation began.

"Ox, I take it you're not home yet, the home phone didn't answer." "You're right, Harold, Vivian and I are in a hotel here in Las Vegas. Vivian has been cleaning up on the black jack table and the security boys are beginning to gather around her. For a while I thought we were going to get pitched out of here. She's earned back about half the cost of our trip."

Jacobs hesitated and then began hesitantly, "Uh, Ox, how did the boat get to Las Vegas?" "Oh, the boat," Ox laughed heartily, "We got off the boat at Galveston and we bought a new Lincoln there and drove here. Yesterday, we got married. Vivian says our kids will be put out because we did it without them being involved, but we got tired of being in separated adjoining rooms. So many times we couldn't get the door between them to open, so we had a better idea, Vivian is now Mrs. Bowman, and I am hen pecked again." Vivian had deduced who was calling, and in the background, her voice responded, "hen pecked, Harold, pay him no heed, the old rooster, loves it." Now both Bowman's were speaking into the phone, and Harold offered his own congratulations. It was agreed that he would now notify both families of the nuptials, so that outraged children could blow off some steam before their respective parents had to listen to them. Then the conversation got more serious.

"Ox, we made a flight the other day on Horizon Air, and it just so happened that the pilots flew over our area on the Teanaway. As you know, you cannot see our shack from the air, but there was a column of smoke like our stove would make coming up. I looked as carefully as I could. I think someone is staying there." "Well, we sure enough didn't rent it out to nobody." "You got that right," Harold responded, "I have to go to San Francisco tonight, and I will be gone for 2 days, but when I get back, I better go have a look, it may be just some hapless, homeless soul, most likely is, but I better look into it and maybe get the sheriff to help me get him or them out of there."

"You know, young pup, Vivian and I are leaving tomorrow to drive home, take us two days so we could get there sooner and have a look." Harold Jacobs now found himself wishing that he had not said anything about the cabin. Ox rarely acknowledged that he was old to a point where many men are feeble or have passed on, and the thought of Ox trying to confront some hobo bully at his age was worrisome. It would not be good, not good at all. "No way," Harold answered, I want to be there, if there is trouble of a physical kind, better that I be there too." That discussion went on for another five minutes until finally Ox promised that he and Vivian would go to Titusville and stay there until Harold had returned.

Harold hung up feeling reassured such would be the case. On the other end of the conversation, the two old grey-heads looked at each other and grinned. Vivian allowed she was dying to try a snowmobile, and so they plotted their venture. Ox and Vivian would share driving the new car a long day and one half. to reach the old barn on the ranch where the Jacobs and Bowman snowmobiles were stored. After some practice runs in an open field, he and Vivian would head up the river road and the two adventurous newly weds would investigate things at the cabin.

CHAPTER 38

Nils Jensen had worked for the State Department of Transportation for five years. In all that time he had never seen anything quite like what had been called in concerning a road hazard at Crystal Springs. Coming up on the area in the state pickup he saw two old free-standing lamps, a mattress and a battered settee that had been dumped, probably off the back of a truck. This junk was left scattered across the highway. A yellow road caution sign had been hit by the sliding debris and was broken. It would have to be replaced. Available repair crews were short handed this date and he was obliged to answer the call alone. He found the scene and watched as motorists ahead of him were getting by the mess by driving out onto the generous shoulder on on the Crystal Springs side of the highway.

Fortunately, traffic was not heavy, and he was able to quickly shove the settee and the mattress into the Crystal Springs yard and then he picked up the lamps and leaned them against the settee. His pickup was too small to haul the junk so he called in a report and a larger truck would come out and pick up the whole lot. For now Jensen would bring the broken sign in for repair so he was about to depart when, by chance, a Washington state patrol trooper stopped to make sure Nils didn't need any help. While he was stopped talking to the highway worker through his open window, he activated his flashing blue light to warn oncoming traffic to be cautious approaching the area.

More to have something to talk about than anything else, the trooper showed Jensen a new picture of Rolf Burnside and also pictures of two juveniles suspected of breaking in to cabins in the area. Obligingly, Jensen took a fairly close look. Then the trooper's radio crackled followed by a flurry of words about a roll over accident east of Crystal Springs. With the flasher emergency lights still active, he did a U turn and sped off As he came abreast of Rolf's parked Blazer, the radio voice said the roll over had apparent serious injuries, and with that the trooper paid no attention to Rolf.

Rolf Burnside saw the whole incident beginning a quarter of a mile away. First, he noticed the yellow flashers of the highway department truck and then the blue ones came on and his blood turned cold. He slowed down and momentarily stopped, hoping not to be noticed, but when the blue flashers went past him at about 90, he heaved a sigh of relief and kept on driving toward Jensen's location. Jensen was lifting the broken road sign intending to throw it into the back of the state vehicle. As the Blazer approached, Rolf forgot the advice he had drilled into his cohorts in training for the kidnapping. He stared directly and intently at Nils Jensen, who just moments before had looked at the same face staring at him from a black and white photograph. For an instant each man had his eyes fixed on the other. Rolf could swear that the highway worker jerked his head forward as if to get a better look. Rolf was seized with panic

Now suddenly, the Blazer was accelerating away. Jensen was not a law enforcement officer. He would not give pursuit as such, but this sure did look like that wanted guy. He tried to make radio contact with his station and the mountains foiled transmission from his location. So he put the microphone back and resolved to try it again a few miles down the road. In the meantime, it was his duty was to get the sign to his station and pick up a new one to replace it, so he drove west.

He had covered about an eighth of a mile when the blast of the air horn from behind took him by surprise. The driver of the eighteen wheel semi coming up from behind was late. Jensen's sixty miles per hour made him feel like he was standing still as the big truck went around him spraying snow melt as he passed. However, when the big diesel came up on the Blazer, passing the 70 mph impediment would have required a much longer stretch of open road and so the truck driver fell in behind the Blazer and had to be content with 70. Within a mile the vehicles encountered a bank of winter fog obliging them to slow down even more. Of all the rotten luck, Rolf thought, now that he was slowed down here came that damned state pick up overtaking the semi behind him. Rolf was shaking with panic. He was not sure whether the state pickup driver really recognized him, but from Jensen's expression, Rolf would guess that indeed he did recognize him. Rolf pondered, was the state worker pursuing him or he just happened to be going in the same direction? Nonetheless the state pick up was behind the semi and continuing to follow. Despite the fog, Rolf increased his speed to 70 and when he felt he was far enough ahead of the truck that it appeared to be only a shadow in the fog behind him, he braked hard and made a sliding turn onto the road that follows the Teanaway River up stream. He would ditch the state man by driving up into the remote area north and wait for a while before resuming his journey to points more remote from the long arm of American law.

Jensen used his radio to report to the Kittitas Sheriff office in Ellensberg just what he had observed and his uncertain guess that the driver was that Rolf Burnside. Although he could not be totally positive, the skid marks turning off and upstream on the Teanaway led him to believe that the Blazer may have turned off although he really did not see that. Jensen could not report that he was sure of anything. It *might* have been the wanted man, although Jensen could not swear to it, the Chev. *might have turned off*, was he sure? No, but there were subsequent stretches of road beyond the fog bank where he could see a mile or so ahead. The semi still could be seen, the other rig could not, so where did it go?

Burnside continued as far up the road as the depth of the snow would allow. The snowfall in this area was less than farther in at higher altitude, and as the road began to climb, slush turned to compact snow, then compact snow steadily deepened and finally the last several miles required four-wheel drive.

Although Rolf was sweating with anxiety fearing he may have been discovered, he noted that there were a number of sets of tracks made by vehicles of various kinds first to houses and later to cabins. Apparently a number of locals lived the whole winter up this God forsaken road. Then it got more remote and there were no further signs of settlement. There were no more tracks. Nobody had been up here during the snowstorm. The Blazer was beginning to high-center in the snow and could go little further. A driveway was faintly visible on the left hand side. He pulled in and thence behind a copse of evergreens completely obscuring his presence when viewed from the road He was well hidden, and if he could stay that way for a few hours perhaps enough snow would fall to foil any effort to track him. He would use his sleeping bag to stay warm and he would lay low until about 3:00 AM. The cops should have given up by then.

CHAPTER 39

Years before Ox Bowman and a gangly young Harold had made a deal with a rancher to store snowmobiles and cold weather snowmobile clothing in a shed next to the rancher's house. They had had their own keys to the shed for years. As Ox and Vivian drove in, Ox explained that rancher Middlestone would be in Palm Springs this time of year, but that he and Harold were free to come and go from the shed. The building was dark and unheated but there were electric lights. Ox pulled Harold's snowmobile outfit from a closet and gave it to Vivian feeling she would probably drown in it, but Vivian, albeit thin, was no midget. She filled it out respectably and she now would be warm enough. Then she volunteered to put on the helmet and she laughed lustily as he helped her get it on and strapped in firmly. Vivian loved adventure.

She did listen to Ox as he went through the safety tips that novice riders can foolishly and sometimes fatally ignore. Vivian had the good sense as befit her maturity, but once she was safely out in the open, she was hell on wheels (or skids as you might choose) and she did the rounds of the 20 acre pasture in front of the house soon feeling at home with speeds up to 30 MPH. Ox got a bit vocal when she drove even faster, and although trying to be careful, she loved getting Ox a little stirred up over her antics. And so now they were off up the Teanaway Road. Oh what fun!

CHAPTER 40

Boomer had been in that box before and he did not want to get in a second time. He decided to hide under the cabin, and it was past 8:00 AM before Cheryl could corner him, drag him out from under the cabin and tape the box closed with Boomer's grumbling and snarling resonating from inside. It was the first time Cheryl had ever spoken so harshly to the cat. Normally she enjoyed Boomer's antics, but today, her calculation of 17 miles to civilization bore heavily on her mind. She wanted to be some where by dusk, and wasting the morning chasing a recalcitrant cat did not make the task any easier. Yelper watched the whole thing with what appeared to be amusement, and now the unlikely trio were headed down the road. Although it was snowing this morning, most of the accumulated snow had fallen earlier and was now settled and firmed up. The outline of the road was faintly visible and she found it easily. Her ankle felt good and she started slogging downhill. She was covering the ground at a good pace. It felt good and her spirits were more like those of a normal youngster at 14.

School athletics and private dance training were paying off. Snowshoes can be awkward especially on rough terrain. But she was handling it very well. Yelper seemed excited and he would run ahead and then run back to make sure Cheryl was following. He probably repeated this antic a hundred times. Cheryl was now straining some above her earlier pace. For hours she had been slogging along in almost total silence but four hours out from the cabin she had pulled the sled a remarkable 8 miles. Now she was pulling harder yet because sometimes, when the breeze was right she could hear the distant rumble of 18 wheelers powering up and down hills on US 97. And she was encouraged; her downward trek had taken her to an altitude where the snow was more compact and now the awkward snowshoes could be removed and stored on the sled. Civilization was out there somewhere! She could hear it! She squealed with delight and did several dancing moves that delighted Yelper and disgusted Boomer. She had been so mature during this seemingly endless odyssey, but now for a moment, she was a child. It felt good. She was sorry she lost her bracelet though and she wasn't sure what she was going to tell her mother or Aunt Sue about it. It did not occur to her that when they found she was alive, a lost bracelet would become the most unimportant thing in the world.

Ten minutes after the dance exhibition, joy was tempered with concern. She had stared out the cabin windows for hours as the blizzard swept down the mountainside, and she knew how vicious it could be. Now heavier snow was beginning to fall again and she just had to get to where those trucks were passing. Fortunately her scare was brief because the flurry of heavy snow was brief and again only a light dusting of flakes was coming down. Her confidence returned and again she was sure she was going to make it if she just kept up the hurried pace.

Boomer would occasionally make a lunging effort to open the top of his box and exit from his prison. By relentless lunging he had weakened the tape and stops had to be made to reseal the box. Each time he grumbled his unceasing complaints despite Cheryl's reassuring voice.

During the same brief flurry of increased snowfall, Jensen told the responding deputy, Robert Salinski, what he had seen. "Could you be sure this was the face you saw last night?" Jensen had to admit that he was not absolutely positive, but he had also looked carefully at the black & white photo displayed by the trooper and thought that resemblance was "real good." "Did you actually see the Blazer turn off?" "Well, no," but the truck effectively blocked his view and that view was from perhaps ¾ of a mile, and at the time considerable fog shrouded the area. Nonetheless the skid marks on the river road were so fresh he would guess that the Blazer made the tracks.

"Maybe so, maybe not," the deputy mused, "Deputies on night duty have broken up drag races there before. The first mile of the river road makes a good drag strip for the race crowd, and they love to lay down skid marks just for the hell of it whether they are in a race or not. Those skid marks may have been made in the wee hours. But, this FBI agent wants to get your story first hand." Jensen was a bit downcast. It was obvious, this deputy was highly skeptical. But his skepticism was short lived. A minute later the radio blared out a message from the Chelan County sheriff. At about 9:30 that morning, a sleepy motorist felt he had better nap for fear of falling asleep on the road. He pulled off onto this campground and saw steam rising up from a pile of something so he drove on in to investigate. He was now so upset he could hardly talk but he managed to communicate that he saw a warm dead body and then he saw a number of canvass bags. He did manage to say that they were just good high quality canvass bags, ordinary enough except for the stenciled words "Federal Reserve Bank, San Francisco."

The Chelan deputies had secured the area and the FBI was on its way to investigate. The deceased could be involved in their case.

Caldwell had only traveled 10 miles beyond Cle Elum heading toward the Leavenworth campground when yet another communication briefly describing Jensen's report came in and he responded that he would visit this latter scene. The campground would have to wait. The Ford Explorer bearing Federal plates changed course again and soon pulled in alongside the State pickup and the deputy's prowl car.

Caldwell first noticed the new Lincoln parked. in a driveway one hundred yards ahead. The auto was facing a small shed and the rear plate area was clearly visible, but no license plate appeared.

Introductions were terse and serious conversation began, Caldwell speaking first. "Whose vehicle up ahead of us there?" "Don't know, it was parked there when we got here and I notice the windows are frosted with the cold so it's been here a while," the deputy responded. Caldwell pressed further, "can we get a registration ID?" It was a question to which Caldwell already knew the answer. Washington State Department of Licenses can answer that question on any Washington registered vehicle within seconds at anytime day or night, and he thought the deputy should already know the ID of the registered owner simply because the car was in an area of suspicion.

The deputy nodded his head in acknowledgement, got into the prowl car and drove on ahead and in behind the new Lincoln. He could be seen on radio and in five minutes he returned. The sheriff drove back and in behind the pickup and brought the information. The car had been purchased, of all places, in Galveston, Texas with purchasers declaring their Washington residency and seeking Washington State registration. Registered owners were listed as Oxford and Vivian Bowman 524 River Street, Titusville; both licensed Washington State drivers, both parties 70 years old. Permanent license plates had not yet been issued. Salinski had pressed Washington's DMV further and could now add that Bowman has a dirt bike and a snowmobile also licensed here. Also there were snowmobile tracks from the Lincoln vehicle heading on into the hills.

This all seemed very vague to Caldwell and God knows there had been hundreds of false leads investigated in this heart wrenching case without result, but even so, some inner policeman sense was stirring a feeling of excitement, and the bank-bag find fueled the fire. Signaling to another federal officer he called, "Hartwell, is my briefcase in the wagon?" "Well, it should be, I've never seen you without it!" Hartwell grinned, and Caldwell responded "Of the thousands of agents that could have been assigned to me, I get a comedian. Bring me those mugs in the side pocket"

Hartwell knew now what his senior was up to. He spread the seven facial photos out on the hood of the state vehicle. Counting from left to right, Rolf Burnside's latest known photo was number three. Jensen had held back from the conversation, remaining silent until spoken to, but now he was center stage. The seven men in the photographs could well have been brothers, the resemblances were good for a legal "line up." "You know any of these guys, Mr. Jensen? Take your time and be sure if you do." Nils Jensen did not need time. His eyes swept the seven pictures and then, without hesitation, he jabbed a finger at number three. The ID was firm and serious questioning did not shake him. He knew what he saw. Jensen added, "he seemed just a bit older than in that picture, but that sure *could* be him! If not it has to be a brother."

It was not certain that Rolf had ducked up the river road, but it was the best possibility right now. "Salinski, you probably know the country better than I do, there are four of us now counting yourself, do we need back up?" Robert Salinski thought about what he remembered from the last time he did any off road exploring in this area and then answered thoughtfully. "If he's in there on a snowmobile, and if the snow is firm enough now, and if he gets wind that we're after him, he could try to go clear over the top and down into the Boulder Creek drainage and lose us altogether. We should be chasing after him right now. The snow could be concealing his tracks already. Let's all get in your wagon after I call for stand by back up to come in with snow mobiles to cover all possible routes out". Caldwell nodded in approval and thought to himself, "Salinski you may grow up to be a good cop yet."

Nils Jensen was excused to report back to his station, and the Explorer headed north up the river road and into the hills.

It was well past noon but there would be no thought of lunch.

CHAPTER 41

The driver side seat of the Blazer had been pummeled by a hundred thousand miles of human bottoms and the padding had been compacted into a state of uselessness. Burnside's rump was squalling for a break. Rolf got out for a stretch and then for nature's relief. Now that the fury of the last storm had run its course and the snow of this morning stopped; the sky cleared. And soon the newest snow was warmed enough that it was beginning to fall off the trees. Standing under the trees offered good cover, but it also offered an incessant cold shower.

No one was around and so Rolf walked out to the road and took stock. The woods had a mystic silence as the wind was nearly still. There was no sound of man either on the ground or in the air.

The temperature, had reached its high for the day and after briefly hovering at 40 degrees would soon begin its evening plunge. It was entirely pleasant and Rolf was thoroughly enjoying the relaxation. It was a welcome change. He had been on the run and in great fear of apprehension for days. Now he was at ease. Things would go right, he just had to bring his brilliant mind to bear and work his way through this. The thought of spending the rest of his life as a rich, mysterious American expatriate and raconteur in a country hostile to the American Government left him smiling. He was enjoying his situation for now.

For brief, pleasant moments, nothing was to be seen or heard. Then something began disturbing the silence of the hills. Coming from half a mile or so away, one could now distinctly hear the faint sound of two air cooled engines. No doubt, they were snowmobiles and coming north up the river valley. At the same time he could sense there was something coming south. Was he being approached from both ways?

Yelper rounded a turn in the road well ahead of Cheryl and the sled when a familiar scent came to his sensitive nose. His dog brain recalled the treatment he received from the various occupants of the old house that smelled so bad. There was the petting and pleasant sounds from the huge, easy-going one, civil treatment from two of the others and the inevitable vicious kicks from the heavy set one; and it was the latter's unmistakable scent that came to him now.

Responding Yelper sought what had always been a dependable refuge. He bounded back to Cheryl and plopped himself squarely between her legs in the same manner as he would have done under the table of the trailer hideout.

"Yelper, you're in the way, move!" Yelper looked up pleadingly and whined. Something was wrong, and it obviously was something down the road where Yelper had been exploring. Doing her best to convey the need for silence to Yelper, Cheryl continued to pull the sled and its angry passenger down the road, but now quietly and cautiously. Meanwhile somewhere down the road there was this funny engine noise that she had heard before. She thought it might be two chainsaws like the ones Uncle Harry had.

Rolf had a pair of binoculars in the glove compartment and now he dug them out and peered at what was coming toward him from 250 yards away. The person seemed to be sneaking along and looking furtively from side to side as it moved down the road. As the distance closed, he began to recognize and the recognition as it became more certain led him to gleeful astonishment. He knew from Wenatchee papers and TV news that all hope of finding Cheryl "Cherry Blossom" Comstock had been abandoned, and yet, by God! That was her! And that damned fool dog too! How had she survived? "Oh, this is rich," Rolf murmured out loud. "She's my ticket out of here. I can drive out and if anybody interferes between here and when I get on a plane in Mexico City, I have a gun to her head. I'll fire a shot nicking her ear if needed to show I am serious, deadly serious, ahh, good plan, good plan!"

Rolf opened a small bag of personal possessions. At the very bottom was the pistol. He had not wanted to use firearms in any part of this caper, but changes of circumstance called for changes of technique and Rolf Burnside was the man for all seasons that could shift with the changing wind and meet each problem with a cunning that left those law enforcement goofs stuttering to themselves. "Ah, good plan, good plan!" Now Cheryl was too close for Yelper's liking and he bolted. In long bounds he sped past the clump of trees where Rolf was concealed and ran and ran.

The hound was hearing something that caused him to go beyond where he could see Cheryl. It was a situation like a fire where a dog senses danger even though not sure what it is. What the dog actually thought, of course, no human knows, but in another 500 feet he came abreast of the two Bowman snowmobiles. The machines were now down in a canyon area and the sound did not transmit up to where Rolf was hiding and waiting for his prey to come closer. Suddenly Yelper seemed to sense friendship in the two elderly black faces coming up the road and he began yapping incessantly and crossing back and forth in front of the noisy machines.

Ox raised his hand signaling Vivian to stop as he himself braked and dropped the throttle to idle. "Hey there young pup, what are you doing up here all by yourself?" Then the barking stopped and Yelper turned and began running up the road with the curious snowmobiles in pursuit. Yelper would look back from time to time to make sure the machines were following him and Ox guessed that something notable was happening. Yelper disappeared from sight ever lengthening the gap between himself and the following humans.

Rolf stepped out from his hiding place and grinned with a malice that belied all thought that this was his own flesh and blood. Cheryl stopped stock still and stared speechless with horror as Rolf advanced toward her. Her whole body seemed to suddenly grow ice cold and shivering. She had run and limped and crawled for miles to evade the wretched menace of this monster and his compatriots. She had been a virtual prisoner for weeks as her injured body healed. She had been deprived of house and home and the love and support of family in a manner that she could not have imagined beforehand. From all of that she had escaped and was now happily trudging along with her two animal friends, and then, suddenly the whole nightmare had returned. She stopped frozen in fear.

"Well if it isn't Miss Lippy with all her God Damned answers for everything. I think you have earned a trip to Mexico little lady. I'm taking charge of you right now." Cheryl was no longer frozen. She turned and began to run but she had waited too long. Rolf grabbed at her and although his grasp was broken by her surprising strength, it was enough to cause her to stumble. Then she was up in an instant and running, and screaming as loud as she could in case someone was near. Now Yelper had returned and for the first time in his life, the wolf's killer instinct buried thousands of years deep in his brain surged to the forefront in answer to the screams of his master. He grabbed Rolf's right leg and jerked backwards with a vicious pull that ripped trouser leg and drew blood. Now it was Rolf that stumbled, falling down in the snow. Heisting his bulky frame back up he reached in his waistband and pulled the pistol out ready to kill the dog, but now Yelper was in front of Cheryl and he couldn't get a shot. "Can't kill the kid right now," he thought, "she is of great value alive and nothing if she's dead. Better to keep up the chase and bring her down on the snow, then kill that damned dog. It would be a pleasure."

Cheryl screamed again and again just as they had taught in school. Then she heard a high pitched male voice, "hold on there friend, what's the problem here? Kids can be bad but you usually don't have to shoot 'em."

Rolf was horrified. Someone, no, two someones had come in behind him. Regaining his composure he turned and began to point the gun at Ox, but in that moment, the young hound chose to continue his revenge for all the kicking and scolding with which Rolf had punished him over the past months. Making a growling sound more savage than anything he ever uttered during his mock battles with Boomer, he hit Rolf's right arm just below the elbow and then he bit down with surprising fury. Rolf lunged toward the old man and his heavy bulk sent Ox sprawling. Paying no attention to the accelerating sound of the machine behind him he screamed, "You're way too old for this sort of thing old man, now just back off or I'll break every bone you have!"

At that point, in a manner of speaking, Rolf's life went full circle. His ears were filled with four cycle air cooled roar and then his legs went numb. All in an instant, the scenery in front and above him began a rotation. First he was looking at Ox as he sprang back with remarkable agility, but then he was looking at the tree tops behind Bowman and then it was the sky that filled his sphere of vision. His gymnastics continued as the trees that had been behind him flashed into full but upside down view for just an instant before being replaced by a white blur as he plunged full face into the snow.

Vivian with less than 90 minutes experience had achieved complete mastery of the snowmobile. She had hit Rolf Burnside from behind at 15 miles an hour and accelerating. In a sequence lasting no more than one or two seconds the front cowling of the machine bent Rolf's legs into the fetal posture and lifted him upwards as Vivian instinctively ducked her head as low as she could. The windshield plastic cracked and snapped but still held most of its shape causing Rolf's body to continue in rotation as the machine passed clear under him and then gravity took over and he fell unceremoniously into a face down belly flop. Vivian made a tight circle coming back around so that she was headed back toward him threatening a second attack.

Rolf raised himself up from a full prone to a sitting position. Rolf was as "old south" as they come. There was total contempt in his eyes as he glared at Vivian saying "Nigger, where I come from they would lynch a black bitch like you for what you just did."

"Oh, really?" she asked with a slight smile, "well my son is a judge in Memphis and every so often he gets to hang a sack full of white trash like you, what do you think of that, Honkey?"

Ox took a minute to regain his composure. It had been decades since he had sustained the pistol shot to his throat in the Randy Murdoch holdup up, and for a moment he was stunned into inaction, but now he was himself again. He managed to pull back on the hammer of the pistol. Taking his time and keeping the barrel steady and pointed at Rolf, he rose up off his prone position with an agility normally attributable to a man twenty years his junior.

Rolf now turned his gaze away from Vivian and looked in Ox's direction as the black man spoke. "I was shot once by a worthless punk like you, and I haven't forgotten what it felt like. I have the gun now and you better believe that if you make one move towards either of these ladies then where the Lord made room for your two eyes, I am going to make room for number three."

Rolf was whipped.

"What are you going to do old man, shoot me right here?"

"Maybe yes, maybe no. First of all, I want to know what this is all about. Who are you? Why are you manhandling this young girl? I need to know why the dog seems to despise you as much as I am growing to."

Cheryl was still shaky from the terror of the past ninety seconds, but even now she felt comforted and relieved by the presence of these two old people so she spoke up.

"He and his henchmen kidnapped me and wanted my dad to pay 10 million dollars for my release, but I got away and I have been living in a cabin up the road."

And from there on the dialogue continued without interruption for ten minutes. Ox and Vivian now began to fully understand the magnitude of what they had stumbled on to, and they were up to the task. They used a rope from the saddle bag of one of the snowmobiles to securely bind up the hapless Rolf. Then they tied him to Ox's snowmobile causing him the ultimate humiliation of walking while every other human was riding. Boomer may have been sympathetic, but nobody else was. As they were taking Rolf into custody, they asked dozens of questions and Cheryl willingly responded. Talking in the rapid delivery style of youngsters in the twenty-first century, some of the detail of the kidnap incident overwhelmed Ox and he would interrupt and ask Cheryl to go slower explaining that his was not the best hearing in the world. Cheryl quickly filled them in about Gerald who befriended her, Arnie who was bent on raping her, and Bart of whom she knew the least except that he was in on it from the beginning.

From Cheryl's description, Ox knew that by unbelievable coincidence his was the cabin that became Cheryl's haven giving her food, heat, shelter and a refuge for her recovery from the injured ankle. But for now, other tasks awaited him and his new bride. Fully understanding what they needed to do, they tied the toboggan with its dissatisfied feline passenger to the rear of Vivian's machine. Ox had already made a friend of Yelper by sharing a still lukewarm beef sandwich and by some talking and petting which Yelper accepted. He indicated he thought Ox was OK. Yelper would trot out the remaining travel distance running first alongside Cheryl and then Ox. Cheryl climbed on behind Vivian leaving Ox free to devote his full time to keeping an eye on the fugitive who was now walking ahead of Ox's machine. Several times Rolf stopped and braced as if to bolt away but then there would be the audible click of the pistol hammer to the cocked position and he would sullenly turn again to trudge on down the road.

Vivian and Cheryl were well behind on the second vehicle keeping a considerable distance between them and Burnside so as to prevent him trying to grab one of them as part of an escape. However, the hope of escape quickly faded from his mind. When he spoke to Rolf, Ox's demeanor was as cold as the deadly gaze on his face. "You make one move different from what I tell you and I'm goin' to empty this little pop gun into your skull. Now move out. We're taking you in."

CHAPTER 42

FBI agents are trained vigorously to assess and react quickly to unexpected situations. It's a talent that has to be developed if they are to avoid the mortal risks of their profession. However, Roger Caldwell could be forgiven for his speechless gasp and pause when he tried to digest what now was coming down the road toward the Explorer. After all, consider how often during a cop's lifetime would he experience seeing two snowmobiles with old grey operatives and one teen age passenger who was dressed like a boy but was obviously a girl running in tandem with a dog alongside and a cranky hissing cat in a box on a sled. To top off the incongruity of it all how often would such an entourage be led by a sullen downcast fat man with his hands tied behind his back?

When Ox saw the oncoming vehicle he immediately noticed the sheriff uniform sitting in the back seat. He quickly put the pistol in his coat pocket so the Explorer passengers would not jump to the wrong conclusion.

Caldwell stopped the Ford, crying out to the skeptical deputy, Robert Salinski, "Nils Jensen was right, sheriff, do you recognize who that is walking? It's Burnside!"

Not recognizing the civilian dressed federal officers Ox spoke directly to Salinski. "Sheriff, I have two people here you might be interested in. The little lady behind me there says she is Cheryl Comstock and that this worthless piece of trash that I have trussed up kidnapped her. So if you don't mind, I would like to deliver both of them to you."

"Oh, by the way," Ox continued, "the trash here was carrying a gun, but my good looking bride here relieved him of it and I am turning it over to you for safekeeping." With that Ox lifted the gun slowly out of his pocket and handed it over handle first and barrel pointing back toward him. He did not want to be misunderstood.

Now the full impact of the incident cascaded down on Rolf. His thin and fragile ego about his own criminal brilliance gave way to a grief stricken reality, and he sobbed uncontrollably. "Oh mother, I tried so hard. It's all so unfair." Later, his weeping became more pronounced as Salinski tore the open the money boxes and showed Caldwell that the money had indeed been recovered.

Caldwell made his introduction and took over the interrogation. He moved as quickly as he could because in Titusville there was a mentally damaged woman and a grief stricken man who even now were accepting the agonizing loss of child. Doctors had warned that Bonnie Gay could possibly be driven into a state of depression as to require that she be kept on suicide watch. Any word of information being developed on this remote country road and then later in the warmer interior of the Cle Elum Police department would be withheld until he was sure of the whole story.

By time he was ready to notify Marcus the day was over. The original drive to Leavenworth would be cancelled and Leavenworth authorities were told to go ahead with processing the campground death scene. They could make appropriate disposition of the body found there and they could examine and test the now impounded Blazer and its bloodied front end.

Cheryl and the Bowmans were hungry and Caldwell treated to supper at the Sunset Café in CleElum. He finally called the Comstock home and the conversation lasted fifteen minutes. Marcus knew then that a miracle had occurred. Cheryl was alive, dressed in boy's overalls, apparently healthy save for some complaint on her part about a sprained ankle that was now in mild pain from her long walk out. Best of all she was in good hands and on her way home.

After the federal and county officers checked in with their respective offices, they formed up a three vehicle caravan. The FBI rig with Cheryl as a passenger was the leader, followed by deputy Salinski with Burnside cuffed hand and foot in the back seat. Agent Hartwell kept an eye on the prisoner in support of the deputy sheriff. Oxford Bowman, followed in his newly acquired Lincoln with Yelper in the back seat and Vivian holding the cardboard box that imprisoned Boomer. Cheryl told her whole story. Speaking into a recorder she related her entire experience for transcription later. The traverse of I-90 and SR 18 would be the last 90 minutes of tranquility that Cheryl would experience for days to come as first the media and then the whole world gasped joyfully at the news of this happy outcome.

There would be a flurry of telephone calls spreading the good news. Everyone in the Cottrell and Comstock families would be happy, joyful and full of conversation. Hazel would be handling the incoming calls to the Comstock home. It would never be silent for the first two days. Reporters called from just about every English speaking part of the world as the story developed.

For now, Yelper sensed the mood and joined in from time to time licking faces and whimpering contentedly. He was delighted to be with two adult humans who obviously liked dogs. He was in a good mood, Boomer was not. Testing Vivian's firm grip several times without success, he concluded that it had been a long day. He had serenaded Cheryl with his most emphatic yowls for hours and he was now finally "yowled" out. He slept until they reached Titusville.

As the three vehicles turned onto SR 18, Cheryl fell asleep.

▬▬▬▬▬▬▬▬▬ CHAPTER 43 ▬▬▬▬▬▬▬▬▬

Cheryl had to be briefed on her mother's depressed, sometimes suicidal condition. The Interrogation room of the King County Sheriff Satellite Station just north of Titusville was chosen for that conference Dr. Myerson was standing by accompanied by an accredited student grief counselor. There was some concern about how Cheryl would face a mother who was convinced that her only child died somewhere in the mountains. The student grief counselor hinted that such a concern was probably not real because kids are far more resilient than adults might give them credit for. She did agree to brief Cheryl to be ready for whatever might be Bonnie Gay's response in seeing her child alive.

The grief counselor had guessed correctly. They were all amazed. Cheryl was alternately astounded and weepy as her mother's medical record and present suicidal condition were revealed to her. She paled when she was made to realize that there were even now plans for her memorial because no one could have possibly survived for all those winter weeks with only warm weather clothing and with neither tent nor food. After all of this was related to her, Cheryl said she understood what had happened to her mother. For a few moments she expressed a remorse and dread that she had caused all this. The counselors assured her that the cause was the kidnapper who was now safely in custody and he would be a threat no more.

Cheryl had a lot to digest. Rolf had disappeared before she was born. He had been so hateful that Bonnie Gay had destroyed all her pictures of him as a means of helping her get him out of her system; and all of that also occurred before Cheryl would be old enough to remember. She grew from babe-in-arms to a teenager with no father figure other than Marcus; and no idea what Rolf looked like or who he really was. Rolf had decided to keep it from her until he could hurt her the most with that news, just as he released her per the original plan, or when he was safely into Central America per the second revised plan. It would take some time for Cheryl to reconcile herself to accepting the nightmare of Rolf Burnside. She had known from age eight that she was adopted, and Marcus had fulfilled the father role for her so completely that she had harbored only fleeting spates of curiosity as to who her biological father was or what had happened to him.

Cheryl, in her maturity responded about as the student grief counselor had surmised. And now she understood that she had a part to play in restoring her mother to total recovery. She also knew that might not happen for a while. The wounds that had been inflicted on this mother's psyche were deep, shattering her very stability and the "cure" might be months away. "Is there anything special that I should say or do when I meet mom?" "No, just be yourself; that will help your mother the most."

Judy Myerson agreed to take part in waking Bonnie Gay. Myerson had learned a lot about life in the Comstock household and after giving the matter some thought she asked Marcus, "do you think Hazel Phong would be willing to take part in this?" "Yes." No doubt, that was a good idea.

In spite of the late hour Cheryl was awake again and glued to the backseat windows and squealing with youthful delight as old familiar sites of her hometown, passed by. She was smiling and bubbling with chatter as they turned into the Hellgraves driveway. It was 2:30 AM. Cheryl was on a renewed burst of adrenalin.

In the darkness, Bonnie Gay Comstock was unable to sleep. She sat on the edge of her bed and stared dully at the carpeted floor. She hadn't shown much emotional response in the past few weeks but she now showed some surprise at the knock on her door. "Hazel, is that you?" "Yes, it's me." "What's wrong Hazel?" she responded, showing genuine concern for someone else even though she cared little about living herself. And now Bonnie Gay recognized Dr. Myerson coming through the door behind Hazel. Marcus had been banned by Bonnie Gay's irrational state of mind weeks before and so he stood in the hallway together with the counselor, and Cheryl herself. "Bonnie," Hazel began, "Dr. Myerson and I have wonderful news." With that Myerson signaled Cheryl to approach. From inside the bedroom, Cheryl's form was in silhouette caused by the lights from the hallway. Hazel was standing beside Bonnie and would say later that she gasped because Cheryl gave the appearance of being an angel with the light shinning all around her. Bonnie Gay did not look up at first, and then she heard the one word that would begin her return to normalcy and happiness. Linguistic scholars rate it as one of the five or six most melodic words in all of spoken English.

"Mother!".

For weeks, success had been on Rolf's side in his mad quest to cause this family grief; but now Bonnie Gay was staring at a living, smiling daughter. At first her mind just could not encompass what had happened. It was almost as though she was sedated to a state just short of losing consciousness. She did not speak, but this was anticipated. Acting on Judy Myerson's instructions, Cheryl began to come closer and as she did she first raised her arms to waist level and then finally rushed forward embracing her mother. That was the catalyst, and for the next ten minutes there was almost total silence save Cheryl's joyous sobs and her mother's ecstatic moans as the whole grip of grief and agony began to release her mind so that it could grasp what was actually happening. Fair to say, it was more than mere words can describe, and there were no dry eyes in the house.

Roger Caldwell said good bye promising to be in touch later to finish up his investigatory procedures. After the quick trip to King County Corrections Center to take care of the bookwork on Rolf as a federal prisoner, Roger Caldwell was alone talking to himself as he often did. "This was a miserable case in a lot of ways, we just looked downright stupid; this guy slipped through our fingers time and again. Only a miracle, literally an act of God, no several acts of God delivered our victim safely. I've never been humbled by a case quite like this one." One development after another frustrated all his best efforts to locate Cheryl and the pressure he felt increased by the agonized expressions of a father who looked at him with pleading eyes and an expression that asked, can't you do something more?

Now a horn behind him honked its demand that he drive on. with its driver sarcastically calling out, "That light is as green as its going to get." Caldwell smiled and obligingly went on the through the intersection and on toward his home. The irate motorist's voice caused him to regain perspective. After all Seattle office had solved an almost impossible case and delivered a live victim and a miracle for a Comstock family that was planning a memorial less than two weeks later. State troopers, County sheriffs and Titusville police had worked the case skillfully. Rodney Griswold contemplated nothing more significant than tire tracks in the dirt, but he took the time to think, imagine, and then think again; Nils Jensen and the sleepy, but curious motorist were classic citizens, willing to get involved. This would be the final important case in his career; December 31st was less than six weeks away. He was content. Damn, it felt good!

CHAPTER 44

It took until well past Thanksgiving for the Comstock family to labor their way through the ongoing inquiries of media and press. There were literally dozens of invitations to appear on various evening and afternoon shows. All but one local program were politely refused and eventually other more spectacular stories attracted news media attention, and the return to familial normalcy could begin.

Christmas was warm enough, but reserved. Bonnie Gay Comstock was by no means totally recovered and both family and well-wishers from the town came and went quietly. Members of the Titusville Police Department called from time to time. The chief extolled high praise for the work of the Seattle office of the FBI and especially Roger Caldwell. Caldwell himself stopped to pay a call. Bonnie Gay wept on his shoulder thanking him profusely. Caldwell was not exactly dry eyed either.

Slowly but surely, the Marcus and Bonnie Gay family would return to a normal life.

Christmas the following year was a different story. Bonnie Gay's former irrepressible energy and good cheer had returned. With Marcus's approval she had invited the whole Cottrell family for Christmas and they all accepted. Sue had taken custody of the bracelet and now it was refurbished and secreted under the tree for Cheryl to open.

Cheryl and uncle Harry Cottrell were inseparable and they both shrugged off Bonnie Gay's accusations that Harry had spoiled Cheryl rotten and was now aggravating that condition by inviting Cheryl to spend the summer on his ranch again. Harry, Marcus Jr. and Marcus III challenged Cheryl to a shooting contest. Mischievous Harry had smuggled in four toy pistols that shot rubber tipped darts intended for a plastic target. Unfortunately, the vulnerability of glass balls on the Christmas tree presented a much more tempting mark. Bonnie shrieked her disapproval but she received no support from other members of the Comstock and Cottrell families.

And there was more to entertain the happy gathering. Yelper and Boomer had adapted to the rooms and hallways of the Hellgraves mansion. Time and again they interrupted the conversation and even their dining by staging mock battles. The carpeted circular main stairway was an ideal stage. Boomer would feign slumber, curled up, with head buried in his paws and eyes closed. Yelper would attack, growling and barking. With eight legs kicking furiously and teeth flashing albeit doing virtually no damage, they would roll one over the other down every step of the stair case and bottom out on the main floor. Then the display was over and each animal would totally ignore the other and they would saunter off in opposite directions only to repeat the whole demonstration sometime later.

Life was good and would remain so for some time to come.

CHAPTER 45

Arnold Sorenson pleaded voluntarily and took an agreed sentence of life with the possibility of parole after 25 years. He was on the ragged edge of serious trouble once when he made a pass at a female guard. Fortunately, she decided to handle the matter on her own. She cuffed him so hard he fell against a wall, and he apologized profusely. She did not report it.

Gerald Graham was found to be totally under the control of his compatriots and though not legally insane he was a wholly subjugated person unable to form intent to commit crime. There was some grumbling around the courthouse as to whether the law recognized such a condition as a defense, and whether a judge could fashion a sentence accordingly. Nonetheless, a much reduced misdemeanant charge was filed, pleaded and Gerald received a suspended sentence. Eventually, the Comstock family found him a suitable apartment in Titusville and gave him a job which he relished.

Eventually, after his mother hired and fired seven different lawyers, Rolf was convicted of multiple counts including murder, kidnapping, bank robbery and forgery. Texas had a good case for non support. Washington, Oregon and California had iron clad cases for conviction of theft, impersonation, forgery of motor vehicle documents and criminal conspiracy; but none of those lesser offenses were ever charged. After considerable inter communication between prosecutors and district attorneys there was something of a subtle, mutual conclusion that from there on they were beating a dead horse. Rolf received a life sentence without parole.

Rolf's reception into the federal prison population was mixed. At first fellow inmates repeatedly urged Rolf to detail his adventurous plan. Ohs and ahs would be uttered by his listeners as he told of actually possessing and handling 12 million U.S. dollars. They were sympathetic: "Gosh, what tough luck, you were that close!" However, Rolf's celebrity status did not last. Prison life soon reveals the true character of new inmates. False airs or assumed traits of intelligence and strength do not survive. Inmate populations always have leaders and the leaders in Rolf's lockup soon pegged him as the phony Harry Cottrell had always said he was.

Sadly, mother's enabling tutelage was inculcated in Rolf's early upbringing to a point that he would assume his own view of things was always right. Literally, her unwavering adulation had ruined him. Whatever event or circumstance that might thwart him in any endeavor, he would always attribute his own failure to the evil of others. It had to be that way because whatever he had done, whatever steps he had taken, his choices were right and his mother was there to assure him that that was so. Immersed in mother's praises, Rolf matured into a blow hard who sounded exciting at first but his boasting was transparent to friends, business associates and other members of the Burnside family. It was no less so with the current residents of his cell block. Inmates frequently dub new comers with prison names that reflect the character of the plebes as the elders perceive them. Rolf was named "Practical Rolf," because he was an impractical dreamer and everybody knew it.

Rolf was constantly hatching one scheme or another to achieve greater privileges or to gain easier assignments in prison work. Many of his plans were not new. They had been tried before. Veteran inmates rebuffed him when he invited them to get involved. But there was some advantage to being on the good side of Practical. Mother saw to it that he received all the money and presents that prison rules would allow, and Rolf would curry favor by sharing what mother sent him. She visited him frequently, and he tried to use her every way he could. Prison staff would cringe when they knew she was coming because every time she visited she would try to give Rolf some special food or toilet articles that simply were not allowed. She incessantly pleaded for assistance in bettering Rolf's situation. Her requests seemed a bit crazier every time she came. Advancing age and her continued reliance on the bourbon bottle subtly took their toll In sad desperation, Ray Burnside took the necessary steps to have a guardian appointed to manage her affairs. After that, Rolf had no visitors, and that "nice Mr. Johnson" at the bank mysteriously moved on to be the assistant manager at a car wash.

And yet, as time passed, an aging Rolf Burnside could actually relish the memories of his disastrous criminal career. Lying awake at night he could tick off the history of his own genius in twisting the tail of the establishment by stealing several hundreds of thousands of dollars in bank money to finance his grand adventure while the best law enforcement minds of the world were totally ineffective in tracking him down. He had created the illusion that he was somebody else and that he, Rolf the genius, lived somewhere in the wilds of northern India. He had successfully changed his identity in

California, Oregon and Washington motor vehicle records no less than seven times. He had learned how to fly. He owned an airplane, and he actually parachuted safely which possibly is more than could be said about D. B. Cooper. He had conned and dominated those boobs. John Parker Bartholomew and Arnold Robert Sorenson so they would do anything he told them to; what morons! Did they really think a genius like Rolf Burnside would share ten million dollars with them?

And last and best of all he had brought that pompous, arrogant wife stealer, Marcus Comstock to his knees. He had him weeping on the phone and begging for mercy. He had him pleading to accept twelve million dollars! The money was great but what the hell? Rolf had other ways of getting money, but man with that ransom deal, Rolf was in charge! The whole world was shivering with fear. By God, they came to know who Rolf Burnside was, Yes sir. The paralysis of law enforcement and the stark terror suffered by the Comstocks and the Cottrells now that was success man, yes sir, that was success. What glorious days they were.

For the first few months, Rolf could garner a party of listeners as he related his successes time and again, but, there was no more to the story after the ransom was returned to Comstock accounts, and eventually the telling and retelling of the venture grew old. The listeners became fewer and fewer and then there were none. Time moved more and more slowly and a cold bitterness settled over Rolf Burnside.

CHAPTER 46

And now it was 13 years since the date of Cheryl's rescue. Christmas was three weeks away

Illness among older members of both the Cottrell and Comstock families would probably prevent some of them from attending their annual winter reunion. The elder Marcus had given up his large former office although he still maintained a smaller one filled with memorabilia of a long and successful career. The older man was still an advisor but seldom a decision maker any more. He had come to realize that at near ninety he really could not contribute any substance to the ongoing activity.

He came to his office almost every day but he held only an honorary position. He would still be informed on the progress of both military and civilian research, but he had to recognize that so much had changed that for him to try to be active would simply contribute an element of incompetence that would get in the way of younger members of the Comstock team. He no longer had a private parking spot. Three years earlier a physician grounded him and virtually ordered that he turn in his driver's license. Over his protest, the company underwrote a private chauffeur That was harder than giving up a managerial position. The office did contain one ten year old memento that gave him joy. It was the picture of him and his foursome as he treated at the bar for his day's achievement of shooting a 96 golf score and topping it off with a hole in one on a 136 yard par-3 hole.

On Thursdays at the Hellgraves mansion Bonnie Gay monopolized Hazel Phong's personal presence. Bonnie Gay wanted none of Hazel's 15 housekeepers. It was not that they were not capable, indeed Hazel paid well and staffed the best domestic help. But there was more than housekeeping. Bonnie Gay worked with Hazel and it was as much entertainment as it was substantive work. They argued and bickered about almost everything, and every argument ended with gales of laughter. The ugliness of the incident now thirteen years past healed about as much as one could expect.

Marcus Sr.'s former office was now occupied by 27 year old electronics engineer Cheryl Comstock, soon to become Cheryl Mortensen. Although fully qualified to apprentice into the research and development structure of the company, she had convinced the family that Comstock had grown enough that it should now establish a marketing division to further encourage sales and to compete against ever-growing competition domestic and foreign. Management agreed. Cheryl proved to be very effective as its manager. The marketing division had proven its worth in this first year, but this December 3rd morning there were other problems. The intercom buzzed and Cheryl heard the familiar voice of the receptionist, "Dr. Millard on line 2."

Cheryl felt a chill go through her 5'-10" frame, she could guess what the news would be. "Yes Harvey, give me the bad news."

"Cheryl, you did the right thing bringing both animals in, but I think you have already guessed what their situation is. Both Boomer and Yelper are suffering with foreign masses in the abdominal areas, and those masses have spread to where nothing can be done really. They are no longer themselves, they both hurt all over. From here on life is just misery with no hope of it ever being different. And I . . . ." Cheryl interrupted, "Harvey, I agree with what you're telling me, let's do it, but wait until I get there, OK?"

Tina, Cheryl's secretary, knew the pets were in the veterinarian clinic, and she had recognized Dr. Millard's voice as the call came in, and as Cheryl announced that she was going out she inquired of her boss, "is it Yelper and Boomer?' "They have been in pain for weeks," Cheryl replied, "the merciful thing to do is put them to sleep." "How are you're going to break it to Gerald?" Cheryl pondered that for a moment and then responded, "I guess I was only thinking of myself, but you know they sort of belong to Gerald too. Is he mowing today?" With that question Tina pulled the drape at the edge of her window and looked across part of the huge greensward that surrounded Comstock Company. "He is just now finished, I can see him turning toward the maintenance shed. Shall I page him down there?" "Don't bother, Tina, I think I will just drive down and pick him up if he wants to be there when it's being done."

Gerald Graham was just locking the doors fronting the mower storage bay when Cheryl drove up behind him. Noticing the sound of her Lexus convertible he turned and smiled broadly, obviously pleased at this chance to talk with the woman that he had loved from afar for all these 13 years. As time had gone by he had first endured the several years of custodial control and then this very woman became his benefactor and pseudo guardian giving him the opportunity to meld into the Comstock building and grounds maintenance crew. In his view it was all a miracle the benefits of which he would extol to anyone who would hear him and for as long as he could get them to listen. His only regret was that as Cheryl matured from an energetic high achieving child into an accomplished executive and company leader, his opportunities to be around her became progressively less and less.

Now they were standing in front of the maintenance shed beginning with Gerald animated and glowing with delight. But as Cheryl began to explain her presence, the gentle giant's child like grin and enthusiastic animation dissolved. In a moment he lowered his head, his shoulders drooped and then in response to her gesturing, he began to slowly shuffle to the passenger side of the sports car. Moving almost mechanically, he strapped himself in.

Boomer and Yelper seemed drugged as they lay on the table, but they did look up enough to see Cheryl and Gerald come into the room. They were obviously aware, but their eyes were glazed over and all of their energy seemed gone. After asking permission from the doctor, Gerald leaned over the table and with his two immense, gentle arms he encircled these old friends and there were emotionally draining moments for Cheryl and Harvey Millard as Gerald whispered his goodbyes with tears literally pouring onto the fur of the two animals. Both of them licked Gerald's face and then Gerald moved away. Yelper now looked at Boomer as though he was more concerned about him than himself. Bonnie Gay had slipped into the room quietly and each of the women placed an arm around Gerald as Cheryl said, "go ahead, Doctor."

Harvey Millard had administered the euthanasia shots many times and did so this time with great skill. Neither animal registered any awareness of the needle's injection. In 15 seconds, Boomer sighed and his mouth opened slightly, but only after he turned his head enough so that it lay on Yelper's paws. Yelper responded laying his head on Boomers neck and then both were still.